The Other Daughter

Sara Alexi is the author of the Greek Village Series and the Greek Island Series

.

She divides her time between England and a small village in Greece.

http://facebook.com/authorsaraalexi

D1534241

Sara Alexi

THE OTHER DAUGHTER

oneiro

Published by Oneiro Press 2017

ISBN: 9781973165279

Also by Sara Alexi

The Illegal Gardener

Black Butterflies

The Explosive Nature of Friendship

The Gypsy's Dream

The Art of Becoming Homeless

In the Shade of the Monkey Puzzle Tree

A Handful of Pebbles

The Unquiet Mind

Watching the Wind Blow

The Reluctant Baker

The English Lesson

The Priest's Well

A Song Amongst the Orange Trees

The Stolen Book

The Rush Cutter's Legacy

Saving Septic Cyril

The Piano Raft

The Greek Village Colouring Book

The Housekeeper

An Island Too Small

The Village Idiots Trilogy

Chapter 1

Dawn slams the brakes on, one wheel on the kerb, yanks the door open, runs to the house and fumbles in her bag for the keys. 'Don't be dead, Mum, don't be dead!'

She leaps up the four steps to the back door, hands trembling. The key won't go into the lock. It's always stiff; she's been meaning to get someone to fix it for years.

'Please don't have left your keys in the other side …' A whispered prayer.

A click, and relief flows as the door swings open and Dawn hurries inside. The silence is thick and the smell of musty carpets mixed with the aroma of old coats, as usual, sticks in her nostrils. Her feet slow and then halt. Her heart thumps in her chest and the sound repeats itself in her ears.

'Mum?' She whispers the word, terrified that if she says it out loud there will still be no answer.

The utility area that connects the back door to the kitchen is narrow: washing machine and freezer down one side, supporting a worktop on which there is a microwave and stacks of tin cans. Once upon a time, when both she and Amanda lived here, and Dad was still alive, these tins were filled with Mum's home-baked cakes and scones. They've been empty for years now. Above the counter are shelves, sagging under the weight of tins of food, some of them three and four years old, probably older at the back.

In the kitchen, she puts her keys down silently on the table, listening. Nothing! Her bottom lip starts to tremble. Her vision blurs and her eyes swim. Once she has passed through a second door, into the hall, the sound of her footsteps is muffled by the carpet, laid on a thick layer of bubble wrap underlay, Dad's clever idea. The popping stopped long ago.

The television room door is closed. That is where she will most likely be. There is no sound of a television.

'Mum?' Dawn calls out, slightly louder. The sound of her own voice ringing in the emptiness calms her, but there is no answer. Taking a deep breath and then clenching her teeth, she opens the door.

'Oh Mum!' She exhales rapidly. 'Oh, thank goodness.' She hurries to her mother's side and puts her arms around her. 'Are you all right?'

'No, I'm not. Look at these poor mites!' Mum is staring at a charity letter, on her knee, which shows photos of faraway places, and little African children so thin it is amazing that they are alive.

'No, I meant *you*, Mum? Are *you* all right?' Dawn backs off and looks her over from head to foot.

'Me? Yes, why would I not be? But these little children aren't, look how thin this one is. Came yesterday, it did. Imagine how they are today.' Her bent finger traces across the picture.

'Mum, I got a call, you fell!' Dawn crouches so they are eye to eye.

'Did I?'

'Yes! I got a call from your window cleaner. John, is it? He said he had to get Jim to help pick you off the floor.'

'Such nice men. John and Jim. You wonder where their parents are.' Her fingers still on the child's face.

'Mum, it's just a begging letter. You can't afford to give away your money. Throw it in the bin. We've talked about this before.'

Mum looks at her with surprise.

'Several times.'

'You want me to put the children in the bin?'

Dawn gently eases the cheap print from under Mum's hand and puts it on the little round table next to her chair.

'Mum, tell me about the fall, tell me about Jim and John.'

'Such nice men. Window cleaners. Both of them. I think they work together. Is it Wednesday already?'

'No, Mum, it's Monday.'

'This isn't your day.' A frown passes across Mum's brow.

Dawn comes on Wednesdays for tea, and leaves after *Midsomer Murders,* reruns of which are on most days. On Fridays and Saturdays she is at Mum's for tea again, and they watch television after that – usually an old film, a repeat. She arrives at five thirty and leaves at nine: the same routine these past sixteen years.

Now she is back on her feet. 'You've dried blood in your hair. Mum, what happened?'

'My head does hurt.' Mum is looking at the letter on the round table.

'I'll get you some painkillers, but you must tell me what happened.' The painkillers are in the kitchen, in the bottom drawer. She leaves both doors open so she can still hear Mum's voice.

'It was the Damart catalogue.'

'What was?' Next to the pills is a half-eaten family-size chocolate bar and a stack of leaflets from local takeaways. She puts the leaflets on top to hide the temptation.

'It was under the door.'

The tap runs cold and Dawn fills a glass and wets a tea towel, takes them through.

'What has the Damart catalogue got to do with anything?' She passes the glass and Mum holds out a curled hand to receive the pills, and then she starts to gently dab at the dried blood with the wet tea towel. Mum does not flinch; Dawn has never known her to flinch at anything. It is almost as if she is disconnected from her body.

'I told you, the Damart catalogue was on the step. I'd been out to the post office, for my pension. Now where is my bag ...'

'I'll find your bag in a minute. Sit still and tell me what happened.'

'The catalogue was wrapped with plastic, and it was slippery when I stepped on it, that was the problem.'

'Oh God, Mum – you didn't fall back down the steps, did you?' Dawn stops dabbing to look in her mother's face.

'I don't think so. I sort of twisted, I think. Which reminds me, there's a twenty-pence piece under the stool by the back doormat.'

'So you fell by the back door?'

'I suppose I must have done. I called out and John and Jim came.'

'Oh Mum, how long were you calling out for?'

'I don't know. I looked around for a bit, not knowing what to do. I was like an upturned beetle. That's when I saw the twenty-pence piece. You can have that, it's under the stool by the back door. I might have had a little sleep, too, I don't recall.'

'John and Jim?' Dawn puts a hand to her own forehead; the pain there is spreading, a dull ache. It might be the beginning of a migraine.

'Yes, they came, they heard me. It took the two of them to get me up. There was no room, you see, not with me lying in front of the washing machine. John, with his long legs, stepped over me. Pushing and pulling, they were.'

'It sounds horrible. I'm so sorry.'

'Why are you sorry? You didn't leave the Damart catalogue under my door. I think I'll write to them.'

'Yes, you write to them, Mum.' Dawn balls the damp tea towel. The cut is really very small and it isn't bleeding any more. 'You want a cup of tea?'

Mum's complexion is not pale, she has colour in her cheeks, but Jim must have been worried at the time; why else would he have called her, why else would Mum have given him her number?

'Oh, that would be lovely. Is it time for *Midsomer Murders* yet?' The charity leaflet slips from the table and arcs to the floor as Mum leans over and reaches for the television remote control.

9

'Too early, Mum.'

'But you're here ...'

'I came out of work early, when I got the call.'

'The call?'

'John and Jim.'

'Nice men.' She turns the remote in her hand, pointing first one end and then the other at the blank screen.

Dawn goes through to the kitchen, fills the kettle.

'I have a new supervisor,' she calls back down the hall.

'Bit early for supper,' Mum calls back.

Dawn opens the bottom drawer and snaps off a line of chocolate, pops it in her mouth. She closes her eyes to concentrate on the velvety sweetness, the instant lift it seems to give her, the comfort. But all too soon it is gone. She kicks the drawer shut to hide the temptation and the kettle starts to hiss.

'No, I said I have a new supervisor.' She goes back into the television room and slumps into the other comfy chair, on the other side of the gas fire. The sofa, on the opposite wall, side on

10

to the television, is piled high with magazines and catalogues and letters from charities; packets of notelets from the RSPCA show cute baby animals, and there are free pens from the NSPCC.

'A new supervisor?'

'She's one of those people who loves the power. I hope she doesn't notice that I left early.'

'Why did you leave early?' Mum is still pressing the buttons on the remote but nothing is happening.

'Because you had a fall, Mum.'

'Did I?'

'Press the red button at the top. I'll make the tea.'

Her shoulders drop as she walks; the threat of a migraine is leaving her. She will take her time to make a pot of tea, let herself slow down, reflect a little.

'Stupid!' She condemns herself for the way she drove to get here. The roadworks were still going on and the light was turning red as she approached. Her foot hovered over the brake. That was when she felt the first twinge of a migraine and she closed one eye in an attempt to alleviate the sensation.

'Traffic lights for a single small hole on the pavement!' she comments, and she drops two teabags into the pot. The kettle clicks off.

There was no one coming so she stamped hard on the accelerator, at the last moment. The red light flashed across her eyes as she passed; a check in the rear view mirror showed the silver car behind stopping. A glance at her phone told her there had not been another call. She would have heard it anyway. Both arms stiff, tightly gripping the wheel.

She sniffs at the milk and pours it into a little stainless steel jug.

All the time she was driving, all she could think was, 'What if it's worse than John said?' The hill drained the car's momentum and the silver coupe that had stopped behind her at the traffic light cruised past.

'Come on!' she remembers shouting, urging the little blue car on and glancing again at her phone. Nothing. 'Keep calm,' she told herself. 'If it *is* bad, John or Jim will have stayed with her. If it's really bad they'll call an ambulance.' She imagined her mother adamant, insisting that she wanted no doctors, however bad the damage.

She puts a piece of kitchen paper on the plastic tray so the teapot and milk jug do not slip and she finds two cups.

Finally the little blue car crested the hill and gained speed, catching up and passing the coupe on the way down the other side. The roundabout at the bottom looked clear. With no decrease in speed she turned the wheel hard and the car lurched, and for a moment she wondered if the near side wheels lifted. Her instinct was to slow down, but she couldn't, she dared not, and so she exited the roundabout as fast as she entered it.

'Just stupid!' she repeats, and she lifts the tray, then puts it down again; they could do with a biscuit or two, after the shock.

Savouring another strip of chocolate, she looks at the calendar on the wall. Two kittens playing with a red ball of wool advertise the local veterinary surgery. The muscles around her heart seem to tighten at the sight. She could have done it, with just a little encouragement. It might have taken her longer than most but she could have been a vet, or a veterinary nurse at the least. She lifts the page to look at the miniature ponies that grace next month's page. But no, she was not allowed to be the one to shine. Amanda got all that glory. On the corkboard by the cooker, there is a new card from Australia. She plucks it free of its coloured pin.

Dear Mum,

The sun is still shining here in Australia, the sun always shines here. The boys are well and send their love, as always. Carl loves high school and is doing well. Lucas is jealous but I have told him he will go next year. They have cut my shifts at the hospital which I guess is a relief. Brax sends his love as always. Love Amanda. P.H.D.

'P.H.D.' stands for 'Please say hello to Dawn'. When Amanda first emigrated to be with Braxton, she would address the postcards to both of them, but somehow, over the years, it turned into an afterthought, an abbreviation. Twelve years, to be exact. It's meant to be a sort of joke, as she *is* a doctor of medicine but does not actually have a PhD. Dawn pins the card back to the corkboard.

She takes the last strip of chocolate and puts the wrapper in the bin, stuffing it under the empty milk carton, then takes the tea through.

14

'I should have been a vet, you know.' She wants to add *if you had given me one second of encouragement*.

'Did I find my bag?' Mum has put down the television remote control and picked up the charity letter again. 'I need my chequebook.' The adverts are on silent.

'You always have so much to give others, don't you, Mum?' Dawn mutters, but quietly enough not to be heard clearly.

'What, dear?'

'Here's your bag.' Dawn takes the bag from behind the sofa.

'I'll just give them a little something.' Her crooked fingers scrabble for her cheque book and pen, both of which she finds with remarkable ease, considering how full she stuffs her bag.

'Mum, you can't afford to. Listen! You don't have the money to be giving it away.'

'I have a house, dear, I'm one of the lucky ones.'

'Yes, but you have bills to pay and food to buy.'

'I'm sure it will be fine.' She starts to write out the cheque.

Dawn wants to swear as she watches the old woman pretending to be all official, notes the sense of power it seems to give her to write a cheque, and then in a moment of lucidity the old woman becomes her mum again and looks up.

'So, a new supervisor. Maybe that will improve your job.' She smiles and tears off the cheque, and puts it in the prepaid envelope.

'I don't think anything could improve that job,' Dawn grumbles, pouring the tea.

'Yes, but you stick with it, girl. It has a pension, and you'll be glad of that in the long run.'

'In the long run,' Dawn mutters, and she pours the milk. Sixteen years have slid by since she took the job. Sixteen years of her life gone in that hideous role.

The television is now unmuted and the familiar music of *Midsomer Murders* fills the room at full volume.

'I do wish they wouldn't mutter, can you make out what they are saying? They mumble.' Mum says the same thing every time she switches on the television. She can eavesdrop on conversations at a hundred metres, but the television she always needs on full volume. Dawn takes her earplugs from the porcelain box that jostles for space with an assortment of family photos on the shelf above the radiator. Carl and Lucas, the grandchildren Mum has never seen. Amanda in her graduation gown. Amanda on a tricycle aged two. Amanda and Braxton getting married on the beach in the Seychelles. There is also a photo of Amanda with Dad and one of Mum and Dad in their twenties.

'You know, you don't have one photo of me here.'

The moment she has said this, she wishes that she had not. Not one part of her wants to hear the excuses that serve to avoid saying the actual words, the real reason why her image is not there with the rest, which is that her mum does not want to see her there. She is a disappointment.

'Why do I need a photo of you when you are here nearly every day? Could you get me my chocolate, please, dear? Bottom drawer, in the kitchen.'

Chapter 2

They watch Chief Inspector John Barnaby solve a crime of passion, with Mum giving a running commentary throughout. Each time the adverts come on she mutes the sound and the images flicker in silence. Justice prevails in the final scene of the drama and Mum sighs, satisfied.

'I knew it would be him who done it. Never liked him as an actor. Shifty eyes.' She turns the television off. 'I'd better get the tea on.'

Leaning to one side, with one hand flat on the round table and the other on the arm of her chair, she shuffles her bottom forward and then, rocking her weight forward over her feet, she stands unsteadily. She's misjudged it and her weight is too far forward; she tries to put one foot in front, to halt the momentum, but doesn't manage it quickly enough. Her fingers fumble to grip the occasional table but it is an unstable three-legged affair. Dawn is on her feet, her hands out, and balance is re-established.

'Mum, you nearly fell again.' She says it as kindly as she can, to counteract the unexpected fury raging in her gut.

'I just missed my step, which is not a fall. Don't exaggerate.'

'Okay, walk to the kitchen then,' Dawn challenges her, trying to calm her own unexpected internal response.

'That's where I'm going. I think I have a nice leek and potato pie in the freezer, or I have some stuffed potato skins that were on offer. No fresh beans, I'm afraid. You didn't tell me you were coming round.'

'Watch each step, Mum.' Dawn follows her mother, arms out, one either side, ready to catch her.

'And a lemon cheesecake for afters.'

'It must be off by now, Mum – you've been eating that for weeks.'

'The lemon cheesecake?'

'Yes.'

'Well, it lasts for ages, doesn't it, in the freezer? Oh, I don't know why but just coming in from the other room has tired me out.'

She grasps the edge of the cheap pine kitchen table and pulls out a chair, but as she lowers herself onto it she misjudges it. 'Oh!' she cries, lurching to one side, but Dawn is there to catch her and sit her upright again.

'You okay, Mum?' she says, and there is the rage again. It makes no sense. And it's very unkind.

'I'm fine.' Mum sits carefully with guidance.

'You nearly fell again!' Dawn squats to look her in the face, forcing her own feelings down.

'I didn't, don't fuss.' She will not make eye contact.

'What if you fall tomorrow and there's no one here to catch you? What then?'

'I won't, don't be so silly. Just give me a moment and I'll get the pie out.'

'I'm worried, Mum. What if you do fall? Maybe the incident with the Damart catalogue has shaken you. Maybe in a few days you'll be fine but right now I think you need someone to be here with you, for a few days.'

'Can you take the time off work? The pie's in the second drawer down in the freezer.' She points in the direction of the back door but makes no effort to stand.

'No, I can't, not with this new supervisor.' Dawn struggles to open the freezer door. It needs defrosting.

'And peas, bring out the peas.'

Dawn puts the pie in the oven and the peas on the stove, and is about to sit.

'Let's not have steerage, eh?' Mum says and points to the cupboard on the back wall where she keeps the lidded bowls and other serving dishes she has collected over the years from charity shops. The pie must be served onto plates before it comes to the table, or else it needs a presentation plate of its own. The jars of mustard, hollandaise sauce and ketchup from the fridge are arranged on saucers, each with a teaspoon. Dawn plays by the rules. Usually she does it without a thought – it's as it has always been, as it was when she was small – but occasionally it strikes her as pretentious. Mother was brought up on a council estate, after all, in the poorest part of Bradford.

'Did you see we've got a postcard from Amanda?' Mum chirps. 'The boys are doing so well at school, top of the class for Carl. I think Lucas is a little jealous, and even though they can't manage without her they've finally cut down Amanda's hours at the hospital. She works such long hours, I do worry that she puts herself under too much pressure.'

Dawn nods and makes the right noises. She stares out of the window at the flat, grey sky. The weather has turned cold and she wouldn't be surprised if there was a frost. It's a way off yet but it's been many years since they had a white Christmas. It would be nice to have a white Christmas, like they had when she was a child. Didn't they?

'I think the pie's burning.' Mum makes no attempt to stand so Dawn gets up and puts the food into the serving vessels. Mum fusses with the cork mats they are to stand on. Then Dawn sits and waits for the complaint that the plates are not hot enough, but it doesn't come today. The food is chewed mostly in silence, with only a brief exchange about the new brand of hollandaise sauce. But as Dawn puts her knife and fork together she notices that Mum has hardly eaten a thing.

'The potatoes and leeks are good,' she encourages her. 'Try them, leave the pastry.' But Mum just pushes her pie about the plate.

The lemon cheesecake has seen better days but at least Mum will eat that; she's always had a sweet tooth.

'I'll just give it a second in the microwave, Mum, so it's not so frozen.'

But today Mum does not eat dessert either, and she demands coffee instead, freshly ground and filtered, but when it's made she fails to actually drink any.

'How much have you had to drink today, Mum?' Dawn asks as they settle back in the television room. The dishwasher hums away in the kitchen – a comforting sound that makes the place feel more lived in.

'Same as usual. A coffee here and there.'

'You drink too much coffee. Have you had any water?'

'You know I don't drink water.'

'Well, you should.'

'Don't fuss.'

'Listen, Mum, I need to go home. There are things I need to do.' This isn't true, but Dawn just doesn't want to be here. She wants her own space, her own things about her. 'Are you are all right, will you be all right tomorrow?'

'I'll be fine. A good night's sleep will see me right.'

'Shall I help you to bed?' Dawn offers.

'It's a bit early.'

'Yes, but – well, there are the stairs.' It's selfish to put her own needs first. 'I tell you what, I'll stay a little longer and then see you up the stairs.'

'No need.'

Dawn settles back into her seat. A repeat of her soap opera comes on and she relishes the chance to escape, even though she has already seen it. But two minutes into it, Mum says, 'Drivel,' and changes the channel to something about a man sailing a raft down the canals to London to deliver a piano. Although annoyed about missing her soap, Dawn is interested in this mad scheme. The presenter is just about to speak to the raft owner himself, who comes from a nearby town, when Mum pipes up again – 'What stupid things some people do!' – and the channel is changed again to some old black-and-white film. The film holds Mum's attention, and Dawn retreats behind a magazine from the sofa.

By the time the film has finished Mum is yawning, and Dawn encourages her up the stairs to bed. She looks old and frail, taking up only part of her half of the big double bed. Dad watches over her sternly, framed in silver on the bedside table; the sheets on his side are smooth, undisturbed.

'Mum, I'm going to make you some sandwiches for lunch tomorrow and I'll leave out five mugs, each with a teaspoon of coffee in them, or a teabag. That way you can keep track of how much you've drunk and eaten, okay?'

'Pass me my book, dear.'

'Did you hear me?' There is a grunt. 'Goodnight, Mum, I'll come after work tomorrow.'

'Hmmmm.' Mum fumbles with her glasses and opens the book.

Dawn's phone beeps, a text from June.

Hope you have 'naughty' reasons for missing pub quiz? Hilary and I failed miserably, as per always ;-)

The new supervisor is pushing her weight around the following day and all the staff are complaining about her, even the canteen staff. On top of that, there are way too many emails in Dawn's inbox, the first of which is about Hogdykes Abattoir, and the annual inspection that is due. She forwards the email to several

25

colleagues – someone else can deal with it. There's a new case for her to look into today – a complaint about a house with too many dogs and rabbits being kept in unsanitary conditions over in Little Lotherton. Dawn has not been there before, and on the map it looks to be out in the middle of nowhere, a single street of mill cottages backing onto the moors and farmland. It actually turns out to be not a million miles away from Hogdykes Abattoir.

'That has to be the smallest village ever,' Dawn mutters to herself as she looks more closely. It's an old map and it shows a stream running down one side of the street. One plot of land is bigger than the rest – that will be where the mill was originally. The cottages will have been built for the millworkers, but who would want to live so far from anywhere in this day and age, and how would they earn a living? She'll have to drive out there to take a look, check out the validity of the complaint. A day in the country, away from Ms Moss, her new boss. Maybe she could even stretch it to a pub lunch.

The little car starts with ease. It feels good, liberating, to be out of the office. The roadmap is open on the passenger seat but she doesn't refer to it for the first part of the journey – she has a good general idea where the village is located.

The route to Little Lotherton takes her out of Keighley's granite streets and into open countryside, along the Aire Valley, following the train tracks that snake along the valley bottom. Hills rise up on either side – sheep in fields neatly divided into squares by dark drystone walls on one side, and the rugged open moors on the other.

Dawn passes through a number of villages, and now she has to stop often to consult her map. She is not the best of map readers.

'Ah,' she exclaims as she eventually crosses over the train tracks. To her right is signposted Greater Lotherton. She wants to go the other way – Little Lotherton is reached by a lane off to the left here somewhere.

'There you are!' Dawn spots the exit, then turns the car off the main road and up a narrow cobbled lane. There's an old red phone box on the corner, of the type that you don't see much these days. Cars are parked intermittently all the way up on the right-hand side, which means if she drives up she will have to reverse back down; the street is not wide enough for her to turn around. She leaves her car at the bottom, and her cardigan flaps in the wind as she climbs out. She should have brought a coat, but the office is kept so warm and it always fools her. She wraps the thin knitted fabric around her. The narrow pavement is made up of large old flagstones, worn here and there for puddles to gather, tidelines showing where these have evaporated again and again. The street is a steady incline.

'Which makes sense if there's a stream at the back of these houses,' Dawn observes.

The cottages are on two levels, built of blackened stone, with tall narrow windows on the upper floors to give maximum light. These are old weaving cottages, built some two hundred years ago. One up, one down, and an outhouse behind. It's extraordinary to think that looms once dominated these upper floors and the families lived in such cramped conditions below.

Near the top is a house that must be the place she has been called out to see. The windows are dark, as if things are piled up in front of them on the inside, and where the front door should be is a wardrobe, which acts as a rudimentary porch. But it is the smell that really gives it away. The stench is nauseating as she approaches and Dawn thinks she might be physically sick. She pulls her cardigan over her nose and mouth but it doesn't help much. The cottages are set back a little from the street, and each has a very narrow strip of garden in front, edged by a low stone wall. Most of these gardens are neatly tended, and one or two are overflowing with flowers. Others are no more than a patch of earth and gravel. There are no flowers in front of the house she has come to inspect.

She leans over the wall and knocks. The wardrobe rattles and inside the house several dogs bark, but no one comes to the door.

'Excuse me?' Dawn calls to an elderly man who is opening a window in the house next door.

'What d'you want?' He eyes her suspiciously.

'Dawn Todman, Health and Safety. Bradford Council. Do you know if anyone's in?' She knows the title she has just given herself is not wholly accurate, but past experience has proved that it gives her the gravitas to get the job done.

'Health and Safety? 'Bout time you did summit 'bout 'im. Hundreds of dogs he has, and rabbits! It's not nice. Not proper.' He seems a little more friendly now.

'Well, I've heard several dogs barking. Where does he keep the rabbits – inside?'

'No, round back.'

There are several cages at the back of the house, rough-looking home-made affairs, stacked two and three high. The rabbits look well enough, except one that is so large it can hardly turn in its cage.

Dawn had a rabbit called Jemima when she was a child – Myma for short.

'Place is overrun with the creatures,' the neighbour grumbles.

'How many dogs are there?' She looks towards the house as the wind changes.' And what's the smell?' she exclaims, holding the sleeve of her cardigan over her nose.

'That's what I'm saying, it's not right. I have to live with that!' The man sounds triumphant. 'That's what happens when you have too many animals inside.'

'Is it coming from the house?'

'So now you can get rid of them animals, and get rid of that bloody Cyril too!'

'I think there might be a need to get rid of the animals if that's what's causing the smell.' Dawn turns, eager to get away from the stench. 'I'll write a report and see what can be done.'

Cases involving animals are tricky. If her feedback to her boss is too strong and it is decided that the occupier cannot continue to live as he is doing, then there is a good chance that the animals will be put down. She must tread carefully.

'Write a report! Bloody typical. You need to get shut of them animals, not write any report. What good will that do!'

'I have to follow procedures, Mr ...?'

'Brocklethwaite.'

'Well, Mr Brocklethwaite, I'll write my report and proper steps will be taken.' She puts her cardigan over her nose again. 'That's bad, isn't it,' she says.

'Aye, and I have to live with it while you go off and write your bloody report.' Mr Brocklethwaite stands on his doorstep, hands thrust deep in his pockets.

Back in the office, Dawn words her report so as to emphasise that the animals appear to be in good health, hoping that by focusing on this she might spare them death. It may be possible to rehome the dogs, although she didn't manage to get even a glimpse of any of them. It's the rabbits that will be more of a problem, she stresses.

How she had hugged and petted her Myma when she was little. Myma – she was her confidante, an ally to whom she had whispered her secrets, voiced her stifled frustrations about Mum, promised that she would become a vet and earn enough money to liberate all Myma's relations at the pet shop.

Dawn looks up from her report. 'I got her when I was seven and she died when I was' – she looks at the ceiling, trying to recall – 'seventeen.' Ten years she had had the rabbit, and she can still remember her heartbreak when she came to feed Myma one morning and found her curled in her bed, her grey muzzle not twitching, her lungs still.

With a sharp intake of breath, she realizes her thoughts have wandered from her work and she looks across at her supervisor's cubicle, partitioned in glass. Ms Moss is on the phone. She doesn't look so fierce when she smiles, but just as Dawn is thinking this Ms Moss catches her watching and the smile is gone, her face blank. She swivels her chair around to face the window.

A glance at the clock on the wall shows that time has slowed down. Dawn reflects that she should have taken longer when she was out, sat in the car a while.

'I have to go out now. If anything urgent comes up, leave a note on my desk. I'll deal with it tomorrow.' Ms Moss emerges from her glass box, pulling on her coat. Her heels click as she marches out of the office.

Sighs are heard from all corners of the open-plan office, and yawns and stretching noises follow. Dawn looks at the clock again. She should go, see if Mum is all right. She waits a few minutes, long enough to be sure her supervisor has definitely gone, and bundles her coat up, carrying it in front of her, pressed against her stomach, hidden by her flapping cardigan, and she takes the door to the toilets. There are no lifts here but there is a staircase, and as soon as the door behind her has swung shut she starts down the stairs that lead to the garage under the building. The place is only half full of cars, which shows how many people leave early, and now she is one of them.

The smell of yesterday's leek and potato pie is mixed with the permanent aroma of old coats and dusty carpets. Nothing has moved in the room by the back door, and in the kitchen the sandwiches sit untouched, their corners curling on the plate on the table; the tea and coffee mugs are undisturbed. She listens, and her hunched shoulders relax a little when she hears the television is on.

'Mum?' she calls out over the sound of it.

'Who's there?' The old voice sounds frightened.

'It's only me, Mum – Dawn.'

Mum is sitting in her usual chair, television remote in her hand. She looks smaller today, for some reason. 'You haven't drawn the curtains? How are you?' Dawn has to shout over the adverts, which Mum has not muted.

'I feel so tired.' She gives the appearance of having melted into the chair.

'Shall I plump up your cushion?' Dawn takes the remote and turns the sound down.

'My back hurts.' Mum speaks in her normal voice; there is no need to shout now the sound is muted.

'Well, judging by the uneaten sandwiches and the coffee cups, you've been sitting here all day. No wonder it hurts. Come on, get up.'

'In a minute.'

'Never mind in a minute, you've had all day. Why did you not drink anything?'

'I did.'

'You didn't.'

'I did.' Her trembling hand indicates a tiny sherry glass on the round table beside her.

'Mum. Listen.' Dawn squats to put her hands on Mum's knees, and looks her in the face. 'You've neither eaten nor drunk anything. I really think the Damart incident has knocked you for six. I'm going to call in a favour so someone can be with you tomorrow and Thursday, then I'll be here for Friday and the weekend and we'll see how you are after that. Okay?'

'I managed fine today, didn't I? I didn't fall.'

'You didn't move and you didn't drink, and you'll be dehydrated. I'll make some tea but you really need to drink more than that.'

She leaves Mum to fiddle with the remote, goes through to check the sideboard in the dining room. This room is rarely used – once a year at Christmas, but not in recent years. A layer of dust shows Dawn how long it has been since she was there to give everything a proper clean. The sherry bottle is almost empty; she will get more. Mum has so few vices – a drop of sherry and a square of chocolate will do more good than harm at her age. She takes a swig straight from the bottle, and then another. A picture of Dad scowls down at her from the wall.

'I don't know what you're staring at.' She pulls her cardigan around her to hide her overhanging stomach. The void is never filled by food or drink, no matter how sweet it is, but it does somehow take the edge off. Mildly curious, she opens the sideboard cupboard, which is filled with glasses, and there is also a bottle of fizzy fruit juice.

'Hmm, how long have you been there?' She picks up the juice and reads the label. There is no sell-by date. After pouring a thimbleful, she first sniffs and then sips. 'It's fine, she'll think it's wine.'

She fills a glass and takes it back through, and to her delight Mum drinks it relatively quickly. A mischievous glint in her eye confirms that she thinks it is wine and that she has been 'naughty'. Dawn takes the glass from the room, refills it and returns it to the round table with a conspiratorial wink.

'See if there's any frozen sweetcorn, dear. I'm not sure what else there is ... Oh, we can have those stuffed potato skins that I got on offer!'

'Your freezer is stuffed, Mum, and the shelves over the microwave are bending under the weight of cans and packets. There's enough food to feed you for months.

'I fancy the potato skins.'

'I'll go and start everything off.'

Once the sweetcorn is waiting in a pan to be heated, and the peas too, and the potato skins are in the oven with the plates, she picks up the house phone and looks in her bag for her diary to find the number she needs.

'Time to call in that favour.' She dials Janet's number. It rings once and is picked up. The television blares into life and she holds her hand up to her free ear.

'Hello, it's Dawn. No – Health-and-Safety-and-everything-else Dawn ... Yes, that's the one ... Yes, fine. I'm so glad. No, actually, I have a bit of a favour to ask in return ...'

She can see Mum through the kitchen door, down the hall, as she speaks, noting the curve of the old woman's spine, rounded by the years, the slight lump at the back of her neck – a touch of osteoporosis – but always a jumper to match her skirt, always jewellery, no matter how cheap, chosen to match the colours of the day. Today she is in reds and browns.

She explains the situation to Janet, who says she will see what she can do, and not to worry – there are ways of jumping the queue and getting things done, and she'll send someone round tomorrow. It seems it was a good call – she knows the right person to ask, and Dawn is assured that what Janet promises will actually happen.

'Okay, Mum' – she turns the television down – 'there's a lady coming round tomorrow to help you.' She crouches in front of her, looking her in the eye to be sure she has made contact.

'I have just jumped the six-month NHS waiting list for you, so don't mess it up.' She says this last part as a joke; she can introduce humour now. Knowing that someone else is going to help takes the strain away and she suddenly feels huge relief.

'I don't really need anyone,' Mum says, standing with some effort and making her way down the hall to the kitchen. 'Is there any more of that wine?' she asks.

'You've had two glasses, Mum,' Dawn teases, delighted that the fruit juice has been drunk. 'Did you bring your glass?' Mum looks back the way she came and sighs.

'I'll get it,' Dawn says. On her way there and again on her way back her phone beeps.

'Damn!' She does not have to read the text to know it is June, and that she has missed her watercolour evening class.

'Damn,' she mutters again.

Sitting down to eat, Mum seems to come to life a little.

'No napkins, dear?' she asks. 'These plates are not very warm,' she adds, 'and can you get out the hollandaise sauce?'

Normally these comments would rile Dawn, but today she is glad to see Mum back to normal.

'So, are we clear?' she says between mouthfuls of potato skin. They are mushy and remind her of baby food. 'To give yourself a break to get over this fall, we've got you in the NHS loop, so let's keep you there. You know how these things are, once you are on the radar then all sorts of services become available, but drop out and you'll be back on the six-month waiting list. We need to keep you in the system. We don't know what the future holds.'

'Can I have a spoon for the hollandaise, please?'

Chapter 3

The first email of the day tells Dawn that she must organise the notices for the man who is living with all the dogs and rabbits, to give him warning that he must reduce the number of animals in and around the house or action will be taken. It would take her but a moment to print them out, put them in an envelope and post them. But if she were to go there again today, maybe she would get lucky and gain access and see if she can get a count on how many dogs there are. She yawns, and it crosses her mind to take her coffee break early and merge her lunch with her outing to Little Lotherton, and basically spend the whole day out of the office, maybe write up her report in the half hour before home time. If she goes to the canteen for her coffee break now, Hilary will not be busy at this hour and she can explain how she came to miss quiz night on Monday, see if Hilary can remember any of the questions. She presses *Print* on her computer and collects the sheets from the printer by the door, and she is almost surprised to find herself stepping into the lift and down to her car. Hilary and the canteen can wait. She needs to get outside, get out of town, become lost in the rolling countryside on the way to Cyril's house.

She was hoping the drive to Little Lotherton would be a mindlessly blank experience, with her maybe even finding a takeaway coffee before leaving the last remnants of civilisation. That way, it might be possible to make the process of waking up fully nothing more than a slow, gentle struggle. The sleeping pill that she took last night at around two in the morning as a last desperate bid to sleep is still in her system. Consequently she is struggling to surface at all. It is not the first time this has happened, and every time she naturally questions whether it would just be better not to have slept at all.

These thoughts kick her mind awake into a sluggish but feverish state of worry. The drive to Little Lotherton becomes a stew of churning over the same concerns about her mum that kept her awake the night before.

'The woman is nearly eighty,' she reasons with herself. 'But the truth is you don't know if it was the fall. What she's experiencing is probably only temporary.' She glances in the rear-view mirror. But then, what if it isn't temporary? What if this is the start of a slow decline? She cannot rule that out. Then what happens? Her mind keeps returning to the fact that she will be greatly inconvenienced – she has already missed quiz night with Hilary and her old friend June, and her watercolour class with the latter, the only two nights she ever goes out, the only two social events she has. This thinking immediately brings a wave of self-condemnation.

'How selfish can you get!' she tells herself. 'Where is your compassion? This is your mother you are resenting!' Mentally she takes control, but her gut is suddenly churning with anger.

Her bag slips off her shoulder as she gets out of the car at Little Lotherton, and her phone jumps out of her hand and under the passenger seat.

'Keep calm, keep a clear head, everything is fine,' she tries to convince herself. 'Just please God, don't let Mum be grouchy with the woman from the NHS.'

She wills her message across the cloud-filled sky to Mum as she retrieves her phone. Struggling to free her arm, which is still looped through the seatbelt, she tells herself again to be calm. Her navy-blue cardigan, which sags a little at the pockets, flaps open with a gust of wind and the seatbelt will not behave, so, leaving the door partly open and the seat belt hanging out, she straightens up and turns around to look over to the house. If she can hand over the paper this could be a quick visit, and there might be time for a pub lunch before heading back to the office.

A foreign woman is standing at the front door, looking like she has just knocked and is awaiting an answer.

'He in?' Dawn asks.

'I am sorry. To whom are you referring?' The woman clearly enunciates her words; English is clearly not her first language. She has a pretty face and her clothes are a riot of rich colours. With delicate fingers she carefully loops her scarf over her head. Dawn checks her printed notes for the man's name. On one of the sheets from the file, someone has written in the margin in pencil *Nickname – Septic Cyril*. Is that what people call him, or is this how he likes to be referred to? Surely not. She wouldn't like to be called 'Septic' – but then, each to their own. Besides, her brain is still foggy from lack of quality slumber and undigested sleeping pills and she cannot think straight.

'Him. Septic Cyril.' Dawn points at the wardrobe and hopes the name causes no offence.

'I'm from Health and Safety.' She knows this title is not exactly accurate but she also knows that it carries weight in these sorts of circumstances and it might just bring the whole issue to its conclusion more quickly.

She blinks slowly and wishes she was back in bed. The whole problem of a few too many dogs and rabbits suddenly seems so tiring and trivial compared to Mum's situation at home. How much help can she get on the National Health Service? The whole NHS is massively under-resourced – what if they cannot cover the hours she is at work? What if every hour she is not at work she has to be there to care for Mum?

'It can't go on.' Dawn did not intend to say this out loud, and she hides her embarrassment by looking down at her notes. 'Him and his animals, people complaining,' she adds, hoping that she doesn't sound too unreasonable. The wind changes, lifting the woman's scarf from her forehead, and the stench blows over them both.

'God, how can you stand so close? Can you not smell him? Mind you, p'raps it smells much the same where you come from.' She does not mean to be rude – it just comes out. She seems to have lost control over her own mouth. It is the sort of thing Mum might say, but for Dawn herself to utter such a thing shocks her.

'I beg your pardon?' The woman is rightly indignant.

What had she meant anyway, Dawn wonders? What little piece of indoctrinated racism had pushed her to say such a thing? Perhaps the drains are open in India or Pakistan, or wherever this woman once lived, but even so it is petty-minded to think that because of that she would be used to such a smell. This is thinking in Mum's terms.

'I'm not racist!' Mum would blurt out, 'but you know what they're like!'

Dawn can feel her cheeks burning. Perhaps she should apologise, but this might just make it worse, and anyway her thoughts are back again with Mum. She looks at her phone to see if there are any messages or missed calls, then drops it into her bag.

'So, is he in or not?'

If he isn't, she will pass by Mum's before returning to the office, check it's all going well. The wind changes direction again.

'Oh my God, the stink!' She pulls the sleeve of her cardigan over the end of her hand and holds it against her nose, waiting for the woman to answer. When she doesn't Dawn tries again to explain herself.

'Look, I don't know who you are but I'm Dawn Todman, from Health and Safety. I've an order here as we've been given to understand that he has a lot of rabbits.' She checks her paperwork to confirm that this is not the first time this Septic Cyril has been challenged about his pets. 'Again,' she adds. 'And if he has they've got to go, again, and we need to limit the number of dogs.' She says all this with her sleeve still over her nose and she holds out a bunch of papers to the woman.

'He is out,' the woman says, maintaining eye contact with a steady gaze.

'Oh.' This throws Dawn, but then, through the remnants of last night's fog-inducing sleeping pills, she realises that this means she could come out again tomorrow to deliver the papers, which gives her another opportunity to check on Mum in the middle of the day! This could work in her favour.

Her cardigan flaps around her as she heads back to the car. However, it is no surprise to her that, at the last moment, with a sudden desire not to abuse her position and wheedle another day out of the office, she pushes the bundle of papers at the woman on Cyril's doorstep.

'Give him these. Have him read them. He'll have to get rid of all them poor animals,' she says.

'No,' the woman in the scarf says. There is neither strength nor aggression in the word. Her tone is quite flat.

'What? Did you not understand me?' Dawn is puzzled, and a little taken aback by this response.

'I understood and I said no,' the woman says, still calm. This riles Dawn; the last thing she needs is someone making her life more difficult than it already is.

'Listen, luv, I have authority here. I'm from Health and Safety.' She knows this is a lie, she has no authority, but the urge to leave and see Mum is growing stronger. She just needs to wrap this up and use the time to make a quick check on how it's all going with the woman from the NHS. Maybe she could phone, but Mum will say whatever she thinks Dawn wants to hear.

The woman outside Cyril's house is staring at her with wide eyes.

'He needs to get rid of them animals and these papers make it so he has to. You don't want to live next to that stink. Do you?'

Dawn sighs out her words; it all feels like the situation needs greater effort than she has the energy for.

'So you give them to him, right?' Dawn pushes the papers at the woman again, but without conviction. She is nearing the point where she no longer cares.

'You are police?' the woman asks.

'No, I work for the government. Health,' Dawn replies, speaking very slowly, and a bit too loud. 'And. Safety. Do you understand?' She wonders how good the woman's English really is; perhaps she does not understand.

'I do not believe you have authority over me, so I give no one papers,' the woman says.

'Oh, for God's sake.' Dawn says, but she is thinking about how she will present her feedback if she has not contacted the owner or seen the dogs. It looks like her afternoon will be spent in the office struggling to justify the time she has spent in Little Lotherton and the little she has achieved. Ms Moss will read it over and then there will follow a lecture about what she should and shouldn't have done to serve the papers. Perhaps she should have just posted them. She raises and drops her arms, the papers flapping against her knees as her hands come to rest. Maybe she can post them now.

'Is there a letterbox in that thing?' She looks over at the wardrobe porch.

The woman steps to one side so that Dawn can see that there is no place to leave her paperwork.

'Anyway, if he's out then what're you doing standing there?' Dawn says. Maybe if she just pushes a bit she can get this woman to be helpful. She rests the hand and her papers on her hip, and tries to tame her hair with the other hand, fighting the wind that whips the loose strands across her face. She should have washed it this morning; it feels lank. Every time it gets to this stage she puts off shampooing in her indecision about whether to dye it blonde again or go natural. Consequently, three quarters of its length is blonde and the roots are a natural mousy grey.

She waits for an answer, but when the woman doesn't reply she suddenly feels exhausted by life and returns to the car. Today she does not have the energy. She will come again tomorrow.

She backs her car hesitantly down the cobbled street, narrowly missing a vehicle parked at the bottom. As she turns onto the main street towards Greater Lotherton, her phone rings and she pulls over to answer.

'Hello? Yes, this is Dawn Todman ... What? I don't understand. Why? ... Oh no – but why? ... But she didn't ask you to come – I did! ... No, sorry, I didn't mean to raise my voice.' Dawn looks out of the window, over the top of the drystone wall and across the moors. A bird hovers high in the air, looking at something invisible on the ground. The cloud-filled sky has turned a beautiful dark blue-grey and the colours of the bracken, in their autumn hues, range from an intense chocolate-brown to a pale straw. With the phone between her shoulder and ear, she rearranges the papers on the passenger seat.

'No, I understand. Did she have any lunch, a drink, anything? ... No, okay, right. No I'm sure you did the best you could. I'm so sorry she was rude to you.'

She disconnects the call and throws the phone towards her bag in the footwell.

'Stupid woman!' she curses. The hovering bird swoops to the ground and is lost from sight.

The first drop of rain hits the windscreen as she starts to drive towards Mum's house. Really, she should call in to work to ask if she can go and resolve the problem, but she doesn't want the supervisor knowing everything about her private life. Mum is her own business, and besides, no one will be the wiser if she just makes a detour on the way back to the office.

'Mum?' she calls out sharply as she pushes in through the back door. 'Mum?' she repeats, dropping her car keys and bag on the kitchen table.

She peels her coat off as she makes her way through to the television room.

'Mum!' Mum is dozing but Dawn has every intention of waking her with a start.

'Hmm, what? What is it?' Mum's head rolls as she lifts her chin from her chest. Her eyes are wide, scared, the irises pale with age. She does not seem to be focusing properly but Dawn is too angry to care.

'Mum, why did you send the NHS woman away?' Dawn demands, hands on her hips.

'That cardigan doesn't suit you.'

'Mum! The NHS lady?'

'Oh, she was fussing, so I sent her home.'

'I called in a big favour to jump you to the front of the waiting list! Six months long, it is. Now what are we going to do? I can try calling again but I think once you are off you are off. Why, Mum? Seriously – why?'

'I don't need their help.'

'Have you had breakfast or lunch?'

'I'm not hungry.'

'See what I mean. Have you had a cup of tea? Drunk anything?'

'I was just going to make tea, do you want some?'

'Mum, it's mid-afternoon, you need to drink throughout the day. Bladder infections are not fun. Oh, Mum.'

Energy flagging, Dawn sits heavily.

'Is it time for *Midsomer Murders*?'

Dawn does not bother to answer. After sitting motionless through two muted adverts she pulls herself up out of the chair and returns to the kitchen to put the kettle on and find her phone. A quick call confirms that Janet cannot pull the same strings twice, but she can get Mum assessed in two months' time. She apologises, but this is the best she can do.

Dawn thanks her, puts her phone away and opens the bottom drawer, remembering as she does so that she finished the chocolate yesterday. She has a little rummage under a stack of letters, mostly bills and cloth serviettes, and is rewarded with another family-size chocolate bar, unopened. Fruit and nut. She must go shopping, get more of the fruit juice Mum thinks is wine, and chocolate and more tins of soup. She needs to get some fluid into Mum or the whole situation is going to get worse.

Chapter 4

There's only a drop of sherry left, so Dawn decants the fruit juice into the sherry bottle and takes a glass and a cup of tea through to Mum in the television room.

'I'm going to ring Amanda,' Dawn says, setting the tea and the fruit juice down on the round table. Mum's feet are up on a footstool. Her crooked fingers reach for the wine glass, curling around the stem and lifting it to her lips. She takes a long drink and when she puts the glass down Dawn fills it up again.

'You can't, she's in Australia.'

'They have phones there too.'

'You can't afford it.'

'Seeing as you sent the NHS woman packing, we need to think of something else, so this is the consequence,' Dawn retorts, but she decides to make the call in the kitchen.

'Amanda? Hi. No, she's fine ... Well, when I say fine, I mean she's still breathing and domineering as usual.' She absent-mindedly picks up a pen and starts to doodle on the cover of an old magazine as she relates events to date.

'So we now have no help,' she concludes at last. 'There's a private agency who will send someone for as many or as few hours as you like but they charge twenty-five pounds an hour. Yes, exactly. I should see if I can get a job there!' She laughs dryly. 'But seriously, I have nothing, and Mum as you know has no savings, just her tiny pension, and she needs that for food and bills, so I wondered if you can manage to pay for the care? I know it's a big ask but ... Oh ... I see ... So the hours they released you from are not an option? ... Oh, that doesn't sound so great. But never mind, Braxton ... Oh, really? You never said in your postcard ... No, of course, you're right – Mum would only have worried. But are you guys all right? If things are that bad, would it not be an idea to move to a smaller house, somewhere cheaper? ... No, I understand the boys have friends and their school, I was just – Yes, of course, I'm not there. Okay, so basically there's no money anywhere for private help.'

Dawn has drawn a moustache and an eyepatch on the face of the minor celebrity who graces the magazine's front cover.

'I understand ... Yes, it's Mum's phone. Yes, it will be costing a lot so I'd better go. Bye.'

She puts the phone back in its cradle.

'So,' she muses, 'your perfect world, in perfect Australia, with your big house and the flashy hospital, is not so perfect after all.'

She looks at the photograph on the wall of Amanda and her children by their pool in front of their enormous house in bright sunshine. It seems so unlikely that she will be struggling for twenty-five pounds here and there, but maybe it's even worse than she said. Maybe Amanda was not telling the whole truth, just like she herself was not. Sixteen years she has been doing her dead-end job in Health and Safety for the promise of a pension, but she isn't stupid, so pound by pound, pay packet by pay packet, she has saved. It's not much, and the amount has only grown slowly, but it's all she has. She has done the sums, and if she keeps saving at the rate she is doing she will be way too old to go back to college to train as a vet by the time she has enough. But the hope keeps her saving. Maybe when she has enough she will travel around the world instead, or maybe – although this is very unlikely, as she will be too old to get a mortgage – she could buy her own place and give notice on the tiny two-roomed flat she rents above the Indian takeaway.

When she got the job, she would have taken any flat going just to get away from home, and she had overlooked the smell of damp and the peeling wallpaper, telling herself that of course it wasn't permanent. But somehow, once she had moved in and the novelty of having her own place had passed, the idea of moving again seemed less and less important to her and – well, she quite enjoyed decorating it all those years ago, and now she is used to the way she has to lift the kitchen door to make it shut, the curry smells starting at six thirty every night, the hum and chatter of foreign voices coming through the floorboards till midnight, the creaking and clanking of the pipes as they perform their nightly clean-up ritual. Those noises were so exciting when she first moved in, making her a part of the world, not isolated from it, and those noises had given her the energy to make the best of the place with a few rolls of wallpaper and a coat of paint. But now the sounds, the groans and creaks, seem to signal age, and it's as if she and the flat are growing old together. After sixteen years, like it or not, it has become home, and the cheap rent has helped her save.

Well, she may have saved, but what she saves a month is not likely to be enough for a home help for Mum. And what she has in the bank is hers. She has fought hard for her nest egg – sacrificed nights out with work colleagues, and a pleasant place to live. It has cost her the finer things in life – new clothes, make-up, professional haircuts – and all for what? Enough in the bank to offer her some hope for her future. No, there is no way she is using her saving on Mum's care. But what else can she do? If she takes time off work to look after Mum she could lose her job and her pension, and her flat. It would mean living back with Mum, and she would have no job.

'God, no!' She draws a scar on the celebrity's forehead. But what else can she do? The only way she could afford to pay for a carer would be if she didn't have rent to pay, but she does. 'I'm not moving in here.'

She looks around the kitchen. There is much more space than in her tiny flat – but her tiny flat is hers, peeling wallpaper and all. Then she visualises the black mould under her sink and behind the bathroom door. Would she really be sorry to move? Isn't it just inertia that has kept her there? Inertia and the cheap rent?

Well, the other option would be to put Mum in a home, but she wouldn't wish that on anyone, and besides, that would mean selling Mum's house to pay for her care. And she's damned if that's going to happen. She has earned her share of this house, enduring years of Mum's put-downs and undermining comments. It doesn't even seem fair that perfect Amanda will get half. What did Mum ever give Amanda besides love and encouragement? Whereas all she, Dawn, ever got, at best, was looks of undisguised scorn. She was not in Amanda's league – not as bright, not as capable and, in short, not as lovable. She is owed the house; it will be the only good thing she ever got from Mum, and if Amanda is telling the truth about Braxton's failing business and the signs of recession in Australia, then maybe she will get to a point when she too needs her half of the value of Mum's house. Mercenary as it may seem, she must stay practical. Besides, it's not like Mum is going to die any time soon. There must be another solution.

'Back to the situation.' She sighs out loud, trying to keep herself focused. 'The house is not going to the government, so no nursing home, which means private help. I don't want to lose my job, or rather my pension, so the only logical solution is I move in here and pay for day care with the money I save by not paying rent. I can always rent a new flat when Mum feels better. A better flat, nearer work so I spend less on petrol.'

She looks around the kitchen again. The house is all right. When Mum and Dad bought it, it was as cheap as chips, but that was a lifetime ago. The area was not desirable back then. But now, what with the new school down the road getting a decent Ofsted report, and the new high-speed trains to both Leeds and Bradford, the town has become a middle-class dream. No, it's not the house that would be difficult to live with – it's Mum. How long has it taken for her to fight her way to feeling like she is worth at least something? How many self-help books has she had to read to even feel that she is good enough to do something normal like going to local evening classes? Actually, that's a good point – at the moment she walks to her watercolour class once a week, but if she moves in with Mum she'll have to drive.

She exhales heavily and blackens one of the celebrity's teeth, bracing herself for the conversation she needs to have about the future. Dawn vaguely recognises the face – it's someone off the TV, a minor character in one of the soap operas. What's his name? Joey? Jamie? Something with a 'J', anyway. Just visible down the hall, Mum is asleep, her chin on her chest, hands neatly folded in her lap. For a moment Dawn freezes, watches Mum's chest rise and fall, waits. Waits some more. Then a little sigh escapes Mum's lips and she rolls her head and blinks.

'Another glass of wine?' she says.

'Mum, we need to talk.' Dawn sits on the footstool at Mum's feet.

'My mouth is so dry.'

Dawn takes the sherry bottle from behind Mum's chair and fills her glass with fruit juice. The sparkly yellow liquid fizzes, and Mum reaches out her hand for it.

'Mum, you need someone to help you during the day.' She sits on the footstool again.

'Nonsense.'

'Okay, you don't, so can you go and put the tea on now, please?'

'Me? Can you not do it seeing as you're here?'

'Which proves my point, Mum. Before the Damart incident you were back and forth to the kitchen at the drop of a hat. Every time the adverts came on you were in there making a cup of tea, unpacking the dishwasher, repacking the dishwasher, planning meals, writing shopping lists, something, anything. You've always liked to potter. Now all you do is sit. So you need help, just for now. I don't want you to get malnutrition.'

The last part is said as a joke but she knows from work that people do – vulnerable people, the elderly.

'Well, I don't think I need any help, but if you insist you can get the woman from the NHS back. If it will please you.'

Dawn pulls a face, bites her lip. Sometimes she could throttle the woman.

'We can't get her back, Mum,' she says with forced calm. 'You've blown it. We're out of the NHS loop. Now it will cost.'

'I've no money,' Mum says lightly, as if the fact is of no consequence.

'No, none of us have any money, so the only way I can see that we can manage is if I stop paying rent and use the money on daycare.'

'Your landlord won't like that.'

'I mean I'll have to give up my flat.'

Mum has the wine glass to her lips but she pauses to say, 'But where will you live?'

'Oh God, Mum, can you not see that we are all stuck? I will have to live here.'

'Live here!' The horror in Mum's voice is evident. Dawn does not trust herself to speak but she cannot curb her fury.

'Well, if you hadn't been so rude to the NHS woman! I called in a favour for you!'

'I wasn't rude and I never asked you to call in any favour. Perhaps you should have asked me what I wanted first, before you play the martyr.'

'Mum, you told her to get out.'

'Well, she gave me a dessert spoon for my soup, which was tepid, and she ate her lunch, pineapple pieces, straight from the can while she walked about the kitchen.'

'Mum, these are not reasons to tell someone to get out, especially as they are here to help you. Did you offer her a bowl for her lunch, or invite her to sit with you? Did you ask for a soup spoon? Did you ask her to warm the soup a little more?'

'Now, just stop it, Dawn. You're getting on your high horse thinking you know better than everyone. You weren't here, and you didn't have to put up with her. D'you know, her name – her real name, mind – was Diamond! Diamond! I ask you. And she had a stud in the crease of her nose.'

Dawn wishes the fruit juice really was wine, because if it was, right now she would finish the bottle.

'What are we going to do, Mum?' She doesn't look up, leaves her head hanging, staring at the cheap rug that Mum bought some time in the last five years, which lies protectively over the expensive carpet that was laid years and years ago. Maybe one day this will be her lot in life too, her small income dwindling, her tastes becoming increasingly questionable, only she has no daughter to look after her. What will happen to her?

'I suppose you can live here.' Mum sighs as she speaks and it comes across as quite unkind, as if she is bracing herself for the offence. Then she changes tack and says with authority, 'Get the mail, will you. That's another thing that Diamond woman didn't do.'

'She's not a servant, Mum. She was here to help you get something to eat at lunchtime and drink enough liquids.'

'Well, the post would have been helpful. And lock the inner door after you've got it.'

Dawn goes into the hall and unbolts the inner door. They never use the front door, and the inner door is only ever opened to get the post. The entrance vestibule smells stale, and the wallpaper, a busy pattern of blue flowers, is peeling off in the corners just enough to show that someone old lives here, someone who lives alone, someone who is past caring about her surroundings. Then, as she scoops up half a dozen large envelopes, Dawn remembers her own peeling wallpaper, and as quickly as the thought arises and sends its tendrils of implication to every corner of her thoughts she kills it, blanks it out, focuses on the moment.

'They're all begging letters, Mum.' Dawn heads for the bin in the kitchen.

'Bring them here,' Mum barks. 'I don't like to see people suffer. Now where's my bag, I need my cheque book.'

Dawn feels the rumble of anger in her belly; adrenaline releases a power that comes surging up into her chest, hindering her breathing, before it courses down her arms and tightens the fingers of her left hand into a fist that scrunches the letters.

'I suffer too, Mum. Every day I work in that brain-dead job having missed my chance to be a vet, not because I wasn't capable but because you made me *feel* I wasn't capable. And worse, you made me feel I wasn't worthy. Every day I still believe what you've taught me, that I'm useless and unlovable. Taught me so well that I believe it to my very core.'

Dawn calls this from the safe distance of the kitchen. And then she adds, as she walks through the hall, 'I suffer, Mum, every day, so what about me, Mum?'

'You? What on earth about you? What are you babbling about? Are you making excuses for your life again? And for goodness' sake don't talk so fast, I can't make out a word you say when you talk that fast. Oh, you've creased them! What did you do that for? Now pass my bag.'

'I'm not giving up my flat to pay for help if you're giving your money away to any charity that asks,' Dawn says, facing her mum. Her hands tremble so she folds her arms to stop them.

'I beg your pardon. It's not your money to decide what I do with it. Pass my bag.'

Dawn doesn't move.

'I said pass my bag!' Her old watery eyes flash, and Dawn twitches, her limbs complying even though she has no wish to capitulate.

'Here's your bag, then!' She dumps it on Mum's knee and leaves the room.

Chapter 5

Last night, after tea – baked potato skins and lemon cheesecake – they watched one of the few films Mum has on DVD. She's seen them all a hundred times but with Mum's memory as it is, each time is as if it is the first. Dawn did a crossword puzzle in an old newspaper and read a bit of the book she has been reading for at least the last five years, from the bookcase by the television. Then she stood behind Mum to catch her if she fell, as she laboured her way upstairs to bed.

'It's my half-day tomorrow, Mum, so if you want to get up late I'll be back to help you,' Dawn suggested as she passed Mum her book from the bedside table.

'Why would I get up late?' Mum barked, and she took out the plate that holds her false tooth and dropped it in the glass of water on her bedside table. The little splash it made caused dark rings to spread on the wooden surface, adding to the pattern of a hundred other such times: white pockmarks of time.

'Goodnight, then.'

'Goodnight,' Mum replied without looking up from her book. The black hole where her tooth should have been was shockingly noticeable, reminding Dawn of the defaced magazine cover, and her age.

Dawn usually rises early on Fridays. It is her half-day and so, for this reason alone, more exciting than the rest of the week. Although she never has anything planned to fill the free afternoon, just having it feels like a luxury. This morning she is eager to get into the office; the whole situation with this Cyril person and his animals needs to be resolved, and quickly, to avoid the animals coming to harm. If she goes in this early, the car park will be empty and she will not end up driving round and round looking for somewhere to park in the street. Even Ms Moss won't be in her glass cubicle yet. Dawn will have time to get a coffee before she settles at her desk and then she will have all morning to find a solution for Cyril's animals. Although, what more can she actually do? She has sent on her account of her visit, and it's just a matter of waiting for a decision to come back from the powers that be and instructions as to what, if anything, they want her to do next. The truth is she has no power – she is just a gofer for those in their own private offices, ones with walls instead of partitions, people with grand job titles and proper salaries. If she was one of those people, with any power of her own, she would help people like Cyril who care for animals – give them a grant, maybe. But people like her and Cyril never do have the power.

Her motivation to get out of bed dwindles and she watches the second hand of her bedside clock move in little jerky spasms around the face, the hour she is contracted to be at her desk moving ever nearer. Finally, she flings the duvet back and lumbers from its warmth. There is still a nip in the air.

Pulling back the curtains reveals a white sky, flat with clouds but bright. It casts a strange light over everything, enhancing the greens of the trees that peek over the shops and houses opposite and turning the tarmac almost blue. It feels like a storm is coming.

If she doesn't shake a leg there will be a storm in the office, too – and there also needs to be a storm in her flat. She must give her notice and pack her belongings. Every surface in the little apartment is crammed. When she first moved in sixteen years ago she intended to live minimally, not buy anything, promising that she would wait until she got the flat of her dreams before investing in quality furniture. So she only bought a bed and a chair and that was all there was in her flat, apart from the couple of boxes of childhood treasures she had brought from home – mementos that were important to have but did not actually need opening. But as the weeks passed, the evenings after work seemed to grow longer and so, one day, more to pass the time than anything, she sat and unwrapped her collection of porcelain cats. Each retrieval brought with it memories of every coin that had come her way – at birthdays, Christmases, and, after she reached thirteen, from her Saturday paper round; it had all gone into her collection. She had hunted down the ceramic figures in charity shops and on bric-a-brac stalls. How she had loved her cats as a child, and would arrange and rearrange them. They were hers, and hers alone. She unpacked the figures in her flat, and arranged them carefully, but without intending to add to the collection.

She found the first addition – a strange, shiny black cat – in the window of the Oxfam shop next to the café where she sometimes had her lunch. Its tail was held so high, green eyes hand-painted on. That was the day the annual works outing was being arranged and, like the previous year, and the year before that, she had already made the decision not to spend the twenty-eight pounds it would cost, for the coach and the meal alone. Besides, she had been to Blackpool as a child and found it rather depressing. It had rained and nothing had been open and

Amanda had been in one of her moods, refusing to talk to her for some reason.

The arrangements for the works outing, and these memories in particular, left her feeling particularly lonely by lunchtime that day. So the china cat was her compensation, at the grand price of one pound fifty. She felt excited when she finished work, the wrapped porcelain in her bag, but she did not let herself look until she got home. Then, trying to capture the same excitement she experienced in her childhood, she ate her tea whilst looking at the bagged animal and surveyed the room to decide where it should go, delaying the gratification of the final reveal! Compared to most evenings, that was not a lonely one. She had mostly forgotten how she had been feeling as she arranged and rearranged the cats, and then it was suddenly time for bed. After this she started to keep her eyes open for lost china cats, and sure enough she came across them every now and again and her collection grew and grew.

'Oh, the time!'

Dawn interrupts her own thoughts and makes a dash for the shower.

It's interesting to be in a hurry. Normally she has so little to fill her hours she is early for everything. But this morning, by the time she gets to work, she feels quite animated by the speed she has driven at to get here on time, and by the dash up the stairs to her floor.

'Almost late,' Ms Moss comments as Dawn marches past the open door to her office.

'Sorry, my mum's had a fall ... I'm having to move in with her. So much to do.' She surprises herself by sharing this information. It feels part of the rush, as if being busy gives her importance, makes her interesting.

'Oh, so have you booked your time off?' Ms Moss says, not looking up from the papers she is reading, pen tapping.

Dawn slows and then stops.

'Time off?' Dawn asks, trying to sound casual.

'Policy. Two full days or four half-days.' The supervisor still doesn't look up.

'Because my mum had a fall?'

'No, to move.' Now Ms Moss looks up with the same expression of pity and false compassion on her face that Mum gives her when she compares her to Amanda.

'I don't need time off.' It's a defensive reaction and the moment it's out she regrets it – a couple of days off would help enormously.

'It's policy, take it.' Ms Moss looks back to her work and a wave of her pen dismisses Dawn.

'Four half-days or two full days?' Dawn deliberates as she searches through the system on her computer to find out how to book the days off.

In sixteen years she has never taken a day off, not even for the worst cold, not even when she had that weird fever a few years back. Her car broke down once and she was seriously late, but that was over five years ago now, when she had the old car. Two full days would be a nice freedom, but she'll need to give a month's notice on the flat so there is no need to rush the process. And besides, she wants to keep an eye on the Cyril Sugden case. She could not bear it if the dogs were put down because she failed to get something done for them, and that big rabbit needs rehousing. Now that's a thought: if she is to move to Mum's house, there is a garden and a shed ... Well, it would be lovely to have a rabbit again, and it would be compensation for having to live there.

The top email, which has been returned to her by all the colleagues she sent it to, is about Hogdykes. It's no surprise – who would want to go to an abattoir, especially one filled with aggressive, sexist men? She passes the hot potato on to another department; she knows she is only putting off the inevitable, but it will do for now.

A new email notification appears on her screen: *Re C. Sugden*. She clicks on the message and reads through it. It seems that there have been more complaints about the poor man – or rather, one person, Mr Brocklethwaite, has been round the other residents in the one-street village and got them to sign his petition. The complaint is mostly about the smell, but the smell has been linked to the animals and it seems that someone has decided that the rabbits must go. To make a decision on the dogs, someone, which she assumes will be her, will need to gain access to the house and report on the conditions that the animals are living in. Dawn is glad she laid more stress on the number of rabbits, which will be easier to rehome than the dogs. The email goes on to say that they have reason to believe that Cyril Sugden is a hoarder and it is well documented that this can attract rats, which may well be responsible for the smell. Attached is a letter that she is expected to print off and send to Cyril, requesting a voluntary clearing of his house. This will be followed by an inspection that will be made by Monday the fifth.

'Inspection!' Dawn scoffs.

What that means is they want her to go and see what has or has not been done and report back. But there is no real pressure; the department is notoriously slow. Although, thinking about it, sudden changes can happen with no warning. Reshuffles are not unknown, and when they happen they leave everyone feeling unsettled. Well, for the sake of the animals she would rather it is her than someone else who deals with C. Sugden. Better to take four half-days off so she can keep an eye on the situation.

She takes her time to print the letter and then heads to the canteen for a coffee. Hilary has had her hair done, and although the style doesn't really suit her Dawn compliments her on it. She's been here, serving in the canteen, even longer than Dawn has been with the council, and she always has a smile and a kind word.

'Hang on a minute, duck,' she says. 'I'll just serve these and then I'll sit with you. I'm due for me break.'

Dawn often drinks coffee with Hilary, and she doesn't care if there are those who consider it beneath them to sit with the dinner lady.

'Aw, will you miss your own home?' Hilary asks, sipping her tea.

'I'll miss my own space,' Dawn admits, but the spare room at Mum's, the room she used to share with Amanda, is bigger than the sitting room in the flat, and she will actually have more space overall.

'Yes, of course you will.' Hilary stirs in more sugar.

'Mostly I feel I have so much to do. I have to pack, obviously. But I also need to arrange to get these women to come round and care for Mum. Now, what is the name of the company – er ...'

'Ladies-in-Waiting? The local people, you mean?' Hilary offers.

'Yes, that's them.'

'Well, you better get a move on – they ask for an initial meeting and then you have to wait until they have someone free for the times you want. I went through the whole thing with my mother not long back. Now she was a difficult woman!'

'Oh, I didn't know your mum was poorly. I hope she's feeling better now.'

'No, but she's a lot easier to deal with! She's dead.'

This makes Hilary laugh, but the sound is hollow and there is a menace to the tone, and at the same time her eyes are misting over. There is such a mix of emotions, Dawn finds she has to look away. Hilary stops laughing; her face is blank now as if it is easier to have no emotion at all, and then she suddenly says, 'Oh, a customer,' and heaves herself up and hurries across to the canteen counter, leaving her tea.

Dawn sips the last of her own coffee, and for just the briefest of seconds she imagines how much easier her own mum will be to deal with when she is dead. And with no warning she is back there again. In the place she never allows herself to think about. The time Mum did the most unforgivable thing a mum can do. Or, rather, didn't do what any decent mum would have done. And why? There was no reason. None at all. If Dawn ever had questions in her mind about her place in Mum's affections, or Mum's thoughts about her, before then – well, after that inaction she had no doubt at all.

76

She had returned home, to her mum, looking for … no, needing – desperately needing safety and compassion. And three years after that, she found her tiny flat that no one else would rent, and she covered over the flapping raw emotional edges left by events and Mum's inaction with a smooth layer of cold, emotionless armour. She made a deal with life: she would ask for nothing as long as life asked nothing from her. She just wanted leaving alone. The horror she had been through, and Mum's reaction to it, had left her believing that she was lowest of what life spat out. For a while she had toyed with cutting her wrists in the bath, but she knew she was a coward and that only added to her own low opinion of herself. To compensate, she was careless when she crossed roads and, early on, shortly after she had returned to live at home, she had even gone abroad with a vague idea of never returning. And here she is again, the same feelings rising to the surface, fresh as they were all those years ago.

'Stop it.' She dumps the cup back into its saucer to break the spell, to get this dark moment to pass. But the feelings persist. Would the Paul Fiddler thing have happened if the damage had not already been done; maybe she would have fought harder if she had had any self-worth at all, if she had not been brought up with such a domineering mother and absent father! And everything since then, her whole life, has only unfolded as a reflection of that situation.

Her body sinks into the chair, and a familiar weight hinders her breathing and sticks her limbs to the spot, dragging her brow down as her will to carry on is sapped.

'You bitch,' she manages to spit out, but quietly, to herself, with images of Mum as she was then in her head. 'You selfish bitch,' she repeats, and this gives her just enough energy to breathe. 'And now I have to take care of you! Huh!'

She must have said this too loudly because Hilary and the suited man she is serving both turn to look at her.

'Everything all right, duck?' Hilary says. But Dawn does not trust herself to speak; instead she nods and quickly leaves the canteen.

Back at her desk, she glares at the phone. She needs to ring Ladies-in-Waiting but the thought of taking any action for Mum's sake sticks in her gut.

'Sod her,' she mutters, and she spends the remaining hour of her working day playing a surreptitious game of FreeCell.

Chapter 6

Dawn doesn't really work for Health and Safety, at least not directly. She was taken on as an admin assistant, and although her job title has not changed, most of her work these days involves doing the legwork for the overstretched Health and Safety department.

When she's out and dealing with the public, though, it's simplest to refer to herself as an Environmental Health Practitioner, or just Health and Safety, and it makes her feel a little bit better about herself too.

Working with Health and Safety does have its advantages, though – over the years she has been given access to just about every database on the council system, and the IT guys are either too busy or too lazy to revoke her access. So, before the end of her half-day, she accesses one of these databases to look up Ladies-in-Waiting; she might just need something to convince them to put Mum at the top of their waiting list. There is a nice little dispute over some illegal building works in their premises on the high street. That will do – with a little jargon she can make that work if she needs to, so at least she is prepared.

The clock creeps round to one and her half-day is done, so she switches off her computer with a sigh.

'She could get worse,' she says to herself in the car on the way to Mum's. 'What if she needs round-the-clock care?'

She's done the maths and worked out that she can afford one hour's care a day, Monday to Thursday, if she moves into Mum's. That is all her rent money will afford. Any more than that and she will be dipping into her savings. Her savings, she has also calculated, are enough to cover thirty-two days' round-the-clock care. It's not an option. She looks up at the house as she parks the car – the house that Mum has always presented as a promise (one day this will all be yours) but with an implied threat (but only if you play your cards right). It's a message, Dawn is coming to realise, that she has totally bought into.

Slamming the car door and wrapping her cardigan around her more tightly, she approaches the door. Maybe she will go in and find her dead, and all her problems solved.

'Oh my God, stop it!' she tells herself as she puts the key in the door. 'Mum?' she calls, lacing her voice with warmth and affection to make up for her harsh thoughts. There is no answer. Maybe the old woman has stayed in bed as she suggested. The kettle is cold and there are no mugs waiting to be washed up. Dawn puts her keys and bag on the kitchen table and walks through the hall. The sitting room door is open and Mum is there, chin on chest, absolutely still.

'Mum?' She feels a little sick. 'Mum.' She gives the shrunken bag of bones a nudge and it becomes a person again.

'Oh Mum, you gave me a fright. Have you drunk anything?'

'Leave me alone.' This is unlike Mum, too direct to be familiar. Dawn feels a little shocked.

'I'll make you a coffee,' she soothes.

'Just leave me be.' The chin sinks again and she is asleep. Dawn blinks a few times and frowns but as Mum continues to make tiny peaceful snoring noises she decides that this is a good time to ring the Ladies-in-Waiting.

The conversation is matter of fact and brief, and to her relief she learns that someone can pop round today, and they could start on Monday if a direct debit is set up.

When the woman arrives two hours later, she sniffs as she walks through the hall. Dawn is offended, but she knows the woman is right: the carpets are dusty, and there is a lingering aroma of old woman. Perhaps a little cleaning is needed. The interview is informal, and Mum acts as if she is entertaining a guest, coming alive, using her hands to express herself as she talks, trying to sit a little taller.

As the woman gathers the notes she has made and the forms she has filled out, she tells them that a different woman, someone called Kelly, will start on Monday, and would Dawn fill out the direct debit sheet before she goes.

'Well, she seemed nice,' Dawn enthuses as she takes a fresh pot of tea through.

'Bitten fingernails,' Mum remarks in condemnation.

'Well, it's not her who's coming, it's someone called Kelly.'

'We'll see.'

'No, we won't see, Mum, I've booked her and she is coming, One hour a day to help you with your lunch and to make sure you've drunk something.' Dawn pours the tea as she talks.

'You've slopped in the saucer.'

'Here.' She puts the cup, saucer and slops on the round coffee table.

Mum picks up the television remote and the theme tune to *Midsomer Murders* blasts out of the speakers.

'Oh, it's him, I do like him as an actor, what's his name?' Mum shouts.

The following day, after waking in her own flat, Dawn is up and dressed early and heads towards the supermarket. It will be busy on Saturday so it's best to go early. She buys dusters and polish, window cleaner and bleach, something she can sprinkle over the carpets and hoover up to make them smell fresh again, and three canisters of air freshener. A box of a hundred disposable gloves completes her purchases, along with tablets that turn the lavatory water blue and four rolls of kitchen paper.

With her hands full of bags she stumbles up the steps to Mum's house, unlocks the door and dumps the lot on the kitchen table.

'Mum?' she calls loudly, and then she marches through to the television room. The curtains are closed, just as she left them, but Mum's chair is empty and is pushed up against the patio windows; an attempt at a barricade, perhaps? She turns and looks back down the hall at the stairs up to the bedrooms. Mum's bedroom door is shut. If she has slept in it might be nice to take her up a cup of tea. Or maybe she should wake her first, draw the curtains and then make tea to give her a little time to surface.

She knocks lightly on the door. 'Morning.' But as she tries to open the door something stops her; there is a sound of wood against wood. Poking her nose through the gap, she reaches her hand in to move Mum's wooden towel rack, which has been pushed up against the door. What on earth went on last night? Did Mum hear something? What alarmed her so much that she went down the stairs to barricade the patio door? And what if she had fallen on the stairs going up or down in the middle of the night?

The door opens fully at last. The air is still and the room is in shadow as the heavy curtains cut out so much light.

'Morning, Mum.' Light floods the room as she draws back the curtains. The bump under the blankets looks so small and for a moment Dawn wonders if she is mistaken, if Mum is actually up and about somewhere, back to her normal self. She is about to leave the room when the lump in the bed makes a noise.

'Hummm.' The bedcover shifts.

'Oh, morning.' Dawn does not trust her senses and moves closer to assure herself that the tiny heap is in fact Mum.

'Do you want tea?' It seems like a safe thing to say. Mum is on her side, legs curled into the foetal position, taking up as much room as a large pillow.

'I think I might stay in bed a little this morning.'

Dawn blinks, and struggles for something to say; never in her life has Mum lain in bed.

'Oh, okay, then,' she manages to say, finally. 'I'll just do a bit of cleaning. I'll bring you a cup of something in half an hour.' And she backs out of the door.

Once she has pushed past her natural inertia the process of cleaning becomes satisfying. Thick layers of dust are wiped away and surfaces are polished until they gleam. The polish smells strongly of wax and honey but Dawn uses the air freshener too, just because she has it. The front room, reserved for guests, gets the sun in the morning, and the armchair by the window has faded to a pale pastel, in contrast with the sofa, which still displays a flowery pattern in deep rustic tones. The tone of the woodwork, too, has softened in the light. Two matching occasional tables no longer match, one a pale brown, almost white, and the other a deep mahogany tone. A small vase she brought back from Greece when she went, hoping never to come back, graces the mantelpiece alongside miniatures of the Statue of Liberty, the Eiffel Tower, Sydney Opera House, the Taj Mahal, the Sphinx, Mount Rushmore, the Burj Al Arab Hotel, the Christ the Redeemer statue in Rio and a soldier from the Terracotta Army, all of which Amanda brought back from her travels and presented to Mum. Dawn dusts these angrily and the Eiffel Tower falls to the floor. She puts it back without checking for damage.

'Mum, you ready to come downstairs now?' She enters without knocking this time, but finds Mum washing at the sink and quickly backs out again. 'Oh sorry,' she calls through the door. 'Let me know when you're done and I'll help you downstairs.'

'No need,' Mum barks back at her.

'Why don't you say "no, thank you", Mum, like a normal person?' Dawn says, but quietly, to herself, and she looks at the watercolours that are staggered on the wall down the stairs. They have been there forever, each so familiar, and yet no one ever really looks at them. She knows they were done by an aunt of hers years and years ago but she has never really given them much consideration. Maybe they are worth something, and if she gets stuck for cash she could auction them off. Come to that, she could auction off all Mum's treen and the corner cabinet, and the nineteen-thirties clock in the front room.

There are more paintings in there, too – ones that Dad collected. It's strange to remember him when he was alive. Even when he was alive, it was like he wasn't. Her memory is of a hunched-over man in a drab dressing gown, moping his way from one room to another. Always in that dressing gown. There was another man, too, of whom she only caught brief glimpses – a man who was almost never there. He wore a white shirt, and always a tie and jacket, and he worked long hours. Mum has never been one to talk about the past, or emotions, or say anything worth actually saying, but Dawn has pieced it together, and it came as a bit of a shock that these two men were one and the same. Both were her father: one when he did nothing but work, and the other when he was depressed. He died of lymphatic cancer when she was thirteen, on the day of the school dance, which she had been so excited about, and because he had died she was not allowed to go. She did not need telling she could not go; a death is a shock. She was not very upset, though; he had never been around anyway, and what difference did it make to her? The word 'father' meant nothing to her, and surely it was better to live whilst she had the chance. Of course, now she can see why they stopped her going: it was a matter of respect. But at the time it had felt unfair.

Yes, she could sell all those pictures and the treen Mum has collected over the years, and all the other bits and pieces: the brass bucket and shovel by the front-room fireplace, the Japanese papier mâché tea set on a papier mâché tray, and Dad's record collection. Isn't vinyl back in fashion? She could put the lot on eBay, get rid of all the clutter around the house.

'Like a vulture,' she comments on her own thought process. 'Leave the woman's things alone.' But no sooner has she said this than a wave of anger and animosity rolls up through her stomach and into her chest. Her fists clench and her teeth bite in a snarl of rage. It is fury that she knows lurks deep in the pit of her being, a violence all pushed down and silenced, an enmity towards Mum.

'She did the best she could at the time,' Dawn hisses through her teeth, trying to believe her own words. But her guts shout back, 'No she didn't!', and the animosity twists around, killing her compassion; it's a war that has been within her, eating her away and allowing her so little rest since that time all those years ago.

'Stop!' she admonishes herself. Then she runs down the remainder of the stairs and into the downstairs loo, where she pours a massive slug of bleach into the toilet bowl and scrubs at the limescale ring at the waterline with the toilet brush. She wishes she could cry. Tears would be such a release, but there is just a knot in her stomach, an unpassable, unthinkable twist in her guts, and then in a moment of warped hatred she flings the brush into the toilet and runs up the stairs. It's time to finally face up to Mum.

'Can you help me?' The words come with a quiver. Mum is sitting on the edge of the bed, so small, so fragile. Her hair, normally neatly coiffured, is flat at the back where she has been sleeping and she has one foot in a pair of tights. The other leg of the tights is twisted around the first ankle and her fingers do not have the strength to pull it free. 'I seem to have got myself into a bit of a mess.'

'Oh!' Dawn is pulled up short. 'Oh, yes, of course, let me help.' And as she bends to assist her she is even more startled to feel Mum's hand on the back of her head, stroking her hair.

'You were always such a good girl.' Mum continues to stroke. The words feel like a balm for her so-recent anger and Dawn's heart softens.

'There you go, Mum, you can pull them up now.'

'Thank you, Amanda.'

She freezes.

'I am Dawn, Mum. Amanda lives in Australia.'

Mum seems to stare at her in incomprehension for a moment but just as quickly she blinks and it passes.

'I think we'll have a cup of tea,' she says as she heads for the bedroom door, unaided.

Dawn makes the tea and they drink it in the television room, but no sooner is Mum's cup half emptied than the old woman's eyes close, and within a few minutes she is fast asleep.

Chapter 7

For a moment she cannot remember where she is and it is the smell, the mix of old carpets and new polish, that reminds her. The bed is uncomfortable, and no amount of wriggling makes it any better; perhaps she should have gone home. But after she put Mum to bed last night Dawn could not stop thinking about how Mum must have fared the night before that, stumbling about in the dark, barricading the doors. She asked what it was all about, when Mum was in her nightdress and safely tucked up in bed with a Horlicks, and Mum garbled half-sentences and huffed out defensive remarks. Dawn got the impression she had been scared and aware that she was too small and frail to protect herself from the imagined danger. Dawn stroked her head as she would a child's.

Rolling away from a spring that is digging into her back, Dawn throws off the covers and watches the dust particles dance in the slice of morning sun that is pushing its sharp fingers through the crack in the curtains. Outside, the garden is shrouded in a ground mist and the sun slithers behind a thin covering of cloud. Dawn can see the Sunday papers, dumped on the path as usual, and she makes a mental note to collect them. Opening the window reveals the day to be crisply cold and she closes it again quickly, the romance of the scene replaced by a shiver. Normally she would make a dash to the shower, but Mum's upstairs shower is over the bath, with cold and hot taps that need constant adjustment to avoid scalding or freezing, and the ceiling slopes so you cannot stand upright under the showerhead. There is a second bathroom downstairs, but that feels too far and too cold, so, pulling on her jeans, yesterday's T-shirt and a jumper, she decides that washing can wait till later. A comb from her bag pulls back her lank hair into a thin ponytail; she must do something with it, get it cut, or treated or something, at least make a decision as to whether to keep dyeing it or not. Her crown shows dark almost to the tops of her ears now. It's not a good look. She tucks her little mirror back in her bag with the comb.

On the landing, Mum's bedroom door is still shut, and with her ear to the door Dawn cannot hear any movement. Yesterday Mum spent most of the day sleeping, which if she is tired is fine, but Dawn suspects it is because she is feeling too shaken by the fall to venture out, let alone drive anywhere, and consequently she is now under-stimulated.

'Not good, not good.' Dawn mutters out her reflections as she patters downstairs.

She puts the kettle on and then goes to dig out the family albums from the bottom shelf of the bookcase by the television, and two more actually tucked under the bottom shelf. She lays them out on the sofa on top of the magazines and makes the tea, and then taps on Mum's door. There is a muttering from inside, coming not from the direction of the bed but from where the old sink is, against the wall. Satisfied that Mum is dressing, she returns to the albums. The oldest one that was under the bookcase is, she knows, of Mum and Dad, and documents their travels around England in a Ford Prefect before she and Amanda were born, in a period they refer to as 'BC' – Before Children.

Picking this one up, she sits in Mum's chair, with her tea. The early photographs are black and white, Mum smiling and so young, and Dad – well, to be honest, unrecognisable. The man she remembers had a long face and always two or three days' worth of grey stubble. Mum sank into years of what Dawn now recognises was depression after he died, and towards the end Dad had been depressed too. Both with good reason – for Dad because he had cancer and he was being cheated of his life, and for Mum because her husband had been snatched from her. She shuts the books and tucks this album back under the bookcase. It will only make Mum miserable to see this one.

The creak of the bedroom door sends Dawn out into the hall and up the stairs.

'I'm not going to fall,' Mum says. She has on a dark-grey A-line skirt and a pale-grey jumper, with silver earrings to match. Always smart. Dawn smooths her own jumper to get out the creases.

'And good morning to you too,' Dawn says. 'There's tea in the television room and I've pulled out the albums for us to look through.'

'Those old things, what do we want to look through them for?'

'Oh, don't be like that. It'll be fun! When did you last look through them?'

Mum makes a small grating sound with her teeth and tries to push past her on the stairs. Dawn backs down the steps and braces herself against the handrail just in case Mum's weight comes lunging after her. When they reach the bottom, Mum says, 'Such a fuss,' and takes her usual chair in the television room.

Five minutes later they are poring over pictures that Dawn hardly remembers. The albums are open on Mum's knee and Dawn sits by her feet.

'Is that me?' A child in knitted trousers and top with a hat and scarf to match is hugging a rabbit around the middle. The creature is so big its hind legs almost touch the ground, which is covered in snow.

'That was your Dad's idea, he bought you and Amanda a rabbit each for Christmas. I told him not to, but he always did as he wanted.'

'I loved that rabbit.'

'Amanda's died and she cried for days and days.'

Dawn does not remember that.

'Did he not get her another one?'

'Oh, he was away with work again by then. When was I even meant to tell him to get one, let alone him find the time to do it?'

'Could you not have got her one?'

This is met with silence. Dawn takes another look at the photograph of herself and the rabbit, at the smile on her face, and thinks she can almost remember having it taken, and that feeling of joy.

'Turn the page,' Mum demands.

'Oh look, that's Amanda, and there's me – and I can't remember *her* name, or *hers* …' She points to the other girls in the photo, who are about the same age as her and Amanda. 'Isn't that June?' The five of them look awkward, in school uniform, half posed, half shying away from the camera.

'That June was always a bad influence,' Mum says, and then her finger reaches out and traces over Amanda's face and she mutters, 'So pretty.'

Dawn ignores the comment about June and is struck by how much Amanda looks like Mum did in the pictures of her with Dad, BC.

'Look, there's Amanda with her gown on.' Dawn turns the page.

'Clever girl. Stuck with her degree, she did,' Mum says.

'I think it was the thought of seeing Braxton that pushed her to keep studying.'

'He should have moved here.'

'Amanda loved the idea of living somewhere hot, Mum. The whole idea of marrying an Aussie and moving halfway across the world. She would never have been happy here.'

'She was perfectly happy here.'

'She was miserable here, and always felt this town was too small! And she had nothing but contempt for her old friends. Does she even keep in touch with any of them?'

'I do not pry.'

'She keeps in touch with no one, Mum.'

'Well, you can talk,' Mum scoffs.

'I still see June!' Dawn's voice cracks into a higher register.

'When she isn't having a normal life with her family.'

'And what is that meant to mean?'

'Nothing. Just that she is busy. She has children and a husband, and can hardly offer you the friendship you need when her life is full.'

Dawn can only stare. Mum turns the page.

'Look, there's one of you and June when you were both single. Wasn't that when you moved into Leeds, into that terrible house that you ran away from? Look at June, every inch the barmaid and you trying to copy.'

'Enough.' Dawn stands. The whole thing was a bad idea and the room is suddenly hot. She needs some space. The hall is no cooler and so she goes outside.

The garden is cool, actually cold, and she shivers.

'Bitch!' she whispers fiercely, and she pulls the neck of her jumper over her mouth as she wanders aimlessly down the edge of the border. The garden is immaculate. For years now the man next door, Mr Sidcup, has been tending it as if it was his own. In fact, he has cut an arch through the adjoining privet hedge, so really it has become an extension of his own pristine patch. Even before the fall, Mum so seldom came out here. Dawn sits down on the wooden bench that Mr Sidcup installed in the far corner last month. It is cold but the blood in her veins is running hot.

'Bitch!' she repeats, and as she recalls the final picture they looked at she also recalls the leggings both she and June were wearing and her anger turns to laughter – sad laughter, with tears. Veronica and Helen were in the picture too, but they looked so much more serious, and younger, at the same time, than she and June. It was their studies at the university that made Veronica and Helen so earnest. June would joke that she too was studying:

anthropology, just not at the university – she was on a practical course, from behind the bar.

Most of their friends at that point were students, and June made life such fun. At the time it felt almost as if they were students too, but without a time limit to bring it to an end. Then again, there was no degree ceremony at the end of three years, either, and no possibility of her becoming a vet without that.

She shivers again and concedes that it is way too cold to stay out any longer.

Inside, Mum is asleep. The photo albums have slipped off her knee onto the floor. Dawn sits cross-legged and opens one at random.

It is an early album and there is a picture of her with the Nine Lives Cat Rescue Team. She is the little one on the end, about eleven years old, with a cat in her arms. Now that was a job she loved – cleaning out after them and cuddling them. She could have happily done that every day, and not just at weekends! It was certainly better than school.

There is another picture of her with her arms folded. Mum took it, trying to make out it was a big event in her life to leave school, that it made her an adult, that she was privileged to be able to walk away – only she had not wanted to leave school.

'There are always things in life that we cannot have,' she can remember Mum saying as she wound the camera on.

'But Amanda is staying on!' That was when she had folded her arms, that moment right there. God, she had been angry.

'Amanda is bright, dear.'

'Well, I can study hard! It's not as if I'm thick!'

Mum had snapped the photo and that was that.

There is one of the café where she first worked.

Mum sprang it on her, informed her that she had spoken to Joyce, and arranged for her to work at the café, serving tea and sandwiches. Joyce was Mum's oldest friend, and her café was in the middle of the high street. Dawn's job was to stand behind a counter all day, pouring tea from a huge metal urn into mugs that she would then put onto the customers' trays. June had landed a job in a local shoe shop, which she hated as much as Dawn hated the café. God, those had been horrible jobs! They felt like life was being sucked out of them, and with no qualifications and no experience she feared this was all she was going to get from life.

Four years she worked there, slowly dying inside, watching Amanda progressing through school and passing her A-levels, and then suddenly her sister was all ready to go off to university. Four years had passed, just like that, and Dawn felt she had done nothing with them for the simple reason that it was the truth. Amanda left home without even a backward glance and the house suddenly echoed with space and silence.

Dawn remembers her last day at the café as clearly as if it was yesterday.

Joyce came in to relieve her, and Dawn slipped out the back for a cigarette. She didn't smoke often, but someone had left a packet on a table, and she palmed them and sloped out of the back door of the café and was surprised to find June waiting for her.

'Hey, you're out early. Brilliant!' June said, pulling on her sleeve. 'Come on.'

'I haven't finished yet,' Dawn countered.

'You have, you've finished for good. Come on, we've a job interview. Give us a fag.'

'But the shops are shutting, where are we going?' she protested, but she followed her friend anyway, so keen was she to get away from the café.

'We're going to Leeds.' June sounded so full of life.

'Now?' Dawn gasped, out of breath, as she hurried after her friend towards the station.

The job was in a bar and the bar was opposite the university. It was full of people their age and it felt like a constant party. The manager was also young, if rather grumpy. He looked them up and down and told them they could have the job.

She is not sure what she would have done had they not got the job. Working at the bar was a dream after the tedious monotony of the café. Perhaps the best part about it was that it was too far and too expensive to travel to every day, so she and June soon found rooms in a grotty student house sharing with Veronica and Helen.

'Anthropology BA.' Veronica stuck her hand out for June to shake, which made Dawn laugh, but June accepted the hand and then turned and shook Helen's hand too.

'Anthropology BB.' June replied.

'What's that?' Helen's eyes widened.

'Behind Bar!' June laughed.

They quickly learnt how to add up whilst pulling pints and mixing B52s, and Dawn copied June's easy banter with the regulars as best she could. It didn't come naturally to her, though, and it often seemed to fall flat or become awkward. But most of the clients were students, the same age as them, and they didn't care. It was like being at a party every night, only they were paid to be there. Of course, there were one or two old locals too. One was particularly pushy with June, asking her out, making crude comments, until one day he'd had one too many and went too far, reaching out to touch her over the counter.

'Oh, sod off, you old git!' June had snapped, unaware that the manager was watching, and the whole bar had fallen silent.

'Actually, I think you're the one who'd best sod off,' the manager told her, and June stormed out.

Later the manager gathered all the staff around him.

'You're not here just to pour drinks,' he said. 'Be nice to the customers. And if you can't be nice then you'd best follow June right now, understand?'

The others mumbled their agreement, scared they would be next out the door, but Dawn stayed silent. Working alongside June had been the biggest perk the job had to offer.

They lost touch for a while after that; June left the shared house and went travelling, sending the occasional postcard, from France, then Greece. She sounded like she was having a wonderful time and Dawn wished she had gone too. The bar job wasn't so much fun any more, and her hours got longer, at first to cover June's shifts, and then two of the other girls left and new girls were not taken on. Soon there were three of them doing the work of six. Dawn started looking around for other jobs, and she even considered getting a day job and going to night school. She had turned twenty four and her life was slipping by more quickly every year.

Then came the events of that night.

Dawn turns the next page of the photo album quickly to distract herself from her thoughts. She leans in towards the page, concentrating, naming the people and things pictured, blocking her mind out, trying to keep the internal wall she has so carefully shored up over the years intact, using all her willpower to stop the memories bursting through.

'There seems to be no chronological order to the album,' she says out loud, hoping the sound of her voice will ground her in the present. The pictures have been randomly placed, held in place by their little sticky corners. It's hard to imagine that Mum spent time doing this, but she knows she herself didn't, and Amanda has just not been around, so there's no other explanation.

She is not sure how, or why, Mum has a picture of the house where she and June lived. There they are – her, June, Veronica and Helen, all looking so young and so carefree, smiling away, arm in arm on the doorstep of the terraced house in Leeds. The house that at first represented true liberation to her. She can remember it now – feeling so alive and young and free.

She closes the album forcefully. That same house became the place she was cut down to size. A darker and more terrifying grounding as to her place in life she could not imagine. She shivers again, but this time it is not from the cold.

Chapter 8

Mum continues to doze, little flutters of air occasionally parting her lips. Dawn puts the albums away and then busies herself with the magazines on the sofa, taking it upon herself to throw out all the ones that are clearly just there because nobody has bothered to put them in the bin. Even the noise of the magazines slapping against each other as the rubbish pile grows does not disturb her, and so Dawn, now in the mood for clearing out, potters through to the room by the back door and stares at the stacks of tins on the shelves.

'Why, Mum?' she says to herself. 'Do you fear starving to death? Or are you hanging on to a piece of the past, a time when you were needed, when you had a role in life, feeding us all?' This last explanation seems closer to the truth.

Dawn lifts down a tin of sliced mushrooms with a sell-by date of September nineteen ninety-eight. She almost thinks it might be worth keeping it, it's so old, but then reminds herself why she is going through all this stuff and tosses it in a black plastic bag that will probably spilt under the weight of everything she will be putting in there. For some reason the image makes her smile.

She continues to fill the bag, and the shelves empty. Very little is in date and as she takes down the final tin, expiry date two thousand and six, the room seems strangely empty.

'Right!' She rolls her sleeves up. 'What's next?'

The freezer is next, and she boils water and sprays it onto bags of peas and mixed veg frozen to the sides. A number of clear plastic bags full of leftovers go straight in the bin, and there are no fewer than three lemon cheesecakes, all past their sell-by date, and four tubs of ice cream, half eaten, and also out of date. It is odd to see the freezer emptying and it makes Dawn think of her own fridge, which seldom has anything in it at all.

She takes the bucketful of ice that she has hacked out of the freezer into the kitchen and puts it down the sink, and dumps the bags in the bin outside the back door. But she is not done – unwanted memories are still trying to push their way through, demanding her attention, and so she faces the kitchen once more and decides to set about the wine rack by the fridge. There are eight bottles of wine there and Dawn cannot remember a time when there were any more or fewer. Her mother never drinks wine with a meal, unless Dawn brings a bottle over. Now she thinks about this, she finds it weird, until she takes out the first dark-coloured bottle to find it is empty, but with the foil covering squeezed back on where the cork once was. The next bottle is alcohol-free mulled wine with a use-by date of over four years ago. This rattles against the first bottle.

The process is beginning to depress her. All her initial energy is now drained out of her, and there is something so sad about an old woman trying to keep her food and wine store full, even if what is there is unfit for consumption. Surely it is better to have the space? She sits heavily on one of the kitchen chairs.

'If there is any alcohol on these shelves then I'm going to drink it!' she announces, and this gives her enough energy to pull out the next three bottles, which are all

101

mulled wine, and all out of date. The last three bottles all appear to be empty, foil tops carefully replaced. On careful inspection, the last bottle turns out to have a glassful left at the bottom, but the wine is sour and she pours it down the sink. The empty wine rack looks barren; she has never seen it that way before.

Was that a sound? She stops moving to listen. Is Mum up and moving about? She jumps to her feet and tiptoes to the door; she is just in time to catch Mum sitting down again, a large sherry glass in her hand.

'Don't blame you, Mum,' she calls out, but as she passes through the hall she finds Mum has put the chair from by the telephone against the inner front door, which is always bolted. She is not sure if she wants to cry with frustration or reassure the old woman. Instead, she goes to the drinks cabinet in the front room and pours herself a large sherry in a glass that, she seems to recall, Dad got free at a petrol station back in the late eighties, perhaps.

'If you can't beat them,' she says, and she takes a slug straight from the bottle before replacing the top and putting it away, then she takes her glass through to join Mum. The theme tune to *Midsomer Murders* is blaring out down the hall. They will watch it together and she will listen to Mum's inane comments and pretend the world is fine.

The next day, after an early morning call to reassure herself that one of the Ladies-in-Waiting is definitely booked to come round, Dawn helps Mum get up and leaves her to dress. Then she takes her down to the television room, supporting her as she lowers herself into her chair, and leaves the remote close to hand.

'Now, do not lock the back door, Mum, because if you fall asleep the woman from Ladies-in-Waiting will not be able to get in to help you with lunch, okay?'

Mum nods.

'And there is a key by the kettle for her to take away, okay?'

Another nod.

'I'll just brush your hair for you, Mum, it's all flat at the back.'

'Oh, stop fussing and go,' Mum snaps, grabbing the remote control and pulling her head away from Dawn's soothing hand.

'Suit yourself.' Dawn says this loudly enough for Mum to hear and stamps out of the room. It feels quite daring; she almost expects to be called back from the kitchen, where she is gathering her bag and coat. She smiles to herself and lifts her head up higher when it is clear she will not be asked to justify herself.

'Oh, and it's Monday, Mum,' she calls as she adjusts the collar of her coat. 'So I'll come after work to make tea, but I won't stay for long as it's quiz night. But I'll stop in after that and help you to bed, okay?'

But there is no reply, and when she looks through to the television room she can see Mum's head lolled forward, her chest lowering and rising; she is fast asleep.

The following morning the wipers swish back and forth, smearing the dirt evenly on the windscreen for the first half mile or so to work. The rain has flushed the fields on either side of the road with green and chased away the cold, and it feels quite mild. She has set an alarm on her phone to call the Ladies-in-Waiting whilst they are with Mum around lunchtime, to make sure it is all going smoothly. Otherwise, she hopes, it will be an uneventful day. Mondays are usually slack. No one has any energy and no one rushes to answer any emails they have received.

She answers some routine emails and plays several games of FreeCell before taking her first tea break. Hilary is busy as, it seems, Dawn is not the only one in need of tea – half the department seems to be in there. Dawn thumbs through a fashion magazine from a couple of years ago and is a little upset to find that even her most up-to-date clothes predate the collections displayed in it. This makes her think of her hair – she really must decide whether to buy more dye or go natural and get it cut. By now its natural colour is probably mostly grey. She is not sure she is ready for such a bold step. Would it make her look like Mum?

'Oh, that was a rush.' Hilary sits next to her and points at a pair of sunglasses in the magazine, with a three-figure price tag.

'I'll get you a pair,' Dawn quips.

'Get three pairs and we'll wear them for quiz night. It will give us an excuse for getting the answers wrong as we won't be able to see what we're writing.' Hilary laughs and then is on her feet again as a new queue begins to form at the counter. Amongst them is Ms Moss, so Dawn slurps the remainder of her tea and sneaks out of the canteen. She can get in another game of FreeCell and then attend to her emails when Ms Moss returns.

The morning drags. She spends a little time trying to pass the email about visiting Hogdykes Abattoir to a male colleague, explaining that he would not be subject to sexist abuse from the workers, but he says his timetable is full, so she forwards it back to where the original email came from. When her alarm goes off it makes her jump. She turns to apologise to a room that is mostly empty – even Ms Moss is away from her desk – and takes her phone out to the hall to make the call.

'How is she?'

'She's fine, she ate well,' the woman reassures her. 'We've had three cups of tea and she's walked to the kitchen and back and been to the loo. Nothing to worry about. I'm just about to go now and she's engrossed in some murder mystery on telly, and seems perfectly happy.'

'Oh, thank you.'

'Okay, talk later.' And the phone purrs.

'So all it took for her to make the effort was for me to threaten to move in with her,' she says to the dial tone. 'Talking of which.' She returns to her desk and starts to type up a letter to the landlord, giving notice. She wonders if she is likely to get her deposit back, and then reasons that, even if she doesn't, twenty pounds is not what it was sixteen years ago.

The afternoon drags, and judging by the fidgeting and sighs from around the room, she is not the only one who is glad when Ms Moss stands and puts her coat on ten minutes early. As luck would have it, though, Ms Moss's phone rings, and after that she takes her time to arrange her desk and in the end leaves five minutes after the hour, to a communal sigh of relief.

As Dawn approaches Mum's, it occurs to her that as soon as she has given notice this will be her hometown again, and she stops at the corner shop where she used to buy sweets after school. The place has long since changed hands and the shop has opened up inside to become a mini-supermarket, but it still has a long counter loaded with sweets to tempt small children. She buys chocolate, wine, sherry, soup and more soup, as well as a box of individual frozen cheesecakes and mini pizzas, and dumps the lumpy plastic bags on the passenger seat. She hums to herself as she drives the last quarter-mile to that so-familiar house, feeling lifted by the glass of wine she has promised herself on her arrival.

'Oh!' She is momentarily disappointed when she remembers she must forgo the glass of wine as it is quiz night and she will have to drive. Or maybe June can pick her up – it's only a little out of her way.

In the kitchen, a used pan, a bowl, four mugs and two teacups wait to be put in the dishwasher. She dumps the bags of shopping next to these and makes her way through to the television room, where she finds Mum fast asleep.

'Mum ...' She gives her a nudge.

'Oh, who's that? Amanda?'

'No, it's Dawn, Mum. How was Kelly?'

'Amanda?'

'No, Kelly.' She sighs out the name. Why is she bothering? She stands and looks around the room to see if there is any other sign that Kelly from Ladies-in-Waiting has been.

'No – Amanda, dear,' Mum mumbles.

'No, Mum, I'm Dawn. Amanda lives in Australia and I'm asking about Kelly from Ladies-in-Waiting who came to see you today.' She speaks loudly and impatiently, and she wonders if she is doing the right thing handing in her notice on the flat, but then she reminds herself that she cannot afford Ladies-in-Waiting if she does not. 'Shit!' she exclaims to herself, quietly, so Mum cannot hear, at the thought of just how stuck she is all over again.

'No, not Kelly. Kelly is sick. The woman who came was called Amanda and she was very nice.' Mum is alert now and sounds like her old self, ready to chat, interested in life.

'Oh! I see. Well, I'm glad she was nice. You got on, then?'

'She talked away, I could hardly get a word in edgeways but I didn't mind. It was nice to have some young life around the house. Someone with a bit of fun and energy.'

'Oh, how old was she?'

'About your age.'

Dawn blinks slowly and takes a long, deep breath.

'Did you say you were making tea?' Mum asks.

Dawn takes another breath and counts to five.

'A pot of tea, or do you mean you are hungry?' she says finally, making an effort to keep her tone even and calm. You know it's quiz night for me tonight?'

'A bowl of soup will be fine, and do we have some lemon meringue pie?'

'I got cheesecake.'

'I don't like cheesecake.'

'Fine, don't have it.'

'Pardon? I can't hear what you say if you walk away while you talk.'

Dawn flicks the kettle on.

'I'm so tired of this!' She folds her arms on the counter and drops her head on them. All of life feels squeezed out of her, as if she had been drained dry, and for what? Because the cantankerous old woman in the next room is her mum? Is that a good enough reason? It's not as if she has been a good mum. In fact, by most people's standards one might say she has been pretty rotten, so why carry on doing this? Why even maintain a relationship with Mum – why not just walk away? She would if it was any other person in the world.

'Because Amanda has fled to the other side of the world and there is no one else,' Dawn tells herself. 'But,' her inner demon taunts, 'you could just leave her.' She could, but how often has she told herself that she stays for the house, her payoff, the carrot Mum has dangled all these years? In these moments, when she is feeling too drained to pretend, she knows that bricks and mortar are not why she is there. The truth is that Mum is another human being who has no one else to care for her. She would be a sad, lonely little old lady who would fall down dead one day and lie there for weeks until the smell of her decomposing body alerted some passer-by. Dawn could not do that to her worst enemy and, a small part of her argues, if she does this for Mum, then maybe one day someone will do it for her. It is a hope that, with no children of her own, has no foundation, she knows, but it is a hope she clings to.

The soup comes to the boil and she cuts a slice of bread in half.

'Here you go, Mum.' She presents the food on a tray with a cloth, a proper soup spoon and a folded linen napkin.

'Put it there, would you.' It is a command.

'"Thank you" would be nice,' Dawn says, loudly enough for Mum to hear.

'Yes, it looks very nice, you're right.'

'Right, do you need anything else? It's quiz night. Do you need the loo before I go?'

'I am not a child!'

'Okay, I'll see you later then. I'll leave my phone on, it's number one on speed dial.'

But Mum is spooning soup into her mouth and it is taking all her concentration.

Chapter 9

The pub smells of chips. Gone are the days of that unique pub smell of stale smoke and beer. Dawn kind of liked that smell somehow; it reminded her of working with June, and the laughter of students, before life became complicated. The predominant sound at quiz night is always women's laughter, competing with the screeching feedback from the quizmaster's microphone.

June waves to get Dawn's attention as she pushes in through the sprung door. Hilary is next to June, a half of lager in her hand, another on the table, and there are two glasses of prosecco in front of the empty chair. It looks like she'll need to get a taxi back to Mum's.

'How's your mum?' June is rolling a cigarette; she will disappear several times in the course of the evening and come back with a waft of cold air, smelling of smoke.

'She seems happy enough with the Lady-in-Waiting who, as luck would have it, is called Amanda.'

'I don't know why you bother. She's a callous, vicious old cow.' June licks the cigarette paper and makes the final twist.

'That's a bit harsh!' Hilary says. 'And you should put a filter on that.'

'Not harsh. That dried-up shell of a woman has a lot to answer for, and you, Dawn, are the last person who should be running around after her, considering what she did. Back off and let Amanda come and deal with it all!' She stands and pats her jeans pockets, finds her lighter and strides off towards the back door.

Hilary sips her drink and Dawn feels her eyes on her. For all the time they have known each other, they have still somehow never quite managed to exchange much information about their pasts. Take Hilary's comment about her own mother the other day – Dawn didn't even know she was dead. Come to that, she didn't know Hilary even had a mother – well, obviously she had one, but alive, dead? She knows nothing about Hilary. Does she have siblings, for example? But asking any questions opens the door to being asked in return and she does not want to go there.

'Are we ready?' the microphone squeals, and someone calls out, 'This little piggy went to market,' which draws raucous laughter. Someone makes that same comment every week. The humour is no longer in the words; it is more the laughter of acknowledgement, that they are all here together, repeating a uniting experience, week in, week out.

'Ready? Yes?' The quizmaster never laughs.

'A bunch of Fag Ash Lils out back,' someone informs him, and someone else opens the door and calls into the darkness that they are about to start, and a big draft of cold, smoky air follows the smokers into the room.

'Right, so tonight, the questions have been set by our Ron.' There is a spattering of applause and a small man in the corner stands and takes a bow. 'So let's get down to it. Number one. For a warm-up, get the grey cells ticking over. There are 10 apples, you take away 3, how many do you have?'

'Oh, come on!' someone heckles.

'Anybody got a recipe for apple pie?' another voice calls and a few more laugh.

'Number two. Now listen up because I'm not going to repeat this one. Lee's father emigrated from China. He has five children, La, Lu, Lin and Lo – what's the last child's name?'

'Isn't that racist?' a voice asks, with a hint of laughter but also a serious tone near the end. The room falls silent; no one knows if it's okay to comment.

'Number three. Is it possible for two kids to be born on the same hour, day, month, year, and have the same parents, and not be twins, and not be adopted?'

The room is silent as this question is absorbed.

'How are the boys, June?' Dawn asks as an aside.

'Ash sprained his ankle playing football last weekend and is driving me round the bend with his moaning that he won't be picked for the school team, and Jake's just got his first girlfriend bless him, not that any of us are allowed to mention it!'

It feels like a safe moment to ask – she can count on June to deflect if necessary – so Dawn says, as casually as she can, 'Do you have children, Hilary?'

'That's why I had to marry him,' Hilary replies. 'One drunken night of him pushing himself on me and a lifetime of marriage. I'm older than you – that's how it was then.' She twiddles her pen and looks at the quiz paper, situation accepted.

June looks quickly at Dawn, who manages to get a drink to her lips to mask her instant reaction.

'I reckon it's possible.' June taps the quiz paper with her finger; no doubt her intention is to distract Hilary's attention. 'They could have been embryos fertilised at the same time.'

'No, this is just an old riddle.' Hilary already seems to have moved on from sharing a piece of her past. 'They are two of triplets.'

'I'm just going to the loo.' Dawn extricates herself and heads out of the back door, but bypasses the toilets and goes to stand with the smokers. She is immediately offered a cigarette, which she accepts, and she pretends she is listening to the other smokers rehash the day's tabloid news but she is thinking of Hilary being 'pushed upon' and how that shaped her life. But more than that, it underlines why she has kept

Hilary and everyone else in the world at arm's length, and why Hilary, who never asks and never offers, is her only new friend in nineteen years: the risk of opening doors to her own past is too great.

Maybe it wouldn't be so bad if it was just the memories of that night that she had to deal with, but for Dawn there was also what happened afterwards. There was her mum! How would anyone understand that? People judge, that's what they do. Remaining aloof is a way of taking care of herself, for now, but it is also how, one day, she will end up entirely and completely alone, when Amanda is still in Australia and Mum is …

'You all right, dear, you look a little pale?' a woman with lipstick painted on wider than her lips asks.

'I think it might be the nip in the air,' Dawn answers quickly, and she stubs out her half-smoked cigarette.

'Best go in then, chick,' a man in a Leeds United football shirt answers.

There is a bit of a shove of people inside, by the toilets, which tells Dawn the quiz is on a break and the bar will be jammed with people wanting to be served. But she is still on her first prosecco, and as she doesn't really want to take a taxi back to Mum's and then have to get a taxi back here so she can drive into work tomorrow, she decides she will not drink any more anyway. June will down anything Dawn leaves and Steve will pick her up if necessary.

'The boring practicalities of life,' she mutters, taking her seat.

'What are?' Hilary asks.

'Drinking and not driving.' Dawn tries to smile, but it's a smile that doesn't reach her eyes as she looks at Hilary. 'Actually, tonight, rather than sitting here not drinking, I think I'll call it a day.'

'But you've only just got here.' Hilary says.

'You okay?' June asks knowingly.

'Yeah, I think I'm worrying about my mum. I would feel better going back there.' And the look June gives her says she knows this is a lie. Dawn gives her a little smile of gratitude for letting it go.

'Well, if it all gets too much, you know me, I'll still be up hours after I get home,' June says lightly, and she picks up her mobile and gives it a little wiggle, inviting Dawn to call.

'Okay, goodnight then. I hope we win.'

'Not likely, we've only answered three of the first five questions and now our prize team player is walking out on us,' June teases.

Hilary reaches for Dawn's second glass of prosecco.

'See you tomorrow,' she says, putting the glass to her lips. And Dawn makes a mental note to stay away from the canteen for a few days, to let the dust of intimacy settle.

She drives back slowly, not because of the half glass of alcohol but because she doesn't really want to go back to Mum's. She knows there is no choice, though; if she went back to her flat and Mum fell on her way to bed – well, it just doesn't bear thinking about.

The rain starts halfway home; it builds quickly and her wipers struggle to keep the screen clear. As she drives, the droplets look like they are curling horizontally towards her. It had been raining that other night too, nineteen years ago. The same sort of rain, thick and drenching, and on that night she had returned from a pub too, the pub she worked at.

He had been in the bar that night.

'No.' She tries to stop the thoughts, but sometimes they just will not stay away.

He had been bantering with her and she had so wanted to tell him to get stuffed, but this was shortly after June had been sacked for being 'unfriendly' so she bore his sexist jokes and his crude remarks, and her defence had been laughter, and she had smiled at him to keep her job. If she had known that her defence was to be used against her, she would have quit that job there and then. That or smashed a bottle over his head.

'That guy on the end is pretty drunk and he seems to like you,' Pete the bar manager sidled up to her to say. 'I'll show him the door if he gets out of hand but in the meantime get him on the Talisker 18.'

'The what?'

He pointed to a bottle high up on the shelf behind them.

'Eleven pound a shot. Good girl.' And he slithered away, but not so far that he couldn't watch her, so she dutifully offered the whisky.

'Talisker 18, what's that then?' the drunk man slurred and she pointed to the bottle high on the shelf. The man eyed the steps up which she would have to climb to retrieve the bottle and he became eager to try a sample. She held the back of her skirt against her as she climbed up, and then she turned and came down facing forward. After she served the first glass, the manager reappeared next to her and put the bottle back. She was naive but she was not stupid and she understood the game that was being played.

'Can you please pass it down again, the man might want another drink,' she requested. Pete smirked in her face.

'And I think I do want another shot.' The drunk man pulled out another ten-pound note. Dawn had the sense to turn to one of the other girls, who was wearing jeans, and ask her to get the bottle. Pete gave her a hard look but as the man had bought the second drink there was no more he could say.

'I'll have another,' the man slurred.

'I think you've had enough,' she answered.

'I said one more.' He tapped his glass on the countertop.

'Best not, mate.' She tried to soften her refusal. Pete started to make his way over to her so she slipped off to the loo, and by the time she came back Pete was talking to another customer and the drunk man had gone. She didn't think about the incident much after that. And a familiar face appeared through the crowd.

'Veronica!' she greeted her housemate. Helen was just behind her.

'Finished our last exam of the year.' Helen could hardly string a sentence together.

'Well, let me help you celebrate.' Dawn took two glasses and filled them up with soda water.

'Whats-at?' Veronica looked at her sparkling clear drink with disdain.

'That is your anti-hangover remedy, which you will thank me for in the morning.'

'Killjoy,' Veronica said, but she drank it anyway and then declared they were going home to get some sleep.

The rest of the night went as normal, followed by the routine of cleaning up and shutting up. But on stepping outside, Dawn found it was chucking it down with rain. Two of the other staff hurried away under one umbrella, and the other two got in a car.

'You want a lift?' Pete asked.

'No, you're all right,' Dawn dismissed him. She didn't trust him. He drove away without appearing to give her a second thought.

By the time she got home she was soaked to the skin; her thin coat was wet through and her denim skirt was a tone darker and heavy with the weight of water. She could hear Veronica and Helen in the shared kitchen but she went straight to her room and stripped off her wet clothes. After wrapping her old and sagging but thick towelling robe that was two sizes too big around her and tying the towelling sash in a knot, she headed to the kitchen for a cup of something warm.

She pushed the door open to find Veronica chatting merrily away to a man with his back to her and so she entered with a smile, ready to be pleasant to whoever Veronica's new friend was. Helen was nowhere to be seen. Dawn put the kettle on and then turned to face him and be introduced.

'Oh Dawn, you know Paul, right?' Veronica said, and Dawn's jaw tightened.

Looking back, she wondered if it was inevitable that it was him? Surely not, and yet that was how it felt at the time. As if she had no control over her own life. Other people determined if she stayed on at school or not, other people decided on the job she got, other people told her who to serve and what, using her – and now here was Veronica expecting her to be pleasant to a man who had made her feel far from comfortable. The drunk from the bar.

Chapter 10

Outside Mum's house, Dawn cannot move from the car. It's a good thing she isn't driving, with the memories coming back in such a rush. Over the years, her memory of the physical pain, and even the fear, have lessened. It should be a relief, but instead this has left the wrongs done to her to burrow away at her subconscious, slowly eroding her foundation, forever threatening her with imminent collapse.

'No!' It comes out as more of a whine than a word, but something has to be released. She folds her hands tightly into her armpits, knowing what might happen. In her flat there are doors with holes punched in the hardboard facing, now patched over with polyfilla. Some of her favourite porcelain cats have met their demise against the walls, she has written off a car, and, when all else fails, she draws out crimson tears that eventually fade to raised white lines on her thighs.

Her head hit the floor. Bam! Her eyes felt like they danced out of her skull and back.

'She was in a bathrobe, no underwear – how much more provocative can a woman be, m'Lord?'

The pull on her belt was so hard that her ribs creaked and bent; she could feel it. Another yank and they would break.

'All night she had been flirting with my client, banter that was witnessed by many, and in the pretence of offering a fine whisky from a high shelf she even climbed some steps in a miniskirt. I do not think I need to explain what effect that would have, we all have imaginations.' The others there, all male, turned to look at her, exercising their imaginations.

'No!' This time the word is a re-enactment and then the pictures flood her vision again. The same old scenes.

'No! What the ...? Veron–' But his hand on her mouth left her friend's name unfinished. His hand tasted salty; for a second the sensitive tip of her tongue could feel all the tiny unseen ridges of his skin, before she retracted it so vehemently she blocked her own airway and began to spasm and cough. The hand over her mouth forced her head back but her need for air was greater, and she lashed out at him.

'According to my client, her back was arched and she gave every indication that she was thoroughly enjoying herself.'

The hand left her mouth. She gasped, sucking in lungfuls of air, the oxygen swimming in her brain, her vision refocusing. His free hand tugged at the neckline of her robe and his head lowered, tempted by the exposed skin, no doubt, and she twisted to avoid the touch of his lips. As soon as his forehead made contact, the pain spread across the arch of her nose and sent her vision swimming.

'I suggest that if this was an attack, as she claims, then surely she would have called out. She did, after all know that at least one person' – he looked down at his notes – *'a Ms Veronica Stillwater was at home, as she had seen her just five minutes*

earlier. Which leads me to my next query. If this was not
something she wanted, why did the defendant not retire to her
room before Ms Veronica Stillwater, seeing as my client, Mr
Paul Fiddler, was in fact Ms Stillwater's guest?' She trembled at
the sight of him, and she trembled at the mention of his name.

After Dawn arrived home and found Veronica with
Paul Fiddler in the kitchen, Veronica almost immediately
complained that she was not feeling so good. 'I'm not
surprised you feel ill! You were very drunk when I saw
you in the bar,' Dawn said.

'Oh shit, the room is spinning, I think I'd best go to
bed,' Veronica groaned.

'Drink some water before you go.' Dawn went to the
sink.

'I'm just going to go. Passing out is the order of the
day.' And Veronica staggered to the door and was gone
before the glass in Dawn's hand was full.

'Well, just you and me then,' he said, slapping his
hands on his thighs, his feet planted wide as he sat on the
two-seater sofa that was crammed up against the fridge.
Dawn turned the tap off and left the glass to drain,
knocking some cutlery to the floor as she did so.

'Well, I need to get to bed, so if you wouldn't mind.'
She retrieved a knife from the floor and wiped it on her
dressing gown and put it in the drawer.

'I realised you wanted to get to bed way back at the
bar, sweetheart.' He stood then and moved over to her.

There were only two people sitting in the seats reserved for
the general public. June sat looking angry but with a hanky to

124

her eyes. With another glance at his notes, the robed gentleman continued.

'The defendant then suggested to Mr Fiddler that they go to bed, I believe.'

Mum's head swivelled sharply at this and their eyes met. The accusation that lay there was sharper than any that she could have voiced out loud.

Time became distorted, her head pounded from the blow, she struggled to regain her vision. It could have been seconds, or several minutes, but as focus returned she found her head was turned sideways, her cheek against the floor. The upturned prongs came into focus first, the curve of the handle highlighted by the ragged shapes of crumbs and dirt on the floor around it.

It was something real, tangible, understandable, and that was what had made her reach for the fork as she came out of her daze. Then the pain, the weight of his hand, his hand on her shoulder, her shoulder pinned to the floor, and – what he was doing! Oh my God, what was he doing!

'She gave no warning. In the middle of this mutually agreed adult act she stabbed Mr Fiddler here' – he pointed at the man dressed in a neat grey suit, his hair cut short and his head bowed – 'with a fork.' He waited for this to sink in, speaking and acting as if performing in a play. 'If she had stabbed him only once – the first blow, in his arm – we could, under very special circumstances consider this a reflex action, as a response to her passion, perhaps.' He waited, almost as if expecting laughter, and a smile played on his lips. None came, and he adopted a serious expression once more and continued. 'Also, would one stabbing not have been enough for my client to realise that he was in fact playing with fire? Allowed him to create a distance between himself and the accused, to keep himself safe?'

She thought she had made contact with his arm but he did not stop. His face contorted, his lips curled; spittle gathered in the corners of his mouth, his breath reeking of stale spirits. She just wanted it to stop. It had not been a decision; her pelvic bone screamed in pain. She punched him again, forgetting the fork still in her hand.

'No, she did not give Mr Fiddler any time. Instead she stabbed him again, this time aiming for his kidneys. It was fortunate indeed that my client, as you can see, is not built lightly, or else this could have been a fatal injury.' She could not steel herself to even glance at him; the thought filled her with horror.

His pupils contracted and the whites of his eyes surrounded the irises as he became still, frozen in position.

Then he looked down on her, the bestial curls of pleasure on his lips fading, the surprise registering. He rolled off her and lay on his back, blinking, obviously unable to understand what had happened. Carefully she tried to sit up, leant on one arm and then felt something in her other hand. She lifted it up to find she was holding tightly to a fork, the prongs smeared with blood. She adjusted her focus and looked past them at his face. He stared at the fork and put his hand to his side. It came away red.

'He did what?' Veronica spoke quietly, leaning her head on one hand, her eyes barely open, her skin a greenish hue. Helen sat wide-eyed, all colour drained from her face, looking at the floor where it had happened just a few hours before. The radio she had brought down from her room with her sat on her knee, its jolly morning talk at odds with the situation.

126

Dawn could not stop shaking. Watching her hands moving by themselves felt unreal. Her bathrobe was still wrapped around her, the belt still knotted. The night before, they had both crawled, he towards the front door, and she towards the two-seater sofa, where she had remained until a nudge from Veronica roused her from a turmoiled half sleep.

'Bastard.' Veronica's voice was muffled as she filled the kettle.

Helen still hadn't spoken.

'I can't stop shaking.'

'Of course you can't,' Veronica said in sympathy, waiting for the kettle to boil.

'I suppose I should call the police but I just can't face it.'

'No, of course you can't, they only make women feel dirty in these situations anyway. Like they deserve it. Forget the police.' Veronica spooned coffee into a cup, just one, for herself.

Helen still hadn't moved, the small radio in amongst the folds of her nightgown gaily announcing a new number one: Britney Spears with 'Hit Me Baby One More Time'.

Chapter 11

Sitting out in the car, Dawn shivers; it's best she goes inside. But inside to Mum does not seem like a good idea right now. In this state she might say something she will regret. Mum will counter whatever she says, and she knows from bitter experience that she will come out of it feeling worse than she started. At least the rain has stopped. But even that is tainted, as if the past is insisting on being remembered. It had stopped raining just as she got back to Mum's house all those years ago, when she arrived there from the shared house, the day after the Paul Fiddler incident.

Veronica and Helen sat with her for hours in the kitchen, and then Helen went quietly to her room, and a short time later Dawn saw her leaving with her bag – just a glimpse, through the door that was open a crack.

'Where's Helen going?' she asked Veronica, who was making more tea.

'She said something about not wanting to stay in a house so full of bad vibes, or something. You know how she gets – anyway I think she said she was going home to her mum's.'

It felt like abandonment. Not that she had ever been close to Helen, but for her to leave like that after what had happened!

'You have me,' Veronica said brightly, dismissing the absent Helen with a wave of her hand. 'And I've asked Cuthbert and Jacky, Cordelia and Harry round for dinner so that will cheer you up. Well, it will take your mind off it, anyway.'

She finished her tea and came over to Dawn and gently pulled her bathrobe more neatly around her neck and added, 'Tell you what, I'll run a bath, that always makes me feel better.' And she all but skipped from the room, content that her solution would wash the whole episode away.

It only took until mid-afternoon for Dawn to realise that she could not face Veronica's dinner party and her student friends, also anthropologists, who might look like butter would not melt in their mouths, neatly dressed and shiny faced, but who were just like any other students and habitually drank themselves into ridiculous states, so Dawn retreated to her bedroom where she could be quiet.

There she stared out of the window, rerunning the lead-up to Paul Fiddler's attack, trying to work out if there was some point at which she could have averted it, trying to work out if she had been at fault, if there had been anything about her behaviour to encourage him when they were at the bar. She began to tremble, first in her fingers but then up her arms; then her whole body felt like it was shaking under her skin. As these thoughts played on an endless loop, it suddenly occurred to her that she should be at work, in that bar, where he would no doubt be drinking, and all remaining strength left her, and her shaking turned to sobbing. She turned from the window and buried herself in her blanket on her bed, but it gave her no relief, and when the doorbell rang and cheerful voices echoed up the stairwell from the hall, followed by

129

the sound of glasses chinking from the kitchen, she felt so distant, so separate and so tarnished that she realised that she could no longer be a part of that world, that house, that town. But no job meant no room and therefore no independence. Either she worked or she went home to Mum's.

Mum's won; she could not face work.

'History repeating itself,' she observes as she gathers her bag and coat and steps into the cool of the night. The lamp in the side window of the kitchen is on, a good sign that Mum has been up since she left for work this morning. Or maybe it has been left on and she never noticed during the day. It had been on when she had returned from the shared house all those years ago too.

'Leave it alone now,' she admonishes herself, and she puts her key in the back door.

'Hi, Mum, I'm back early,' she calls out. Bag and coat are set down, and she heads straight through to where the television is blaring loudly. Mum's chin is on her chest, her hands neatly folded in her lap, chest and shoulders rising and falling together in slumber. Dawn sighs, takes the remote from the round table and flops into the second chair.

News, politics, a drama that she's seen before, cookery programmes, more cookery programmes. No wonder we're all so fat, she reflects. She pulls down her jumper to cover her ever-spreading belly, which reminds her that she has still not made a decision about her hair.

'Dye or cut?' she mumbles to herself. And as if the powers that be have heard her, the cookery programme takes a break and the first advert is for hair dye. The girl is all smiles and white teeth, the sun in her hair.

'Yeah, as if life is like that.' And in that second she makes the decision to get it cut and get rid of the bottle blonde.

She changes the channel: more news. A serious man in a shirt and tie says, 'However only nineteen point three per cent of the students actually responded to the survey, which showed that sexual assault was experienced by one in–'

She clicks away. 'Of course they don't respond. The world doesn't change.' She spits her words out, quietly and with control, but she cannot help thinking that, had the Paul Fiddler incident happened now, in today's world, maybe – no, definitely – she would have been seen as the victim. The world *has* changed. Compassion would have flooded her way; she would have been offered therapy and support. That's what they seem to do these days. These days the authorities would sweep her along a road of care and attention and unlimited assistance … 'The sort of response you would expect from your mum, perhaps?' The restraint in her voice grates her throat.

'Oh, you're back.' Mum rouses herself. 'Cup of tea and bed, I think.'

Dawn gives her the remote control and potters back to the kitchen. The bottom drawer is empty of chocolate. The kettle rattles away but does not boil quickly. With an impatient step, she takes one of the individual cheesecakes from the freezer. It is resistant to her spoon and the little bits that do come away are too cold to have any taste. She resorts to a knife and cuts slices, spooning these up into big mouthfuls. It is gone in seconds. She checks the bottom drawer again but even with a thorough search there are no secrets to be found.

She lays the tea tray and takes it through, but Mum is asleep again, the remote control having slipped from her knee to the floor.

'Come on, Mum, you're best off in bed.'

'What, no tea?'

'I'll bring you it in bed, you're falling asleep.'

'Oh, okay.' And with unsteady legs she stands and then turns.

'What are you doing, Mum?'

'I'm putting it against the patio doors.' She pushes at her chair.

'Why? It wouldn't stop them being opened. They slide. And the towel rail against your bedroom door – what's going on?'

'Oh, I don't know. I guess I get fearful.'

'But a towel rack is not going to stop someone.'

'But it will clatter as it falls over.'

'And then what?'

Mum's eyes widen and her dry lips part. She seems to have lost so much height since her fall, or is that an illusion?

'I don't know.' She answers like a small child, and Dawn knows this is the problem; Mum feels like a child, small and weak. But unlike a child, she is aware of the terrifying possibilities of the worst that could happen.

'Come on, Mum, let's put you to bed.' Dawn does not want to think about these things herself either. 'You don't need to be afraid of the night, I'm staying here now.'

'I'm not afraid.' It is almost her old voice – sharp, but the power is gone. 'And why are you staying here? I wasn't aware we'd agreed that.'

Dawn closes her eyes and nods her head, willing herself to have patience.

'Ladies-in-Waiting, Mum. I could only afford them by giving up my flat, remember?' And she must remember, too, to give in her notice.

'I don't know why ...'

'You fell, Mum.'

'Well, seeing as you're here you might as well help me to bed. Bring my tea up, will you?' And she walks as sedately as she can to the door, holding on to the mantelpiece and the arm of the second chair for balance until she can reach the door handle, from where she makes a lunge for the end of the bannisters. It is almost written in her footwork that it is just a matter of time before she falls again.

In bed she sits regally but looks as small as a child in a nursery. Dawn puts her mum's tea by her bed and passes her book to her.

'I don't think so, not tonight.' Mum passes the book back and ignores the tea and, using her arms and taking her time shifting her legs about, she awkwardly turns on her side, away from Dawn. 'Oh, my back does hurt since the fall,' she moans.

Next morning, an email about Hogdykes Abattoir is in Dawn's inbox – again! This time she just deletes it – best to say it never arrived. There is another email too, and her reaction to this one is to gather her bag and coat.

As the door swings closed behind her, her phone rings and the animated person on the other end gushes for a moment before Dawn realises who it is.

'Okay, that is good.' Dawn is in the stairwell now on the way to her car, phone pressed against her ear. 'So she was actually eating her lunch when you arrived and there was no need to help at all?'

She scrabbles in her bag for her notebook and, with the phone tucked between her ear and her shoulder, she writes in big capitals *GIVE NOTICE*. As she listens to Amanda from Ladies-in-Waiting telling her how Mum also went to get the post from inside the front porch, unbolting and bolting the inner door, and how, even after sitting down to open her letters, she had got up again to make herself a coffee. Unfortunately, however, she did not drink it all.

Amanda talks about her client as if she is a performing dog, but the content of her report is good, and Mum sounds like she is getting back to normal. Dawn scrawls a big question mark after *GIVE NOTICE*, and puts the notebook away.

'Well, thank you for calling, that's all very good to hear.' And with that, she pockets her phone and feels lighter on her feet as she descends the stairs to the car park.

So far the day is going remarkably well.

One of her superiors – not Ms Moss – has sent over an email saying that they had received a call from a very distraught member of the public over a certain Cyril Sugden and his animals, demanding that the council evict both him and his dogs and rabbits. The email went on to say that some action must be taken, and that they must be seen to be taking the complaint seriously, and that it is 'imperative to ascertain' whether there is any validity to the caller's complaints. Dawn is no longer intimidated by this sort of language. If anything, these days it makes her chuckle, as if the person writing has stopped being a human being and has become a machine, or has suddenly graduated from Eton, and is using all the pompous words they know, trying to establish their superiority. The email added that someone must visit the property to find out how many dogs this Cyril Sugden has and whether they can be considered a nuisance. It's one of those hot potato emails, passing the responsibility down the line. Dawn welcomes it, though, because it gives her an excuse to be out of the office, and besides, it is best that she goes herself; someone else might overreact to the situation and that could be disastrous – for the animals! In short, the email gives her all the authority she needed to make another visit with a clear conscience, knowing that she could back up her absence if necessary, prove that she was not taking advantage of her position. Not that anyone really cares what she does except the newly appointed Ms Moss, and even her spark of energy will be extinguished in a month or two. That's the way it goes working for this council.

The high street in town is packed with shoppers, and Dawn crawls along, behind a brightly coloured hatchback with a *Baby on board* sticker in the back window. The cars coming the other way are driven by flustered mums, and little old ladies peering over their steering wheels, driving painfully slowly. Today's phone call to Amanda from Ladies-in-Waiting has given her such hope. It almost sounds like Mum is back to her old self and does not need their support, and consequently that Dawn need not give notice on the flat. But even if Mum is making a recovery, it might be better not to stop Ladies-in-Waiting too soon and then have her fall again. No, best keep them on, for a month at least. She works out again what it will cost.

'Four hundred and twenty five pounds for the month. I am most definitely in the wrong job!' It is a big lump to come out of her savings if she doesn't give up the flat. But maybe if she does give notice, and it turns out that Mum makes a full recovery, it will be for the best anyway. In the bitter light of day, the stark and embarrassing truth is that nothing but inertia has kept her in that flat. Now she is forced into the possibility of change, she can be really honest: she never really liked the place, not even at the beginning. At the start that's what it was, or at least what it was supposed to be – a beginning, only she never made the next step, somehow. Well, it might be nearly two decades on, but maybe she will do it now.

'You've never failed unless you give up trying,' she quotes to herself, checking her rear-view mirror as she slows to a stop at a pedestrian crossing. As she waits for the people to cross, she peers at the window of an estate agent's, only to be beeped at by the car behind.

'All right, keep your hair on!' she shouts at the driver through her mirror as she sets off again.

Once she's clear of the granite buildings and surrounded by hills and trees, work seems a long way away. It is good, as always, to get out of town, and she delights in the grey clouds that scurry across patches of blue. The trees behind the drystone walls on either side of the narrow road are all bent over by the prevailing wind and the moors beyond, display shocks of deep sage green of the tough short grass and the rustic browns of the ferns. It is cold but she opens the window a crack and slows down, and she's rewarded with the call of a grouse, with its staccato 'come on, come on ...', as it glides over the bracken, close to the ground. She breathes deeply, filling her chest, at the sound. Born and raised in the town, and yet her affinity is with the country.

'What? Brrrr, come on, come on, come on,' the grouse teases and taunts her. What she would give to live somewhere like Little Lotherton with bird calls like this just outside the window. But isn't that how most people feel? The trouble is, she would have to work from home or something. With a job like the one she has, where the hours are not flexible, her commute time would double at rush hour, and it's a fair drive as it is. It just wouldn't be practical.

'In your next life,' she promises herself.

The wheels skip on loose stones as she pulls off the main road and onto the single lane in Little Lotherton, with its mill cottages in a line reaching up to the top of the hill. Not only would everyone have known everyone back when the mill was working but they would have worked and played together as well.

'How nice that must have been. Peaceful.' She breathes out the words as she parks and gathers her notebook and her bag and wraps her cardigan about her. Hopefully she will not be outside long enough to need her coat. The seat belt gets stuck in the door again but she takes her time to release it and locks the door.

Cyril's house looks still, but as she approaches, the door of the cottage next to it swings open and out strides Mr Brocklethwaite. She instinctively knows it is he who is the anonymous 'distraught member of the public' of the complaining email.

'Dawn, isn't it?' he says as she draws nearer. 'Well, come through t'back. I swear he has more rabbits than ever!'

Dawn looks at the wardrobe where Cyril's front door should be. It seems impenetrable, with no knocker, no bell, and for a moment she has no idea of the best way to go about this task. She accepts Mr Brocklethwaite's offer to go through his house, even if it doesn't seem like the best approach, somehow. He holds the door for her and she tries to not to appear nosy as she passes through Mr Brocklethwaite's single downstairs room. But she gets the impression of horse brasses by the fireplace and dark floral material on high-backed chairs. Like an old-fashioned pub. Mr Brocklethwaite leads her through.

'He's letting the evidence go!' Mr Brocklethwaite calls to her as she steps out of his back door. He is puffing, out of breath, he is so excited.

And there is a man who, she can only presume, is Cyril. His eyes are red-rimmed as if he has been crying and he is staring at one of the empty cages, the door of which swings open. Memories of her own rabbit rush upon her and her heart immediately goes out to this man and his situation. Well, she *says* man – and indeed, he is an adult, but there is something very boy-like in the way he is sitting on the low drystone wall of his tiny garden, and she wonders if he is challenged, or just a little slow.

She was called that at one time, or rather she overheard one of her teachers say it to Mum: 'It's not that Dawn is stupid, she has a brain. It's just that she's a little slow.' At the time she didn't understand what it meant, but over the years she has come to suspect that what the teacher was seeing was damage – the damage done by being brought up with the belief that her thoughts were of no significance. When she was a child, everything was decided for her: what to wear, what to eat, who her friends were, who could come back for tea and who could not, and even what to think.

'Eat your beans, you know you like them. And I have your favourite for dessert.' But she had never liked beans and the dessert was Mum's current favourite. Only relatively recently has she come to realise that the effect of this has been to make her mistrust her own thoughts and feelings, and that in the past it seemed safer to wait for the adults – teachers, bosses – to tell her what to do, even if they sometimes got annoyed at her lack of initiative.

She hopes she no longer does this, but as she has this thought her focus wavers – she cannot concentrate as a piece of her past demands to be recalled, an event from when she was around seven years old.

'Why haven't you got your coat on, you know we're going!'

She had woken feeling unwell and by breakfast she felt positively sick, so she asked to take her porridge out into the garden, where the sun was flooding the grass and a beautiful day was unfolding. She did not ask to go into the garden because she wanted to be outside, however, but because she thought she might be sick if she ate the porridge, and not eating it was not an option. She knew what Mum would say: 'Don't be silly, of course you don't

139

feel sick. You like porridge. Stop making a fuss.' So going into the garden gave her a chance to ditch the lumpy glutinous mass under a bush and avoid the argument.

She doubts Mum was ever aware that she engaged in this controlling behaviour. But it was no less destructive for that..

With the memory fresh in her mind, she looks more closely at Cyril, takes a step towards him, attracted by the recognition of a kindred spirit. Is he crying? Maybe he finds life a little overwhelming; well, she can understand that too. Whatever it is that she recognises in him, she feels her fighting spirit rise to prompt her to stand up for him and his obvious love of animals.

The foreign woman, the one who was outside the front door last time she came, is there. Her brightly coloured clothes are all pristinely ironed and arranged. Everything about her is neat – her long, shiny black hair, her scarf drawn over her head, the tiny studs of gold in her ears and nose. She looks like the sort of woman who is always in control of her life and, having once taken control, has nothing left to do but to stick her beak into other people's business. Dawn pulls her sagging, bobbling cardigan around her more tightly and holds her sleeve over her nose against the bad smell coming from Cyril's house. Maybe it was her, this neat little woman, who wrote to the council demanding this poor man be evicted.

'Hello, again,' Dawn addresses her. 'Got yourself involved, have you? Typical.'

'I do not know what you mean by that?' The woman seems quite affronted and Dawn wonders if she has got it wrong, although it still seems highly unlikely that someone so neat and trim would be a friend to someone

140

like Cyril. His tweed jacket has several holes in it and the collar, where it stands away from his neck, is shiny with dirt and age. His shirt has many spills down the front and his rough wool trousers are torn at the knee, and both trouser legs are frayed around the heels. No, it is unlikely that he and this woman are friends.

'Mrs Todman, he's let 'em go. Look, half the cages are empty,' Mr Brocklethwaite complains.

'Why is this a problem?' the neat women asks. 'You yourself said that you wanted to get his animals out. What was that word you used? Evicted. Well, they are evicted. Time to be happy.' She smiles at Mr Brocklethwaite but it seems getting the animals evicted may not be what he wanted after all. It certainly does not seem to make him happy.

'Look!' Mr Brocklethwaite turns to Dawn, demanding her attention. 'Look, a rabbit with young 'uns, and look at the size of that one. It's too big to even turn around in its cage. Is that not enough?'

Dawn looks back at the cages. The nursing mother appears quite content as its two young ones feed. The big one does look a little too fat for its cage, and she might suggest to Cyril that he gets a bigger space for that one. Mr Brocklethwaite points with a stabbing finger to make sure she is looking and she finds this a little annoying.

'I don't think two rabbits and some babies is going to be enough to get an eviction order.' She pulls her cardigan more tightly around her. The wind off the moors is refreshing and clean, if cold, but she wishes it would blow more constantly to keep the smell of the house at bay. The grey clouds part and the sun makes its way out, a warmth to it. The wind changes direction and it's a relief to be able to drop her hand from her nose.

'What about the smell, then?' Mr Brocklethwaite demands.

'Well, I for one am grateful the wind is blowing the way it is right now,' she says. 'But yes, we can look into that. But it will take longer. Perhaps the best option is to get in touch directly with the landlord. Do we know who that is?'

Dawn looks at Mr Brocklethwaite. It is intended as a challenge, a sort of 'if you don't, stay out of it' message. She is aware this is childish and she is not proud but she is so used to people telling her how to do her job that the defence is almost automatic. People being upset and blaming it on her, as if her job gives her a magic wand to rid them of all they suffer and if she doesn't do it, it's because she's malicious or something.

'You are talking as if Cyril isn't right here!' The neat woman's voice comes out high-pitched.

Mr Brocklethwaite looks first at the woman and then at Dawn. She doesn't want to catch his eye and so looks at the ground, where there is a pattern of paw marks, as if one rabbit after another has scampered its way to freedom. She is glad to see this – at least they won't be put down. She looks up and sees Cyril, who is scanning the open moor, and this confirms that the little fluffballs have got away, that they are safe somewhere away on the moors.

Mr Brocklethwaite begins to say something but then starts to cough. The wind is changing again and Dawn inches away from the back of the house towards the moor path, back the way she came.

Mr Brocklethwaite's coughing continues; he seems in some distress, as if he cannot breathe, and it is Cyril who slaps him hard on his back, with a big open hand. Mr Brocklethwaite nearly falls forward with the force, his flat cap shifting over his forehead. Cyril obviously does not know his own strength.

'I – I could have you done for assault,' Brocklethwaite stammers, putting his hat straight. His face is red, blood vessels showing in his eyes as he regains his breath. Cyril blinks rapidly.

'Oh, come on!' Dawn's exasperation at the situation escapes her, through the bunched-up sleeve that she holds over her nose and mouth. 'Let's not get ridiculous.' And she steps through the gate and heads back towards Mr Brocklethwaite's house. She has something to report. The rabbit numbers have been reduced. That will look good for her, as if she made it happen. For now that is enough; the situation needs to be contained. The tension between Brocklethwaite, Cyril and this woman, whoever she is, is too tense to risk pushing to find out how many dogs there are today. She will go over one day when she has not been summoned and have a quiet word with Cyril.

Mr Brocklethwaite seems to have recovered; his airways are clear. 'You're right. We should get in touch with the landlord,' he commands, following her towards his own house. 'But you know what, I've just realised summat.' Mr Brocklethwaite seems very pleased with himself suddenly and he steps into his house first. 'He was renting off Archie and Archie died – what? Must be ten year back.' Dawn takes a final glance at Cyril, just to check he is all right. He is still looking away towards the moors, a tear on his cheek.

'So what are you saying?' She follows Mr Brocklethwaite inside, trying to focus. She might have to find out more about this Cyril.

'I'm saying he might not be a legal tenant, that's all. Who's he paying rent to? I can't think why I didn't think of this sooner.' Brocklethwaite sounds excited again.

'Well, if that's the case he cannot stay.' The words are stated very seriously by Dawn but she is not connecting with them; she is still thinking of the tear on Cyril's cheek. When was the last time she cried? When her rabbit died?

'You'll take a sherry with me and t'wife before you head back then, Mrs Todman?' he asks. She does not like the way he says her surname – 'Tod-Man'. And she is a Ms, not a Mrs. There is no man in her life.

'Dawn, me name's Dawn,' she replies.

Chapter 12

'I made pizzas,' Mum greets her as she comes in after work. She is sitting at the kitchen table, a book in hand. The scene is normal, and Mum seems like her old self, and Dawn feels instant relief. And yet, there's something odd, something not quite right; but she cannot put her finger on it.

'Fantastic,' she answers. Not that she wanted pizza, but just for Mum to be back to normal enough to get tea ready is great. She sighs and puts her bag and coat on the table.

'Hang it up,' Mum is quick to demand. Dawn does as she is told, hanging her coat on a hook by the back door where four or five of Mum's jackets are neatly arranged, each with a matching bag. This is just a small proportion of Mum's collection; she has always loved clothes and often, when Dawn has been struggling for money, she has resented her mother's extravagance. But today the sight of the jackets, the bags, makes her happy. Mum's idiosyncrasies are all to be celebrated. She is recovering from the fall and the world is well.

'So, how long before it's ready?' Mum must have only just put the pizza in the oven as no aroma is leaking into the kitchen yet.

'Soon – it's been in for ...' Mum looks at the clock on the wall, twisting in her chair. 'Oh, I'm not sure, I can't remember when I put it on.'

Dawn opens the door of the oven cautiously, ready for the blast of heat, but there is none. Oh well, that's easily done, an oversight; that could happen to anyone, couldn't it? But Dawn's heart sinks as she peers into the oven to find a single mini pizza still in its plastic wrapper and on its foam board.

'Mum?'

'What?'

She draws the pizza out.

'Is it done?'

'Oh Mum, the oven isn't on and you left the pizza in its wrapping.'

'Oh, I thought it felt strangely plasticky.'

'Could you not see?'

'I couldn't find my glasses.'

As Mum says this, Dawn realises that this is what is odd about the scene – Mum is sitting at the table reading, but without her glasses.

'So why have you got a book in your hand?' she presses, confused now, and with a sickening panic rising in her chest.

'Not sure.' The words are clipped, defensive, the conversation is over. Dawn takes a second pizza from the freezer, unwraps both and turns the oven on full.

'Peas or mixed veg?' she calls out, digging through the bags at the bottom of the freezer. Mum continues to sit, book in hand.

'Oh, neither, I think, I'm not very hungry.'

Dawn closes her eyes. So much for the recovery. She returns to set the table, and Mum perks up, issuing orders as if Dawn is fourteen again.

'I think we'll have a tablecloth. And let's put mats down, we don't want the table any more marked than it already is.'

The implication is clear: any marks on the table are due to Dawn's past omissions.

'I do hate people who never lay the table properly.' This last remark is an indirect request for side plates and butter knives, even though there will be no bread served with the cheap frozen pizza. Glasses of water are filled and placed on the table, but Mum will not touch a drop. It is all one big, theatrical fantasy. Dawn used to think everyone did lunch, tea and dinner in the same way, laid out their tables out like this – banquets without substance – with their cheap cutlery and chipped plates. Every meal a protracted ritual.

The clearing-up process is the same – everything in the dishwasher, every napkin in the washing machine, every place mat and surface wiped so the kitchen looks untouched, before the kettle has boiled for after-dinner coffee. It was only when she started watching soap operas on the television that Dawn became delightfully enlightened and liberated enough to have her tea on her knee in her own flat, laughing to herself at the irony – mirroring exactly what she was watching the actors on television doing, and enjoying it all the more for that. At first it felt as if she was doing something naughty.

Now a microwaved frozen dinner on the knee is part of her daily routine.

'Oh, my back does hurt,' Mum moans.

'You said that the other night. Do you think you banged it when you fell? Do you want a paracetamol?'

'Yes, I think I do.' Mum shifts uneasily in her chair.

Dawn consciously flattens her raised eyebrows; Mum never takes medicine. She turns the oven down a little and goes through to the downstairs bathroom. The last time she looked, there were two packets of painkillers there, which have been there forever. Better check that they are not out of date.

'Mum, have you moved them?' There is a bottle of aspirin, empty, and a new bar of soap. Under the sink is a cane wastebasket and under a toilet roll core she spots not one but two packets of pills. She takes them as evidence. 'Mum, these were in the bin, did you flush them?' She looks at the sell-by dates.

'No, I took them.'

Dawn stares at her for a moment.

'Not all at once, don't look at me like that. I mean I've been hurting since my fall. Is the pizza done yet?'

'So she's been taking them since her fall?' June asks later at night class. It is watercolour night.

'It seems so. She's got through two packets, and that means she's been taking quite a lot. Did he say to mix ochre or yellow cadmium or lemon yellow in this?' She scrubs at the colours with her paintbrush.

'Cadmium, but only a little. Look, I put way too much. So if she's in so much pain why has she not told you before? Did she go for an X-ray after her fall?'

'No ... Oh bugger, I've put too much as well, what a mess. It never comes out like he shows us.' Dawn looks around at the others in the class and is relieved to see that most of them seem to be struggling too.

'Maybe you should get her X-rayed.'

'You know what she's like, she wouldn't go if I suggested it. I got so excited today when I thought she was her old self again. It was such a relief.' Dawn wipes her mixing tray clean with a tissue and starts again.

'Not that her old self was a joy to live with either,' June comments. 'Look, my tree looks like a cloud.' She starts to giggle, Dawn joins in at the sight of her tree, but the rest of the room is quiet so they do their best to keep their mirth muffled.

'I thought he sponged the green on?' Dawn says.

'Oh yes, you're right.' June borrows her sponge.

'No she's never going to be a joy to live with. I'm already finding the whole thing depressing.' Dawn dips just the tip of her brush into the yellow and adds it, and this time the resulting colour looks right.

'Well, you don't want to get stuck there,' June warns as she dabs away with a sponge; hers is beginning to look like a kindergarten picture and June is giggling away to herself.

'Don't worry, I have a plan. I'll keep Ladies-in-Waiting on for a month, and then I'm going to get the sort of flat I always wanted. I'm going to use the whole thing to my advantage.' Dawn's trees only look slightly better than June's, and neither looks anything like the teacher's demonstration.

149

'Good for you.' June looks at her, watercolour forgotten. She flings the sponge down. 'Sod this, it's almost break time anyway. Come on – let's go use the computers and look online for a flat for you.'

The others in the class are still working away. This class has only been going for three weeks and they don't really know each other yet. She has spoken to a man called Jim who looks like he is struggling as much as they are. Judy, an older lady, is doing quite well but tonight she doesn't look satisfied, and the two girls, not much past school age, Mercedes and Cat, aren't doing well either. Their pictures are a worse mess than her own, but they don't look like they care and they spend the whole time talking quietly to each other.

She doesn't know any of the others by name. June refers to one of the men as a hipster on account of his beard, and has nicknamed one of the girls 'Squirrel' because she is so petite and does everything with quick nervous movements. Then there is a married couple who are so nondescript that they have called them 'Boring One' and 'Boring Two'. But no one else looks like they are going to take a break right now and Dawn hesitates to be the first.

'Come on.' June stands and encourages her to follow her out of their side room and into the main library. The computers are still switched on although the library is closed to the public.

'Sit here,' June says, and they sit side by side.

June finds an estate agent's website. 'Oh, look at this one.' She clicks on an image of an enormous modern flat, with a price tag far beyond Dawn's budget.

'I'd need to win the lottery for that,' Dawn laughs.

'We could rob a bank,' June chuckles.

'Put in a cap on the budget,' Dawn suggests.

As they scroll through the list Dawn is surprised to find there is more choice than she had ever imagined, and for more or less the same as she is paying now. Many of the places look newly painted and beautifully finished, and she starts to get excited and consequently giggles.

'Maybe you can move somewhere near me,' June says, and Dawn's heart gives a little flutter.

She looks at June to see if she really means it – June has Steve and her boys, her own family, and has no need of anyone else, surely? June is engrossed with the images and doesn't notice. But she sounded serious, and Dawn begins to feel she really can do this and that, actually, she has a friend who will support her through the whole process.

This thought is quickly followed by another thought, or rather a feeling. She is not a child moving back in with Mum. She is an adult, and she is just moving in to look after Mum and then get herself the flat she deserves. This new flat, she decides, is really going to be a new start for her.

Some of the others start wandering out into the library's main hall too, and Judy and Hipster and Cat seem to be drawn to them, presumably wondering what they are laughing over.

'What are you guys doing? Checking out a dating website?' Cat asks as she draws closer, and Dawn feels herself immediately curl up inside. The pictures of the smart flats on the screen are so at odds with how her life is, she feels a fraud for even looking.

151

'Dawn here needs somewhere to live,' June says, as if this is the most natural thing in the world, and she moves her chair a little to make space for the others. Typical June, all inclusive. They gather in close.

'That's a nice one,' Judy says, and she points to one Dawn could easily afford. 'Make the pictures bigger,' she suggests, and June clicks for more details. 'Hmm, it's a bit small for you, perhaps?' Judy says, and Dawn turns to look at her, thinking she is joking, but she is not even smiling. Judy sees her as being worth a bigger space!

'That one, two down.' Mercedes points. 'That looks like you.'

The one she is pointing at shows a light-filled room with one wall a beautiful shade of blue. Is that how Mercedes sees her? A woman with a spacious sun-filled room and pastel colours? That is the sort of flat a proper person lives in, one who has a proper job and friends and – well, a life. She glances at Mercedes, who flashes her a smile and then looks back at the screen.

'I think that one.' Cat points at a picture of a shiny new bathroom, the sort Dawn thought they only had in hotels. She has never imagined that she could rent a flat with such luxury, and the shock is that Cat sees her as the sort of person who would live somewhere like this. Cat, this relative stranger, sees her as being just as valid as anyone else, purely by default.

'Tell you what, if you rent that I'll be round for a cup of tea,' Hipster says.

'Forget tea, I'll be round on bath night,' Squirrel pipes up. 'My power shower is bust.'

And the group laughs. Dawn experiences a curious sensation; these people all have the potential to be her friends. It is such a lovely feeling that for a moment she forgets her dark secret, the past that she cannot tell of, squashes it back down so she can hang on to the pleasant feeling.

'Yes, I could see you in there, it would suit you,' Cat adds, endorsing the choice. They all seem to see her as being worthy of a nice flat and Dawn finds her eyes misting over, she is so very touched by their kindness.

'Come on, you lot,' the tutor calls to them. 'I know some of you are struggling but let's have another go,' he goes on, and the group breaks up.

The second half of the lesson goes much better, and the group seem to have bonded and are now talking freely and giving each other tips. The class might work out even better than the pottery course she and June took some five years ago. That was the last really good group.

'Well, that was good,' June says. She is in her car and is talking to Dawn through the open passenger window. As she speaks, she picks up a bag of apples that has fallen into the footwell and puts it on the seat. 'I'll see you Monday,' she says. 'We're going to quiz night next week, right? How about I pick you up from your mum's and then you can have a drink or two?'

'Sure.' Dawn hesitates to get into her own car, savouring the evening. It has been a good night.

'Oh, and when you do get to the point of seriously looking for flats, let's do it together. I mean it! Get something near us, okay?' and she starts her car. Dawn waves but June is already concentrating on pulling out of the library car park and onto the road.

153

'Come on, Mum.' Dawn starts the routine, because that is what putting Mum to bed feels like already, as soon as she gets there. Mum seems to have melted into her chair, small and unmovable.

The television blasts away and when Dawn clicks it off the silence rouses Mum.

'Come on, Mum, let's get you upstairs,' she says, and the old woman needs no persuading. Really, she should insist on Mum having a drink before bed but, with a yawn, she decides it is easiest just to tuck her up and leave the challenge of forcing tea down her till the morning.

But once she has closed the door to Mum's room, Dawn realises she does not feel as tired as she thought. In the silent kitchen the kettle seems to take ages to boil so she stirs the hot chocolate mix with a little cold water as she waits, breaking up the lumps. After grabbing a magazine from the television room sofa, she takes the hot drink to bed. Whether she feels tired or not, she needs to sleep or she will not function at work.

Tomorrow she must definitely write a letter to her landlord giving notice. Flat-hunting with June will be fun.

She flicks through the outdated periodical and lingers on an article about women's rights in the workplace. It seems the glass ceiling still exists, according to the statistics it quotes. With economic booms, recessions, the boat people and wars in the Middle East it seems that no one has noticed how little has changed since Germaine Greer wrote *The Female Eunuch*. Or so the article says.

'Too right,' Dawn mutters as she flicks over the page, leaving the rest of the article unread. There is no need to know the details – just consider her own position. Everyone's gofer. She is just used as cannon fodder by her seniors, sent out to do battle and soften the enemy, as it were. After all, what does she do? Endless rounds of facing off against landlords and chip shop owners, threatening them with the charges that could be pressed against them unless they make the changes demanded of them. And for the most part they do the bare minimum, and the situation is the same a few months later. Her job is pointless and without any satisfaction, and she has no real power. It just allows those further up the chain of command to say they have done something. Maybe she should think about changing her job too? But Mum's wise words ring in her ears: a job in the council is a job for life, with a guaranteed pension.

She turns back to the piece and recalls the other article that she read, the last one that prompted her to take action.

'Cosmopolitan has a lot to answer for,' she mutters, but then wonders if it was *Cosmopolitan*. Maybe it was *Woman and Home*, or even *The Lady* magazine. It was a long time ago, and it's not as if it matters which magazine it was. It was a week, maybe two, after she moved back home and, when she read it, she began to realise that the whole incident with Paul Fiddler was not going to fade as easily as she had at first hoped. Saying her final goodbyes to Veronica and leaving the shared house had not given her the new focus she had hoped for (she never saw Helen again after that glimpse through the door crack). The academic year was over, and they all had to move out of the house – Dawn too, even if she wasn't a student.

At first the walls of her childhood home felt like a protective cocoon against the world and she did not have the strength to step outside. Even Mum's snideness felt safe in its familiarity. But that article had challenged women who were sexually assaulted and did not report the crime. This, it suggested, was unfair to other women, and left violent men roaming the streets unchecked. So harsh and condemnatory was the author's tone, Dawn wondered if it was supposed to be tongue in cheek, but she soon reasoned that the magazine would not risk its reputation in such a manner. No, the author was serious, and, as if ice water were flowing through her veins, she realised she was reading the piece through guilty eyes. But to step outside her own emotional chaos and do something for the good of others seemed like too much to ask. She flung the magazine in the bin and pulled the duvet over her head. In bed the world seemed safe, and that's where she had spent most of her time since her return home.

'Dawn, are you in bed again? This isn't a hotel, you know.' Mum at least had the decency to knock and not just barge straight in.

'Just getting dressed,' she lied.

'Two weeks you've been here now, and when are you going to get another job?'

'I am applying.' Another lie. She had not told Mum about Paul Fiddler. There would have been too many questions, no real sympathy, and maybe even blame. Instead, she had lied and said she wasn't needed at the pub over the summer holidays; she had told the truth about the shared house, though, which was no longer available. But as far as the real reasons were concerned, she kept them to herself. If Mum knew, it would never be left alone, picked at like a scab until it would never heal at all.

'Well, I would like you to clean the bathroom, please. It gets dirty a lot quicker with two people using it, and I found hair in the plughole, so if you wouldn't mind.' The sound of her footsteps told Dawn she was walking away, the *clump, clump* of her tread on the stairs.

'Guilt, always the guilt.' And the article came back to mind. Maybe she was still suffering because she felt guilty. Not that she had done anything to encourage the attack, God knows she had not.

Maybe, she wondered – maybe reporting the whole thing might prove cathartic …?

It was this thought that took her to the police station.

As she pushed the doors open, she felt nervous and curious at the same time. She had never been inside a police station before, although she had often passed the place, which was just off the high street, while walking to school as a child. There was a nursery next door in those days, growing bedding plants and organic vegetables. Now, of course, it was all houses.

The police station itself was a small place, detached, with a carved stone Victorian porch, built for the days when the local bobby would have lived there with his family. Inside was all Formica, glass and plastic plants, totally at odds with the elegant facade. There was no one behind the little window but on the counter was an old-fashioned bell, which she tentatively rang. No one came, and Dawn waited, assuming they must all be busy. She sat on a long wooden bench opposite the counter that looked like it had been rescued from the church up the road.

She looked at the notices for missing cats and dogs, surprised by how many there were, and she did not hear the policeman approaching down the corridor until he was just a few yards away.

'Can I help you?' he asked.

'I ...' she began, but then she wasn't sure how to word what she needed to say, or even whether this was the right person to say it to. 'I need to report a crime.'

'Right.' He sounded weary as he went round behind the counter and started tapping at his computer. 'Name?' He also sounded very official.

She told him her name and address and then he asked what crime she wanted to report. It was all so heartless and she had to force herself to say the word rape, wondering if this was such a good idea after all. At this, the policeman stopped typing and looked up at her.

'One minute,' he said, and he disappeared into a back room. A few moments later a policewoman came out from behind the counter and led Dawn into another room at the back.

Once she'd outlined the situation, the policewoman was sympathetic but obviously frustrated, and Dawn felt that she was a nuisance, wasting everyone's time.

'You should have come straightaway,' the policewoman said. 'There'll be no evidence now, d'you see? People will have taken baths and showers, cooked and cleaned ...'

The bruises were there, of course, but they had faded to a dirty yellow and looked far from alarming.

'Your word against his,' the policewoman said, and she sighed. Dawn wished she had never come, but it was too late now, and the process was out of her control, or so it seemed.

Her bed, later that day, seemed to have increased in softness, warmth and comfort, and when Mum called her for her tea she did not move; she could not move. She was curled up tightly in a ball and could not uncurl. Veronica had been right. At least to a degree.

From that day, life became pointless to Dawn, or to be more accurate she accepted that the world saw *her* as pointless, and Mum became increasingly impatient with her. She no longer knocked and would burst into Dawn's bedroom day and night, demanding that she get up and do something.

'I had this with your father and I'm not going through it again. Self-indulgent depression never helped anyone. Here, take the polish and a duster and join the real world.'

Dawn shakes her head and screws up her eyes to dispel the memories. Dwelling on them will not change the past; she needs to let go.

'Let go.' She says the words out loud and turns off the bedside light, knowing that the hours will creep by and sleep will not take her till the early hours of the morning. Several times she dozes off and pieces of the past mix with events of the day.

The event of the day that keeps returning and churning round and round in her head is the offer of sherry from Mr Brocklethwaite when she went back through his house, an offer she had politely refused. But he was so insistent that she drank it anyway, standing in his kitchen. Mrs Brocklethwaite, a shrivelled little woman, had been polite but had left the room for some reason and Mr Brocklethwaite had used that moment to impress upon Dawn just how grateful he was to have her on his side. His hand patted first her shoulder, then her waist, then slipped around as if he was inclined to pull her in for a hug. She had broken the stem of the sherry glass, so hard had she slammed it on the kitchen counter before storming out, with Mr Brocklethwaite shouting after her that the glass had been a wedding present from his mother.

'It seems this is your lot in life,' she tells herself in the dark, realising that until just now she had pushed what happened with Mr Brocklethwaite from her mind. She has become expert at that. Ignoring, covering over, burying – all great tactics to erase the need to process events. Is that what Cyril does, too? Are his animals a distraction from the things he doesn't want to think about? She can understand that.

Sleep comes just before the first ray of sun touches her curtains, and she is taken off by a hundred fluffy rabbits into a warren of the softest down.

Chapter 13

Over the next three days, Dawn discovers a new enthusiasm for her work. Rather than reading through countless pointless emails, she forwards them to a selection of colleagues and focuses on finding out as much as she can about Cyril. There is more than she expected about him. Housing has a file on him, and so does Health and Safety, as does Community Care. It seems he was in a children's home and then a psychiatric hospital, but there is no mention of parents. The psychiatric ward, under the charge of a Matron Jan, speaks well of him, and the reports describe him as damaged rather than a broken man, someone who would respond well to a stable environment and loving kindness, perhaps; unless she is just projecting, Dawn thinks, there is a certain fondness in the way it is written. After the psychiatric hospital was converted into executive flats, it seems Cyril was put back into the community and assigned a string of care workers, each for a short period, with no continuity at all. Most recently he has been given a job at Hogdykes Abattoir.

'God, how heartless!' Dawn exclaims when she reads this, thinking of his obvious love of animals.

Since his release into the community he has made claims against the council no fewer than three times, each time saying that he tripped on a poorly laid paving slab outside his house and injured himself. In each case he was awarded substantial damages. For some reason this pleases Dawn, as if Cyril got a bit of his own back on the system.

His last care worker stopped seeing him several years ago and it seems Cyril has slipped through the net since then, which Dawn thinks might not be such a bad thing. She tries to find a mention of his landlord but no name comes up. The name 'Archie Sugden', however, appears several times, and it seems that this Archie lived with him in the house in Little Lotherton for some years. Presumably some relation, although it is a common surname so she cannot be certain.

Dawn becomes engrossed in researching Cyril's case and the days fly by, but she is still glad she booked Friday off.

At the end of the week, she rejoices in the fact that she has the whole glorious day to herself and it is a rare luxury to lie in bed after seven in the morning. She writhes about on Mum's cotton sheets and tries to get back to sleep again, but the thin curtains with the cartoon yellow-and-blue flowers, which have been up at the window since she was a child, do little to block out the sunlight. Giving up on the idea of sleep, she just lies there, feeling the weight of her body against the sheets.

She runs through her mental checklist and is delighted to find she has done all she needed to do this week. There wasn't much on the list, but all of it was necessary. She gave notice on her flat, finally, and she responded to a demand from Ms Moss that she give Cyril notice to voluntarily clear his house. Judging by the tone, Ms Moss wanted to make it clear that, unlike her peers, she did not mess about and that she expected results. She used the word 'hoarder' liberally and said she had received an email addressed to her personally suggesting that rats were becoming a problem in the area. Dawn could almost see Mr Brocklethwaite sitting down to write the letter, after the sherry glass was broken. It would be his way of paying her back.

She also knew that what Ms Moss wanted was a shot over the bows, a way to try to make something happen with very little effort – just send a letter to the hoarder. Basically, it was a threat: you clear your mess or we will come in and do it for you! So she spent most of one day carefully wording a letter to Cyril, explaining that it was necessary for him to clear a few things from his home and that she would have to come and check that he had done it. It had to be official, of course, but she softened it as much as she could.

Yes, everything is done, and she can lie in bed for as long as she likes … Except that now she needs to get up to use the toilet.

Once up, she decides that she might was well make tea, start forcing liquids down Mum as soon as possible. The sooner she starts, the more chance there is of getting enough in her before it's bedtime again.

'Mum.' She taps on the door. 'You want tea?'

'Oh, my back hurts,' comes the reply through the door.

'We really need to get you X-rayed, Mum. You might have done some damage when you fell.' She has not been given permission to open the door yet.

'Hospital? I'm not ill,' Mum answers.

'I'll make you a cup of tea.' Dawn gives up and heads down the stairs.

By ten, Mum is up and in her chair, a second cup of tea by her side.

'Have a biscuit, Mum – you ate so little breakfast.'

'I wish you would just stop fussing,' Mum snaps, and then she frowns.

'Your back bad?'

She doesn't answer, but she tuts her disapproval; Dawn tightens her lips to try to stop herself saying something she might regret, but for once the words will not be stopped.

'Oh, I give up!' she shouts. 'I've moved in here to try to make your life easier, and you do nothing but make snide comments, and refuse my help – well, sod you, Mum!'

The television room door slams behind her but bounces open again as she runs down the hall. There are so many things she could be doing rather than pandering to Mum's bad temper. 'Well, forget you,' she calls down the hall from the kitchen. 'Get your own tea. I'll stop fussing, all right.'

She snatches up her keys and leaves the house. She pauses by the milk bottle on the steps, decides it is not her responsibility to take it inside and, after slamming the door of her car, drives off at speed.

She immediately has to slow down at the junction.

She should go back. The woman is in pain. Pain is never fun and makes everyone grouchy. She must persuade Mum to go to the hospital and see what is wrong with her back, or at the very least try to get a doctor to come out to her. 'Not that they do that these days,' she growls.

After turning right, she finds she is on the road to her flat. She will take the next left and turn around and go back to Mum's house. But her temper drives her forward and she doesn't turn.

'I'll just pack up a box or two. I can't be there for her every minute! It will give me a chance to calm down.' Her breathing is still heavy, the anger still raging.

The door to her flat, by the entrance to the restaurant, seems dirtier than usual and it smells of urine. Someone has left a small black bag by the door, knotted at the top and with the silhouette of a dog printed on the plastic. The signs may make people bag their dog poo, but what's the point of that if they just leave it on the street?

'Why can't they put them in the bin?' Any other day and she might pick it up, or find a stick and poke it into the gutter, but today it is not her concern.

She takes the steps up to the flat as fast as she can, eager for the insular calm of her own space.

She is greeted by the smell of damp, the result of her not having been there for days. It's rained a lot recently, which won't have helped. With no one to open a window or move the air around, and the heating off, the place feels neglected. It may be her furniture and her ornaments, but overall the flat feels abandoned.

Slowly, the sight of her ornaments begins to take over her senses. It is not that she had forgotten how many she has – she knows that the ceramic cats are lined up everywhere – it's just that in this moment they are no longer individual items; they are just clutter covering every surface, and there are even clusters of them on the floor. There are also more glass vases than she recalled. She knows that recently they have become a bit of an obsession for her; if she sees them in charity shops she appreciates their beauty and decides she must have them. The blue vase that she saw as something so magical when she bought it now looks like a piece of tat, with a chip on the rim, and too chunky to be considered elegant.

'Stuff! I've filled my life with stuff.'

She sighs and is about to flop into her chair, which is what she always does when she gets home. However, this time she stops herself and goes through to her bedroom. The lace cover on her bed today looks like something an old lady might choose, the lace-edged pillows appear cheap, and the room does not hold the charm she thought she had instilled in it. In short, it looks like an advert for a second-hand furniture shop, and a low-quality one at that.

She pulls down a couple of flat-pack boxes from the top of the wardrobe. Where to start? The china cats, the vases, the lacework linen? She pulls a suitcase out from under her bed. That makes the most sense. Pack up her clothes – she will need them.

After a couple of hours she has packed her suitcase and boxed up most of the vases. She may have spent good money on them but they are going back to the charity shop. The clock on her wall tells her she has left Mum for too long. As an apology for her eruption earlier she will get a couple of salmon steaks for lunch; Mum will like that.

She goes up and down the stairs, carrying boxes to the car, and, finally, bumps her suitcase down the stairs before locking up and heading for the supermarket.

'Mum, you want a nice cup of tea?' she calls as she lets herself in. The kettle is cold, so Mum has not made herself a drink. The television is quiet and a peek through the door confirms that Mum is not there.

'Oh shit.' Now she feels really bad. Where on earth is she? Has she left the house? Has she gone back to bed? Dawn runs up the stairs and pushes open the door, and she is partially relieved, but mostly dismayed, to find that Mum has indeed gone back to bed.

'Keep it light,' she counsels herself.

'Hi, Mum, guess what I've done? I just took three boxes of stuff I no longer want to the charity shops. How are you doing?'

There's no response.

'Sorry I shouted, Mum ...' She hadn't meant to apologise.

'Shall we get you up?' She speaks as kindly as she can. 'I got us some salmon steaks for lunch, your favourite.'

And then she tuts; it's the sort of thing Mum would say to her.

'I might stay in my dressing gown today.' Mum's voice is weak.

'That's not like you. Come on, I'll help you get dressed.' She opens the wardrobe. The wardrobe is enormous, built in down one side of the bedroom, wall to wall. When Dad was alive his suits took up half the space, but now it is all Mum's clothes – three racks of colour-coordinated outfits with matching handbags and more shoes than a person could wear in a year. It is a mystery how she managed to put together such a collection on her pension.

'What colour are you in the mood for?'

'I think my hot water bottle must have burst.' Mum is pulling her nightdress away from her legs.

'But you didn't have a …' Dawn turns away from the wardrobe and runs her hand over the sheets. Then she washes her hands in the bedroom sink in the corner. 'I think we might have to get you some new pants, Mum. They have them now, very comfortable. Very discreet, you know, for moments like this.'

Mum has pulled her nightgown off and stands naked before her. Dawn has never seen Mum naked before. Her curiosity about the folds and wrinkles causes her to stare for a moment, but she shakes herself free and guides Mum to the sink, and puts a flannel in her hand.

By lunchtime Mum is clean and dressed and sitting at the table in the kitchen enjoying her salmon steak, but she is very quiet. No mention has been made of the lack of side plates or water glasses. But nor does she complain about her back.

'I think I'm done,' Mum says and she stands to clear away her plate.

'This salmon's good, isn't it? I always think it's more tender if you wrap it in foil rather than grill it. What do you think?' Dawn says.

It's not so much a noise as a feeling of the air being suspended. The slap is Mum's hand on the table edge. Dawn's fork hangs motionless for a moment by her parted lips. Then, fish still impaled on it, it clatters to her plate as she lurches to her feet. Mum is falling – her head sinking, sinking – the table grows longer and it takes many steps to circumnavigate it. Dawn holds out both hands, her arms too short to reach, and with a gentle thud Mum's knees meet the floor. Her eyes are wide, her mouth a little oval as she falls forward, her arms useless.

Dawn catches Mum's head just before it hits the floor. One hand is on her shoulder, the other arm shoved under her chest, Mum's nose against her bicep.

'Mum!' They are both on the floor, one of Dawn's legs twisted uncomfortably beneath her, Mum slumped in her arms.

'Oh dear,' Mum manages to whisper.

'Mum, are you all right?' Dawn cannot move; she is pinned beneath a weight which is heavier than Mum's fragile frame would lead her to expect.

'My legs ...'

'Mum, I'm going to lay you down, let me do it, don't struggle.'

She manages to wriggle her leg from under the dead weight. She grabs her coat from the back of the chair and balls it up to support Mum's head.

'Shit, shit, shit.' The mantra comes unbidden. 'Mum, I'm going to ring an ambulance.' But Mum does not answer. 'Shit, shit, shit.'

She has to scrabble in the balled coat under Mum's head for her phone. 'Sorry, Mum.'

Finally, she finds it and stabs in nine-nine-nine.

'Hello – yes, ambulance, yes, my mum's collapsed …
Yes, she is conscious … I don't know. No, I won't move
her … Yes, she is breathing.' She gives her own address
and then corrects herself and gives her mum's. 'No, I
won't move her … Yes I understand.' The phone is then
discarded on the tabletop.

'Mum, it's fine, the ambulance is coming.'

'I'm fine, dear.' She sounds far from fine, and makes
no attempt to move, just lies still on the kitchen floor.

Dawn strokes her hair, just as Mum did for her as a
child, when she was ill.

'You'll be fine, Mum. Are you comfortable enough?'
The white hair is so fine now, thinning but soft.

'Not really.'

'They say you are not to move.'

'My foot.' One foot is twisted awkwardly under the
calf of the other leg. As gently as she can Dawn untangles
the limbs and lays them out.

'Better?'

There is only the smallest grunt of a reply but Dawn is
on her feet – the approaching siren tells her that the
ambulance is here already. Opening the back door, she
dithers, half in, half out. She does not want the ambulance
people to waste time going to the inoperable front door.
Two people in green, bags in hands, approach.

'Here,' Dawn calls, and she rushes back to Mum.
'They're here, Mum, you're fine. They'll look after you.
Mum, are you awake? Mum?'

Chapter 14

She looks just like any other old lady lying on the hospital trolley in admissions: wrinkled, grey-haired and withered. It is strange to see her there, so human, so fragile.

'Ward Four,' the porter tells her as he starts to push the trolley.

She asks no questions, her mind racing and yet blank at the same time. The strip lights come and go overhead, alternately lighting up Mum's face and casting it into shadow. She seems to be aging with every second.

Without warning the trolley swerves sharply sideways under a big sign that reads *Ward 4*.

A nurse looks up from the reception counter.

'A Mrs Iris Todman,' the porter announces, in a manner that suggests they have arrived at a ball. It has been years since Dawn heard anyone address Mum as Iris. She is always Mum: Mum to her face, Mum in Dawn's head and Mum when she talks to June or to Amanda in Australia. The Ladies-in-Waiting even referred to her as Mum.

'Last room on the left,' the nurse says, and she looks Dawn up and down, emotionless.

There are four rooms on the ward – two to the left and two to the right. There are four beds in Mum's room, but only a single bed in the room opposite, occupied by a skeleton of a woman, her mouth open; she has no teeth and is as still as death.

The trolley is wheeled alongside an empty bed and two nurses bustle through the doors and draw the curtains around them, obscuring Mum from Dawn's view.

'Hello, dear.' The woman in the next bed is up and sitting in her chair.

'Hello,' Dawn replies and the woman begins to sing a Christmas carol, in a thin, high voice, almost in tune.

'Excuse me.' The woman in the opposite bed lifts a hand, trying to get Dawn's attention. 'Can I go downstairs now? I need to let the dog out ...'

Dawn glances out of the window. They are on the ground floor, and a door in the corner of the room leads out to a neatly tended square of garden with a bench under a tree. There's no one in the garden.

The curtains swoosh open and the porter wheels the trolley away, followed by one of the nurses. The other nurse adjusts Mum's pillows. The enormous hospital bed dwarfs Mum's thin frame.

'The doctor will be along to see your mother in a minute, and we'll need to take some blood.' The second nurse smiles and leaves.

Mum seems resigned to the situation, sunk into the pillows, her hair matted on her forehead. It is most unlike her, but Dawn wonders if she will bark at her for fussing if she combs it to make it a bit neater. The mum she knows would be horrified at how she looks.

'I'll just straighten your hair, Mum, the doctor is coming round. He'll be able to tell us why your legs collapsed.' With a comb from her bag she carefully straightens Mum's crown and fringe. Mum does not seem to care either way – she doesn't react, just lies there.

'How long do I have to stay here?' she asks, so quietly it startles Dawn.

'Oh, they just need to check you out.' Dawn's intention is to reassure her, but she is not sure if this is for Mum's benefit or her own. She smooths the sheets and the thin cover, and then there is nothing more to do but wait. She sits in the chair by Mum's bed, right next to the first woman, who is still singing carols. She seems a happy soul.

'Do shut her up!' the woman opposite grumbles, and Dawn turns towards the singer, who carries on with her song, unconcerned. The fourth bed, directly opposite Mum's, is also occupied, and the woman in it is fast asleep. Dawn turns back to find that Mum's eyes are closed and her lips parted, a gentle whistle of breath coming in and out. She does not seem out of place in this room, and to Dawn this is startling. She fidgets in her seat, trying to get comfortable.

Hours seem to pass, and the doctor does not come. Dawn's stomach begins to grumble. Finally, a nurse, a young man with a pleasant face, bounces in, a grey cardboard kidney dish in his hand, with a syringe and an empty vial in it.

'Hello, Mavis, give us a song,' he says to the woman next to Dawn.

'I'm a Geordie girl,' she tells him.

'Can I let my dog out?' the woman opposite asks. Her name is printed in large letters above her bed: *GLADYS*.

'You're in hospital, Gladys,' the young nurse tells her. 'Your son is taking care of your dog.'

'He's a booger,' Gladys retorts.

Right' – he turns to Mum – 'let's take some of your blood, Iris, check if it's blue or not.' He chuckles at his own joke. 'Hello,' he addresses Dawn. 'I'm Tristan, one of the nurses here. I'll be here for ...' He consults the board at the end of the bed. '... Iris, for the next few days.'

He flashes her a broad smile, and Dawn is encouraged by his false jollity. Or maybe it's not false, and this really is his manner? It might get tiring if one were exposed to it all the time, but in this grim setting it is a tonic. He draws the curtains around the bed, excluding her again whilst she digests the reference to the next few days. What does that mean?

Behind the green curtain, Mum gasps, a tiny, enunciated 'oh', and then the curtain is drawn back again and Tristan leaves with his kidney dish. Dawn notices that the vial is now full of blood.

'Right, it looks like they are going to get to the bottom of why you are so tired, Mum,' she says. 'They'll do a blood test, and that will show up anything wrong.' Dawn pats Mum's hand, just as Mum did for her when she was poorly.

'Tea's up.' A woman in a purple overall and a purple cap pushes a trolley into the room. 'Hello ...' She leans forward and reads the sign above Mum's bed. '... Iris. Nice to have you with us. Cup of tea?'

Dawn finds herself catapulted back to the clinic.

TEA, a sign read over the ancient urn that looked as if it had been there longer than the Portakabin itself. There were no cups, no plastic beakers, just an empty space beside the urn that told of its redundancy. But it was better to let her eyes rest on this than anywhere else. A toddler was on the floor, dirty-faced, nappy and no shorts, playing with a food-encrusted toy car. The mother – black PVC skirt, yellow off-the-shoulder top – ignored the child, the dark shadows around her eyes framing her blank stare. Next to her was a thin girl curled up on herself, all long, awkward limbs. Her T-shirt was torn at the shoulder and her trainers were coming apart.

'Dawn Todman?' A round woman briefly appeared at the door and left again without waiting for Dawn to reply. Dawn stood and walked to the door, conscious that the cabin's fragile shell reverberated with every step.

'Todman, Dawn?' the round woman asked a second time. They were now in the hall by which Dawn first entered. There was a second door off this on the other side of the reception window.

'Yes,' she admitted.

'Been here before?' The woman studied her clipboard.

'No!' Dawn said in horror and the woman smirked.

'STDs are more common than you think. Come this way.'

It had taken everything she had to force herself out of bed to go to that clinic. Mum's constant refrain had pushed her there. 'What's *wrong* with you?' she demanded several times a day, and Dawn began to wonder if there really was something physically wrong, and then the

175

'Yes, I'll be along in a minute, I'm doing the rounds.' Tristan smiles at her, reassures her, but immediately turns back to his list, sucking on the end of his pen. It seems that Mum's pain is not his priority, but then he has a whole ward full of people in pain.

'He's coming, Mum, with painkillers,' Dawn reassures the old woman that Mum has become. Mum makes no response, her eyes closed.

Half an hour later, no one has come, and Dawn looks out into the corridor, where there is no sign of any nurses at all. She could ask at reception, but as she approaches she finds one nurse on the phone and another frowning over a stack of paperwork. The place gives the impression that it is very understaffed.

'Did you ask?' Mum says on her return.

'I'm a Geordie,' Mavis announces.

'Excuse me, can I go and let my dog out?' Gladys asks.

Mum pulls a face that tells Dawn she is in pain, so once again Dawn ventures out into the corridor, but now there are no nurses on reception either. Eventually she finds the staff gathered for a meeting in a side room, consulting clipboards. Should she knock and ask for help, or will they see her as one of those people who just don't know their place, who think their own ills are always more important than others' – a complainer? They might even resent Mum for that and care for her less. She looks at the clock on the wall. It's been over an hour now since she spoke to Tristan.

The corridor is silent and she hovers outside Mum's room, unsure what to do. Then, with absolute clarity, she knows. She will do what Mum did for her when she needed her most.

Chapter 15

The days merged into one another, and Dawn lost track of the time she spent in bed, safe under the covers. And then, one afternoon, the bedroom door burst open.

'Now I understand!' Mum wasn't just barking – she was shouting and waving a piece of paper in one hand. Her other hand held an envelope. Dawn watched her through the folds of the duvet.

'What kind of girl are you?' Mum ranted. 'You're no daughter of mine, and then to come up here and have me worry about you moping around when all along you are just terrified of what you've done!'

Dawn pulled the duvet from over her head and struggled to sit up, trying to make sense of Mum's words. 'What?' she managed uncertainly. Her pillows slipped to the floor and she sat back against the wooden bedhead, which was hard and unforgiving.

'You want me to read it? I think I should, out loud, so we are all clear about what you have done.'

'What?' She could only repeat herself.

'"Ms Dawn Todman is summoned to court on the twenty-seventh of the month." Does that ring a bell?' she asked and then she let the hand holding the letter flop.

'Court.' Dawn repeated the word. She dreaded the very idea of standing in a room full of people and being forced to admit what had happened to her. But she must press charges, if only to keep others safe from Paul Fiddler. It was the least she could do, and only right. He must account for what he had done!

'Court? Is that all you have to say? Are you ridiculing me? Or are you even crazier than you seem? If that's your response then I suggest a plea of insanity.'

Mum stood there, waiting for her to say something. Dawn sat up, her legs over the edge of the bed, her hair tousled, her bedclothes scrunched up beside her. Mum's words were not those of a woman who has just found out her daughter has been raped. And why was she talking about a plea? It was not Dawn who was on trial.

'Why in God's name?' Mum continued, 'I mean, is there ever an excuse for stabbing a man?'

'What!' Dawn's body stiffened.

'With a fork, apparently!' Mum rolled her eyes, as if she was passing comment on the fact that Dawn had not even managed to stab the man adequately.

'Mum ...' Dawn began, desperate for her mother's love, her empathy, her understanding.

'First your dad moping around and then dying on me, and now you stabbing people. Thank God for Amanda, else I would begin to think it was me!'

And she turned on her heel and dropped the letter, which floated to the floor as she stormed from the room.

Dawn picked it up, still not comprehending. It was addressed to her.

'What are you doing, opening my mail!' she shouted at the closing door, but the words printed on the letter drew her in. Her charge of rape against Paul Fiddler had been met with a counterclaim of GBH.

'So long ago – why does it not fade?' Dawn says to herself.

'I hurt,' Mum says.

'There's no one in the corridor.'

Mum groans, using all her strength to turn over, trying to get comfortable. She heaves her weight onto one side. Moves one leg, then the other, struggling. Dawn does nothing to help.

The letter lay against her bedside lamp, staring at her. Other letters came too, from a solicitor she had never heard of; all were opened and propped against her lamp, with a bowl of soup next to them, or a slice of toast, a doughnut, a sandwich. She would read the first line and leave the rest, then eat a mouthful of the food. In the quiet of the night when not even a dog barked she would venture to the toilet, just the once, but only to pee. She was not eating enough for anything else to happen. During the day she remained half asleep, curled up under the covers.

Mum stopped shouting at her, stopped even talking to her on the occasions when Dawn was awake when she came in. Once she complained about the smell of the bed linen, and the duvet had been wrenched off, stripped, re-covered and thrown back on. At one point Dawn made the Herculean effort, in the dead of night, to change the bottom sheet, but failed to do it right as the sheet she put on was a double and her bed was a single. After that she would wake to find both duvet and cotton sheet wrapped around her, pinning her down, adding to her nightmares.

'It's tomorrow, then,' Mum announced one day, before stamping out of the room.

Turning onto her back, Dawn stared blankly at the ceiling. For a moment she wondered what, exactly, was tomorrow, and then realised the only thing it could be was the court date. But she had nothing to fear, had she? Whilst she was locked in her cocooned world of duvet and sleep, Mum had been opening her letters, serving her food, changing her bedclothes, taking care of her. In her moment of need, when she could not function, when life's arrows had crippled her, Mum had taken over, had become something like the mum she always had been to Amanda. She had looked after Dawn, her firstborn, hadn't she?

The next morning Mum knocked on her door early but didn't come in. It was an alarm call of a knock, and Dawn peered into the half-light to find clothes laid out at the end of the bed. A dismal dark-brown dress that Mum had once bought her and she had never worn was there, with her work shoes. Really, she should shower. Best, in fact, if she showered. Her legs could hardly carry her slight weight and when she got there Mum was in the bathroom, so she waited, and when Mum emerged she did not say a word to Dawn, just looked at her. Dawn used all her strength and will to undress only to find, when she finally stepped under the shower, that all the hot water had gone and all the conditioner had been used.

Her hair consequently frizzed up, and the only way to tame it was to tie the mousy-brown bush back in a tight bun. A younger version of Mum stared back at her out of the bathroom mirror. It felt deserved.

'Taxi's here,' Mum called, and with heavy legs and a firm grip on the banister Dawn made her way downstairs. Mum handed her a coat and without a word they went to the waiting car.

Mum hurried from the car and up the steps to the court building when they arrived, to get out of the rain that had started falling. But Dawn walked, looking up at the sky at the big drops that shot down at her. There was nothing left to care about; today any last pieces of remaining dignity were to be publicly stripped from her.

The building was vast, with high ceilings and pillars that lined the corridors. In front of them was a large cork noticeboard with printed sheets pinned to it, and it was here that Mum found her name and worked out where to go. A man in uniform stood outside the door they were to go through but he told them to wait on a bench alongside a man with a tattoo on his neck and a woman who was so thin she looked like she might snap with every hacking cough that rattled her frame. Most of the space was taken up by a very large woman with a young face and three toddlers who fidgeted and whined.

'Bang, you're dead,' one said to Mum as she perched herself on the end of the bench. Dawn remained standing.

'Dawn Todman,' the uniformed man called, and she was ushered into a small room. 'You'll be seen here,' he said, then left.

There was nothing in the room, no poster or painting on the wall, no adornment of any kind, just two hard chairs facing each other across a small table.

The door opened again.

'Dawn Todman?' A man in a black robe came in as he read her name from a sheet, and then he looked up at her. She had no idea what he expected to see but she clearly wasn't it. He tried hard not to look her up and down but he failed to cover his surprise.

'Dawn?' he asked. The whole process had stolen her voice. She felt too terrified to speak out loud.

'Yes, this is Dawn,' Mum said, rescuing her.

'Dawn Todman?' He clearly did not believe it.

'Yes,' she managed to say, finally.

'Oh, I see – er, well, your solicitor hasn't given me much to go on ...'

Dawn looked at Mum for an explanation. Who was her solicitor, and why had he not given this man much to go on?

'What solicitor?' Mum snapped back, and Dawn felt her heart leap, as if it was to be ripped from her chest.

'Mum?' she managed, but she received a silencing look.

'Who is this solicitor?' Mum said and Dawn felt she had fallen into a nightmare.

'There were letters,' the man said sifting through his briefcase. 'You did receive them, they were recorded. How many times did you see your solicitor?' He spoke directly to Dawn.

'I thought Mum ...' She did not bother to finish the sentence. Surely Mum had been dealing with it all? Mum knew that she had been unwell, unable to move from her bed, knew the state she had been in, *was* in. It was what any mother would do, protect her young. Of course Mum would have seen the solicitor, fought her corner, kept her safe. Even the smallest dog snarls at someone who tries to harm its pups.

'What?' Mum countered, looking from Dawn to the man and back again.

'Look, a charge of GBH is serious … I presumed … Well, never mind that now, I see you assert that he attacked you?'

'He raped me.' Dawn felt tears squeezing from the corners of her eyes. This was not how it was meant to be. She was taking Paul Fiddler to court to do what was right, not to have to defend herself.

'I've read the statement that you gave to the police, but you did not go straightaway and – well, it's easy to assume a lot from that … especially if you include the stabbing. I'm sure you see what I mean …'

His voice wavered and he spoke in stops and starts. Dawn suspected he had only glanced at her case before he entered the room. She blinked and stared at him. His hair was fine and well cut; his skin held just a touch of a tan. He was clearly a man who lived well. Why would he be bothered about her? Why would anyone? She should never have started this whole process.

The man in his robes shuffled his papers some more and then looked up at her with an apologetic smile.

'I think I'll ask for an adjournment. I think we can, maybe, sort out some sort of deal.'

He muttered the latter part and Dawn wondered what he meant by a deal, horrified that it had come to this. Wasn't it she who was the victim? All her focus was now on Mum. Mum had hung her out to dry, had done nothing. She had not protected or even aided her in this matter. She had opened the mail to satisfy her own curiosity, but what happened after that was of no importance to her at all. This man in his black robes would decide her fate – another man making choices about her life.

Dawn put her hands out to use the table to steady her quivering legs, but it was not enough – she sank down and it was fortunate that the chair was there.

'Oh my goodness! Are you all right? … A glass of water in here!' the robed man called out through the door, but he had not tried to help her. Mum stepped towards her and patted her arm, which lay motionless across the table.

Chapter 16

Dawn's world shrank to the size of the hollowed-out space she made for herself between mattress and duvet, a nest in which she could lick her wounds. Mum no longer brought food, so in the cold light of the moon she would sneak down to the kitchen and eat half a tin of cold baked beans or a slice of bread. No mail was brought either, and nor was there any on the little table by the door with the stack of free newspapers.

At one point Mum brought a man up to see her, and he tried to talk to her, but she could not surface. Had she signed something? Had Mum thrust a pen at her, forced her hand to close over it, or was that a dream? It was *all* a misty dream.

Under her bed she found a box of books she had as a child, and she read them again. They were about happy children with animals, horses that lived in their houses, a girl who lived on a farm and raised ducks. With the familiar words came the memory of hope, the long-lost belief that one day she would be someone – someone with her own life and her own animals, and in those fleeting seconds she was happy. But then morning would come and reality would crash in on her. Sleep was the only real comfort.

Slowly, so very slowly, though, she emerged. An hour or two each day she was awake in the daylight until one morning she woke and stood up, just like that. Her body gave her no warning, it just did it, and her feet took her to the window and she looked out on a day that was full of sunshine. She couldn't feel it – it was someone else's day, someone else's sun, but she was on her feet, and that was something.

'Ah, so you've decided to rejoin the world, have you?' Mum was in the kitchen, putting on her coat, when Dawn padded in on bare feet and filled the kettle.

'I have an eye appointment,' Mum added, and she left the house.

By day the house looked so different. Everything lost in time, all the furnishings a little shabbier than she remembered, and she wandered around touching everything, familiarising herself once more with objects she had known all her life until, in the sitting room, on the sofa, by the television, Paul Fiddler's face stared back at her. A black-and-white picture, a smiling portrait with the headline *All Charges Dropped, Local Journalist Celebrates*.

She snatched it up and read on.

Our own local journalist Paul Fiddler has recently been put through the mill by false accusations from local girl Dawn Todman.

There was a small photograph of her, her lifeless hair half covering her face, dark under her eyes. It could not have been a worse picture.

An out-of-court settlement has seen all charges against him dropped, and we are glad to have Mr Fiddler back on the team.

'Arghhh!' She let out the guttural cry as she threw the tabloid across the room and sank to her knees.

'Now, where is Iris Todman?' A rhetorical question from a young man who was blonde, blue-eyed, tall and handsome. He made Dawn think of the posters idealising the Aryan race in WWII. But this modern young fellow wore a mauve shirt and chinos, complemented by a stethoscope around his neck.

He picked up the notes hanging on the end of Mum's bed. 'I have the results of your blood test, Iris, and it seems we have some kidney issues going on.' He looks down at her chart. 'I'm going to prescribe an intravenous painkiller to make you a little more comfortable, and I'll hook up a drip to keep you hydrated. Okay?' He looks at Dawn and smiles. 'There's something we just need to touch on, though – we ask everyone who stays with us as a matter of course.'

Mum's eyes widen. Dawn's lips part.

'What did he say?' Mum asks.

'He wants to talk about something.' Dawn speaks loudly.

'Yes, it's just a matter of course, just a general question – we need to know about resuscitation.' The young doctor pauses. 'Some types of resuscitation can be very, er ...' He mimes, one hand on the top of the other, violent shoves, downward through the air. 'Because as we get older all our bones get more brittle.'

He taps his chest. Dawn wonders if he is shaving yet, his skin is so smooth and taut.

'We all need to know if we are on the same page with this.' He shuts his mouth and the muscles around his lips tighten.

'Mum, do you want resuscitating if anything untoward happens? Just that it can be rough,' Dawn says loudly, near Mum's ear.

'In the case of heart attack, for example, only about fifty per cent would, you know, still need a bed, and afterwards, they do not usually leave hospital, not from this ward.' He looks at Dawn.

'You mean because of her age?' she says quietly.

'Yes. It can be very traumatic.' He does not lower his voice but he speaks directly to Dawn.

'Best not, then,' Dawn says. How did they get from Mum's legs giving way in the kitchen to this? 'Best not then, eh, Mum?' she says loudly. 'Okay?'

'Yes, I think not.' She can tell Mum is trying hard to sound in control, pushing the conviction into her words, but her eyes are wide, a rabbit caught in the bright light of mortality. Does she really understand what is being asked?

'Okay. Great.' The young man replaces the clipboard and takes hold of either end of the stethoscope around his neck, his manner cheerful. 'I'll see you in a bit. We might take you for an X-ray, though, Iris, just to check out your kidneys.' He adds this as if suggesting an outing, and then he hurries from the room with the spring of youth in his step.

'Am I going to have to stay in?' Mum asks.

'It looks like it.'

'Did they say how long?'

'They've not said anything.'

'Hello, Iris.' The woman in the purple tabard is back, no trolley this time, just a notebook. 'There's shepherd's pie, or chicken and mash, soup of the day or a sandwich?' She waits, pen paused. Mum looks horrified.

'You'll need something to eat, Mum. What do you fancy?' says Dawn. 'Tomorrow I can bring you food in but for today we'll have to make do.'

'I'll put shepherd's pie down, shall I, Iris, I think you'll like that. Now, my Geordie girl.' She moves on to the next bed.

'Which is a point, Mum – I'm starving. I haven't eaten all day and I think I need to phone Amanda, to let her know you're here.'

'You're going?'

'I need to eat and sleep, Mum, but you'll have a nice dinner, have a sleep, and I'll be back. It's Saturday tomorrow.'

Leaning over her, she kisses Mum's forehead just below the hairline, and before anything more can be said she leaves the room, hurries out of the ward, eyes darting in search of exit signs in the soulless corridor. She hurries to the exit and, once outside, sucks in air that is untainted by smells of urine, or sickness, or disinfectant.

It's been a while since she used public transport, but as she arrived at the hospital in the ambulance she has no other way to get home. It's a relief to find the buses run every five minutes and they are reasonably direct. It does not take much longer than it would have taken her to drive to get back to Mum's.

She is a little surprised, but pleased, to find Mum's back door locked. There's a sense of satisfaction that she had been together enough, in the middle of her panic, to remember to secure the house. The air inside is still, as if the rooms are on hold. They seem to know their mistress is absent.

With the kettle popping into life she picks up the phone. It rings for a long time.

'Hi, Amanda? Yes, I know, sorry – yes, I know the time difference, sorry, but it's Mum. No, no, she's fine – well, sort of fine. Actually she's in hospital. Her legs gave way ... No, they've not said anything yet, they are keeping her in tonight ... um, hmm hmm, yes ... I just thought I would let you know ... Of course, as soon as I know ... I think it would be a bit premature to book a flight ... Yes, I understand, let's see what tomorrow brings. No, I'm fine, thank you for asking. Er, Ward Four ... Me? Hot bath and bed for me. Yes, love to all the boys.'

The house sounds even quieter after she puts the phone down. The silence reflects back at her from all Mum's bits and pieces. The treen on one shelf, the pottery collection on another, wooden boxes collecting dust, and, high up on the dado rail, plates interspersed with glass animals. She has the greatest urge to clear some surfaces, make a little space, but she pulls herself up short. Is her flat any better? She has no right to judge. But it's not that she is judging, it's just so claustrophobic.

She goes through to the television room and gathers all the magazines from the sofa, new and old alike, and takes them outside and dumps the lot in the recycling bin. She cannot remember the last time she saw the sofa bare. Before Dad died, maybe? It must have been so on trend in the sixties – orange velvet, tasselled brocade along the bottom. The sun has faded parts of it and there are rich coloured squares where magazines have been stacked summer after summer.

Dawn stares at one of the squares, hand on hips. She will spend tomorrow at the hospital; that will be a duller-than-usual Saturday, but hopefully Mum will be out by teatime, so she must remember to buy something to eat for tomorrow night and Sunday lunch ... Or she is bound to be out for Sunday lunch, even if they keep her in again tomorrow night. Then on Monday – well, Monday is a bank holiday so that works well, and then she will see if Mum needs more hours from the Ladies-in-Waiting. Mum will have to help with the cost, and so will Amanda, no matter what she says.

'One step at a time.' She sits heavily on the empty sofa, feet up on the footstool, remote in hand, and switches on the TV, then immediately turns down the volume, just in time for *Midsomer Murders*.

Armed with a flask of soup, a pack of home-made sandwiches, a multipack of crisps and a bottle of fizzy white grape juice Dawn strides purposefully down the hospital corridor, still reeling from the price she had to pay to park her car for the day. She might take the bus tomorrow if Mum is to be kept in tonight. But that is a negative thought that she pushes away.

'There's no reason to keep her in, they only did it last night to cover themselves.'

'Pardon, dear, are you talking to me?' a man on a Zimmer frame asks. He is edging out of a door marked *Ward 6*.

'Sorry, no, myself – I talk to myself.' She hurries on, breathing in the smell of antiseptic as she passes each ward.

The doors to Ward Four are propped open and a family is wandering in, looking lost. The boy has a bunch of flowers in his hand, the girl a pink envelope.

Dawn passes them at the reception desk and continues to the second room on the left.

'I'm a Geordie girl, ding dong merrily on high.'

'Excuse me, can you tell me when I can let my dog out?'

'Nurse. Nurse?'

Mum's bed is a mess of sheets, the light-blue cover twisted up in a heap, and there is no Mum. A spark of panic sends Dawn back into the corridor, where the nurse from yesterday – Tristan – is coming out of the room opposite.

'Where's Mum … er, Iris?' she asks him. Oh, please don't let the worst have happened, it was only her legs that gave way.

'Iris? Same place. Next room, bed on the left.'

'She's not.'

'She is.' He leads the way and then with a gesture of his hand displays Mum's bed and leaves. Dawn stares at the messy bed. There is a movement. Surely not? Another twitch. But the bedclothes are almost flat. No one could be under there. She lifts the cover back and, sure enough, a tiny, meatless shoulder pokes upward, a mess of white hair.

'Mum?' The tiny bag of bones moves again and Mum's face appears, but it is not her face; her mouth looks sunken, her cheeks hollow. 'Mum?' She can think of nothing else to say; nothing else would make sense.

'Amanda?'

'Dawn.' She is not offended; the whole situation is so extreme. She looks around to get her bearings and on the side cupboard is a glass, and in the glass is an upper set of dentures. She looks back at the old woman. She does look different but it is definitely Mum.

'Shall I help you sit up?' On the cupboard top there is also a mug with two handles, holding a milky liquid waiting to be drunk. 'There's a cup of tea here, Mum.'

Dawn untangles the sheet, finds Mum's arm, puts her own under her armpit. 'Ready?' she asks and then she lifts. Mum weighs nothing at all and ends up sitting so upright on the pillows Dawn wonders if she should pull her down a bit again.

'Tea?' she asks. Next to the bed is a drip, and a tube has been plastered into the back of Mum's hand. Her hair is flat on one side and messy on the other. Dawn picks up the comb and tries to tame the hair but it will not sit flat where it sticks up and will not bounce up where it is lifeless. In the pit of her stomach she resists the evidence that Mum is so small, resists the reality that behind Mum's normally coiffured exterior she is just a little old lady like any other – shrivelled, vulnerable and mortal.

'Tea?' The woman in the purple tabard is back with her trolley.

Dawn resigns herself to the fact that it is going to be a long day.

Chapter 17

Dawn spent three years on the dole after the incident with Paul Fiddler. At first, she was considered by the dole office as sick and had to make no effort to get her fortnightly money. The dole money went straight into her account, but she did not need it anyway – she was eating nothing and spending nothing. She had lost a great deal of weight, and if she needed anything it was clothes; those she had hung off her, if they stayed in place at all. At one time this would have been a reason to celebrate but she just didn't care, and only idle curiosity guided her onto the bathroom scales. Then there was the first back-to-work interview at the dole office – an energy-sapping, humiliating experience full of questions and veiled threats about what would happen if she didn't make the required number of job applications. Halfway through the interview the man looked up at her and said, 'Aren't you that Dawn Todman that had her picture in the papers?' It felt like a knife through the heart. How much of the rest of the world knew about her and was judging her? Who else would look at her and see the mugshot from the papers? She felt exposed and desperate to hide, get away, as far as possible.

On her way home she stopped outside a travel agent's window, full of pictures of happy people in faraway places, and on impulse she booked an escape to Greece. The dole money she had saved was only enough for a week, but it would be a safe place, where no one would recognise her, no one would have formed an opinion of her before she opened her mouth. At home everyone had her labelled: a rape victim, a criminal, someone who would stab someone with a fork, or lie to the police. Nothing she could do would change these opinions.

She was so upset she even tried to talk to Mum about it. But Mum's reaction was typically unhelpful.

'No one will remember you in a month,' she said, dismissing Dawn's concerns. 'I can't believe you paid good money for a holiday! And where do you think the money is coming from to feed you?'

'I used my dole money. There's still some just sitting in the bank – tell me how much you want and you can have it,' Dawn answered, promising herself – again – that she would not confide in Mum any more.

'I have to tell you what I want? You know, something asked for has nowhere near the same value as something given,' Mum snapped.

The guilt nearly swamped Dawn. She should not have booked the ticket, it was selfish. When she was next forced to the dole office she went by the bank and drew out two hundred pounds, which she left on the kitchen table. It disappeared and was never mentioned, but the griping about her Greek holiday lessened too, and the day came and she climbed onto the bus that took her to the airport where the package group was gathered, and then ushered onto the plane.

After a week spent wondering why she was there, she passed a *fourno*, a bakery, and it was the smell of the bread invading her nostrils that catalysed her reaction. It was as if something was awoken in her and she could finally feel the sun on her skin, and with it came the promise that life could be good. Naturally she did not want to go home, but the holiday rep prompted her to pack and her wooden legs responded to being ushered onto the bus for the airport.

That feeling, the twinge of hope, lasted barely a day back at Mum's house. As soon as she got back, Mum started pushing harder than the man at the dole office ever had for her to get a job.

'This one.' She stabbed her finger at the newspaper. Now that is what you want,' she said over the noise of the television. 'Once you get a job on the council they never sack you. At worst they would move you sideways. And you get a pension, which at your age you need to think about.'

'What do you mean, my age?' Dawn exclaimed. 'I'm twenty-eight, Mum, it's not exactly old.' But she felt old – she felt old and worn and battered.

'I'd already been paying into a pension for ten years when I was your age,' Mum began, and Dawn closed her ears and tried to imagine how she would feel working at the council. It would not be fun like the bar job, but maybe, after the Paul Fiddler incident, she had no choice.

Without asking her permission, Mum rang about the job, pretending to be Dawn, and a bunch of forms came in the next post. Mum opened them and laid them out on the kitchen table, along with a biro.

'Mum, will you please stop opening my mail.'

'It wasn't your mail, it was mine. I was the one who rang them.'

'But it's my name.'

'I applied in your name. You want the job. I mean, you were going to do it, weren't you? Most people would be grateful if their mother took an interest.'

'But Mum, you can't use people's names like that, pretend to be someone else.'

'Iris Dawn Todman. It's a revision of my name.' And Dawn had given up and picked up the pen and filled out the first page. Name, address, previous employment.

'Oh.' She stopped, pen poised.

'What?' Mum was immediately behind her, looking over her shoulder.

'This one.' She pointed. '"Have you ever had a criminal conviction or been arrested, even if you were not charged?"'

'Ignore it,' Mum said dismissively. 'Tick no.'

'But that's lying.' Dawn looked at the back of Mum's head. She had turned back to the sink and was washing up a coffee mug.

'The system lies.' That was the closest she ever got to knowing what Mum actually felt about the whole affair with Paul Fiddler, and the court case. Then the mug was left to drain and, after drying her hands on a tea towel, Mum snatched the pen and put a cross in the box, then passed the pen back.

Did Mum give it a moment's thought after that? Dawn did, every time she wanted to push herself in the job, climb the ladder or complain about her treatment by her superiors. Any time she wanted to answer back to anyone at work. Even when her payslip was wrong, once, she dared not speak up. The lie was like living with a sheet of tar under her feet, holding her down; all it would take would be a little push and the lie would come to light and be seen by all, sticking to her every movement. She could not the stand the thought of a new accusation.

'Oh yes, you were the "rape victim" who stabbed that poor man,' they might say. 'And now you've lied to get a job, I hear?' Greed, sex and violence; it fires the curious, the prim and the wishful thinkers. Everybody seems to be one of these, or a combination of the three. That's what sells papers; that's the content of almost every Hollywood film. Who wouldn't be interested? Who wouldn't point at her and gossip about her for all the wrong reasons if they knew?

'What time is it?' Dawn asks. No one answers. Mum blinks.

'Once in royal David's city stood a lonely cattle shed ...'

'Is my son here yet?' Gladys asks anyone who will listen.

The day drags on and on. And on. A late lunch at the canteen provides a little relief. Floor-to-ceiling windows provide a good view, over the hills, the moorland in the distance, a glimpse of freedom just out of reach beyond the tinted glass and the sense of duty.

Dawn buys a newspaper at the shop by the main entrance and spends the afternoon reading out loud to Mum. Mostly the news is dull but on the third page there is a spread about a man who is floating a raft to London to deliver a piano. There was something about him on the television just recently. Mum has nodded off by this time so she reads to herself.

It seems he is a young man, younger than herself, and his raft appears to have grown since the television snippet – it has elongated, and become substantial. The purpose of the piano and the raft are in debate. Some say it is an art piece, others that he is delivering the piano to his girlfriend, as a token of his love. Either way, Dawn feels hooked by the romance of it all. There is a picture of the piano, which looks a little worse for wear, and a snapshot of the man himself, Neil Campbell-Blair. There is something of the gypsy about his looks; that or he just needs a haircut. By his feet is the cutest little dog and in his arms is a cat. The caption says the dog is called Bushy-Mush and the cat Fuzzy-Pants. Dawn smiles, and considers that she likes him more and more. If she knew people like him, life would feel far more interesting. Mum stirs and reality storms her senses.

'You hungry, Mum?' she asks. Mum has eaten less than a quarter of her lunch, and the bread slowly curls until it is time for tea, by which time Dawn has read out loud everything but the obituaries. At eight fifteen she can bear it no more, and as Mum is asleep again she kisses her head and tiptoes out, getting home half an hour later, bottle of wine in hand, just in time for the nine o'clock film. Tomorrow she must get on with packing up her flat.

'In which book would you find the question "Why is a raven like a writing desk?"' The voice booms over the speakers.

'So she's still in hospital? Why?' Hilary asks as she scribbles down the answer. They are in their usual seats, glasses littering the table.

'Apparently when she had the first fall she damaged her kidneys,' Dawn says. 'Are you sure it was *Through the Looking-Glass* and not *Alice in Wonderland*?' She bows over the sheet to read Hilary's rounded handwriting.

'*Alice's Adventures in Wonderland*,' June corrects her. 'How badly has she damaged them, then?'

'They've not said, but they took her for X-rays and things and discovered she has a heart murmur too.'

'Oh.' Hilary pulls a face and rubs out *Through the Looking-Glass* and adds *Wonderland*. 'That doesn't sound good.'

'You need to slow down, though,' June warns her, and she pauses to take a sip of her lager. 'You've been at that hospital every hour God has sent you.'

'Not every hour. I've moved out of the flat.'

'Really?' June has a froth moustache.

'Yup. I gave my ceramic cat collection to Cats in Crisis, the bed was picked up by Age Concern and the television is in my bedroom at Mum's house.'

'Wow, you've been busy.' June wipes off the foam with the back of her hand.

'How do you feel about leaving your flat?' Hilary asks.

The young man who serves behind the bar delivers a pint to the quizmaster. The women at the next table start heckling him.

203

'Well, he might not be Alice but he is a wonder!' one voice shouts.

'You can peer in my looking-glass any time you like.'

'You want to fall down my rabbit hole?' another calls, and the quizmaster starts shushing them, hissing into the microphone, which squeaks back at him. Others join in, some trying to be witty, others attempting to restore order. As the proceedings grind to a standstill Hilary puts down the pencil.

'The last time I went into my flat it no longer felt like it was home. In fact, the drabness made me wonder how I had lived there so long.' Dawn chuckles, but she hears her own sadness.

'Time for a new you, I would say.' June has sympathy in her eyes.

'Are you coming back into work this week?' Hilary asks.

'Why, are you missing me?' Dawn quips, and then she adds a laugh, to shield herself from possible rejection.

'Yes,' Hilary replies with a serious face and Dawn's heart takes the smallest of leaps.

'Silly cow, of course she misses you. How else would anyone stay sane working there?' June banters.

'Well, the answer is yes, of course I'm in again, I only took my half-day on Friday off but next week I've taken a half-day off every day. So I'm in but not for long.'

'That will feel like a holiday,' Hilary says.

'Not really. I'll be in the hospital when I'm not at work.'

'Are they keeping her in all week, then?' June asks.

'No idea, it's all very vague.'

'They don't know half what they think they know,' Hilary says.

'And Amanda, what's she doing?' June asks.

'What can she do? She phoned the ward, though. Tristan the nurse said she had called.'

'Ah, for a doctor-to-doctor talk. She probably knows more than you?' June says, looking in her bag and pulling out her cigarettes and lighter. But there may be some truth in what she says and Dawn makes a mental note to call Amanda again and find out.

'Outside which New York building was John Lennon killed?' The quizmaster calls out, silencing the banter in the room.

'I'm going for a ciggy.' June stands.

'It was the Ohio,' Dawn says. 'Wasn't it? It was some state name.'

'The Dakota,' Hilary says, and writes it down, not waiting for an agreement. 'So what are you up to at work, anyway – same old, same old?'

'Actually I'm going to spend this next week investigating a bloke whose neighbours are trying to get him kicked out. He has animals and they stink. But the neighbours are the usual old busybodies, can't stand one of them, so I'm sort of on the side of this Cyril. Anyway, I thought I might find out what I can about his landlord, see if we can't get him some help.'

'Beats serving up slop in the canteen,' Hilary says, and she draws a circle all the way around the edge of the quiz sheet as she waits for the next question.

'He looks like he's not been given a break in life – you know, kicked until he is broken. It's easy for people like that to keep getting kicked, and other people don't help because they see the shabby clothes, or smell them, and they think they're not worth the effort. So unfair.'

'All anyone needs is a little kindness,' Hilary remarks.

'Okay, and here is the tricky one now, this will sort the wheat from the chaff. What does the phrase "amor vincit omnia" mean?' The quizmaster struggles to pronounce the Latin words.

Chapter 18

'Hi, Amanda, thanks for calling me.' *For once*, she adds, inside her head. 'No, no change. Well, actually she looks a little better, she doesn't look so small ... No, small – I said small ... And I think someone has done her hair. Yes, I've been every day ... Well, it's up to you. It's a long way but she'd be delighted to see you ... Yes, I understand the boys need you. I'll explain ... Yes, she knows you would have come if we'd known she was going to be in hospital this long but I don't think anyone knew that. It's a week today, isn't it? ... No, you're right, a week and a day. You talked with the staff didn't you? ... You keep breaking up. No, she's not on a drip now. Nothing as far as I know, but they did ask if she'd choked on anything since being in hospital. I'm not sure why, do you know? ... Oh, pneumonia, they haven't told me that. I didn't know you could get pneumonia by choking.'

Dawn is paused by the sink, a pan in one hand. The kitchen floor is littered with pots and pans, more than enough for a family of ten. 'They've put her on intravenous antibiotics? Oh, they didn't tell me that's what it was, I thought the drip was to rehydrate her. Is it serious? It's just like a bad cold, isn't it?'

She puts the pan on the floor and takes another out of the cupboard under the sink. This dislodges a baking tray, which falls with a clatter.

'Sorry, I'm clearing out her pan cupboard. Half of it's been put away dirty. So it could be serious? ... Ah, I see ... But as you say, she is a strong person. ... I'm trying not to worry. Me? Well, I sort of feel in limbo land. It's a waiting game but at the end of the wait is the problem of how she will be cared for once she's back home. Perhaps you could come back then – you know, when she gets out ... So we can sort out what to do ... Sorry, I didn't mean to sound snappy. I think I'm tired. All I do is work, drive and sit in the hospital. It's exhausting ... Okay, we'll talk later, then. Bye.'

She looks at the clock on the wall. She'd better get over to the hospital. At least there is the Sunday film on television tonight, something to look forward to.

Monday. Inspection day. A part of Dawn hopes Cyril has managed to clear enough from his house, thin out his dogs a little, so she can give positive feedback and get the council off his back. Last week's investigation into the identity of his landlord proved fruitless but with only working half-days there was hardly time to do anything after answering emails. Although, to be fair, she did take rather longer breaks than usual in the canteen, chatting to Hilary. She discovered that they have a mutual love of walking and, although she is not quite sure how this happened, they have agreed that they will walk every Sunday morning once Mum is out of hospital. Take it in turns to plan the routes, end up in a pub for lunch.

'Right!' She stands and leaves the breakfast things; she'll deal with them after work – something Mum would never do.

She sends a text to Ms Moss to tell her that she intends to go to Little Lotherton first thing and then turns her phone off so there can be no argument. 'Let's see what we can do for Cyril.'

She pulls Mum's back door closed behind her with a last glance at the dirty plate and knife still on the table. It's early, earlier than she would normally set off for work, but with the excuse to get out into the country and a sense of purpose, why not set out early, take her time, enjoy the day? It feels like she has been cooped up in hospital and at home for months, not just a single week or so, and she needs to see distant horizons, regain a wider view of life, watch the clouds a little and hear birds calling.

The tyres crunch on the loose stones between the cobbles as she turns off the main road and up the street in Little Lotherton. Halfway up, blocking the way, is a skip that is filled to the brim. It's a blustery day with the wind changing direction every few seconds but today there appears to be no smell of Cyril's house mixed in, only fresh clean moor air smelling of gorse and ozone. Maybe it will rain?

Something about Cyril's house seems different but she cannot immediately spot what it is. Certainly the place seems tidier than the last time she visited, and her heart fills with hope and she starts composing the memo she will write about her visit in her head. The skip must be a good sign, surely?

The front door sports neither bell nor knocker, so she thumps on it with her fist. The sound seems to echo within, almost as if the whole house is empty. Has he moved? She checks over the skip for signs of what has happened. Did an eviction happen without her being informed? Has she been left out of the loop because she only worked half-days last week?

'Good morning, Mrs Todman,' a voice says as Dawn peers into the skip. It isn't Cyril's door that has opened but that of the house next door, and the neat woman from last time steps out, wrapping a brightly coloured scarf over her hair. The bracelets on her arm jingle.

'My husband has gone round to open up for you.' She points to Cyril's house.

'Is this all from the house?' Dawn asks, still eyeing the skip.

'Yes.' The neat woman smiles, teeth very white, her eyes creasing up, a softness in her features.

'There must be nothing left!'

'He has very little furniture now,' the woman agrees, still smiling, and it seems clear from her manner that this woman is Cyril's friend after all, and not a nosy neighbour like Brocklethwaite.

'Well, if that Mr Brocklethwaite doesn't get his way and get Septic Cyr ... er, and get Cyril evicted, then there are several routes he can go down to get some furniture. There's lots of help available for that sort of thing.' This is something she could definitely help with; she knows all sorts of strings to pull to provide aid, lots of places where there is surplus furniture just waiting to be given away.

'Oh.' The woman seems caught off guard. 'Aren't you helping Mr Brocklethwaite to get Cyril evicted?'

'No,' Dawn replies as emphatically as she can manage.

'Oh,' the woman repeats, and Dawn wonders if Brocklethwaite has been a bit too handy with her too.

'Aye. He's bit of an octopus after he's had a sherry,' she discloses, and then wonders if she has said too much and tries to smile, but doesn't quite manage it. But then, Brocklethwaite did what he did. He did not behave like a gentleman and that's no reflection on her. 'And his wife only just in the kitchen as well!' she adds.

Cyril's front door opens a crack and a man who can only be the neat woman's husband pushes past the dogs that have gathered around his legs. He is shorter than his wife, and has the kindest of faces, and dark shiny hair that flops over beautiful eyes.

'Oh yes! The porch! It's gone!' Dawn says, realising why Cyril's house looks so different. 'So much better, and no smell. He's not done all this by himself, has he?' She pats one of the dogs that sniffs at her legs, and scratches it behind the ears. The husband invites her into the house.

'We all helped,' he says. His accent is less pronounced than his wife's and Dawn cannot be sure where they are from. India, perhaps, or Pakistan.

'Well, the transformation is amazing. I have to admit I've not been in here before, but I saw it through the windows, what looked like stuff piled high to the ceiling, and the stink.'

The dog pushes its nose into Dawn's hand and she pats it and then holds the animal's head against her leg. 'Who's a lovely boy, then?' she whispers and then says to the couple, 'Well, I don't think anyone can complain against this. But, I don't know about all these dogs. How many are there?' She uses this as an excuse to bend her knees and encourage each dog to come and sniff her and she fusses over each one in turn. She should get a dog, or a rabbit perhaps.

'That's Coco, she's Zaza, Sabi, and Blackie Boo is the black one. Teddy Tail, Gorilla Head and Mr Perfect.' The man introduces each in turn. The animals are all so lovely, but dogs are not easy to rehome, and if it turns out they cannot stay here ... Dawn sighs at the thought of them spending ages in a cage at one of the RSPCA centres, and if no one can be found to take them on – well, it doesn't bear thinking about. A leaflet went round the department recently – two hundred and eighty dogs a day abandoned in the UK, and animal charities pushed beyond capacity. She tries to recall the figures – a completely healthy dog, every two hours, didn't it say? She doesn't want to add to that statistic but she reminds herself she is here to do her job.

'The trouble is, if they get out they'll go around in a pack. People find that intimidating.' She crouches down to look Gorilla Head in the face. 'Have they all been to the vet recently?' She feels around the dog's ears and under its chin, and it makes a whimpering sound, loving the attention, and Dawn pats its flank before standing again.

The woman exchanges a glance with the man. 'I am afraid we have no idea,' she says.

'Hmm.' Dawn crouches in front of Zaza and feels the dog's ears and neck. 'Well, they've no ticks, they're not scratching and they all seem pretty healthy. What's the rabbit situation?'

The woman tightens her mouth.

'What is it?' Dawn asks.

'Nothing.' The woman is lying, that's clear, and Dawn pushes through the dogs to the back door. There are only two cages left, and in one of these is the big rabbit. Dawn's heart goes out to the poor thing, stuck as it is, with no room to move. Something needs to be done for the rabbit's sake.

'Well, it's not a health and safety issue but that big one needs a run, or something,' she says. She should be saying this to Cyril himself, not to his neighbours, no matter how well meaning they are. 'Where is Cyril, anyway?'

'He had a fall, and has broken his leg, so he has been recovering at our house while this one was being cleaned,' the man explains.

Dawn looks first at him and then his wife. She wasn't expecting that. Her own mum never even took care of her when she was in desperate need of a little kindness and yet here these people are, looking after someone who is only a neighbour; how does that happen?

'That is very kind of you,' she says finally, and, taking a good long look at the woman, realises that she may be small but she is one of these powerhouses that makes things happen. This thought gives her the confidence to report that Cyril's situation is well in hand, because it will be!

She nods her head vigorously at the woman. 'Right. Well, I'd better be going. I'll write up my report based on what I've seen. Tell Cyril that he has nothing to worry about as far as I'm concerned, except he might have to reduce his dogs' numbers. The RSPCA can help him find new owners.'

But as she turns to leave, she feels she has lied to them, so she stops and adds, 'On an unofficial note, and I'm not saying this as a Health and Safety officer, mind, this is just from me – if he wants to relieve himself of the big rabbit, well, I used to keep them when I was little. It might be quite nice to have one again.'

She feels her cheeks grow a little warm, but she has started now so she might as well press the point. 'It might be better for the rabbit as well, because I have a little garden at mine and I could make a run. Or a dog, maybe I could take a dog?'

Having an animal would at least give purpose to her Mum's garden, and when she gets her own flat – well, she will deal with that when she gets to it. Patting each one of the dogs again, she makes her way back to the front door, where, as she opens it, she is startled to find Mr Brocklethwaite standing with legs wide, elbows out, sleeves rolled up, hands on hips, with an angry scowl on his face.

'Ah, Mrs Todman,' he growls, then bellows, 'Have you evicted him yet?'

Chapter 19

'He can't stay.' Flecks of spit glisten on Mr Brocklethwaite's lips.

Dawn is brought up short at the intensity of his anger.

'Can I help you?' The man of the husband and wife team steps forward, presents a resistance to this vile man's wrath, for which Dawn is grateful.

'I don't see what you have to do with this. All I want to know is when is he going?' Mr Brocklethwaite pushes past both the man and Dawn and into Cyril's front room.

'Well, buckets of blood!' he exclaims, coming to a sudden halt. 'What on earth happened here? Has he gone already?' Mr Brocklethwaite chortles and he grins in a way that reminds Dawn of the picture of Paul Fiddler all those years ago in the newspaper. Arrogant, confident, self-righteous – a bully. Her anger seethes through her veins. Never again. Never again is someone going to abuse or bully her, nor anyone else she knows. People like him need walls putting around them.

'No, Mr Brocklethwaite,' she says, facing up to him. 'He's not gone, and I'll not recommend that he goes.' She pulls her shoulders back, clenches her fists; she is ready.

'Aye, I thought you might change your tune. You give a man the feeling that you're friendly but you're not.'

Dawn can hardly breathe; she wants to snarl. God, she wants to slap his silly face! How dare he?

'Mr Brocklethwaite, if you are referring to the other day–' she starts, but he does not let her finish.

'Oh no, let's not go there.' Mr Brocklethwaite dismisses her with a wave of his hand. 'You were quick to take me sherry, though.'

'You've got a nerve!' Dawn spits back at him, and she suddenly doesn't know what she might do; her fists ball even tighter. No one is going to get away with pushing her about, not this time.

There is a movement to her right, and out of the corner of her eye she sees that the small man, his hair now swept back out of his eyes, has moved to stand by Dawn's side, and then his wife closes in on her other side, bringing with her a faint smell of rich spices and light flowers, and her bracelets jingle as she moves. Their allegiance is plain, and a calm sweeps over her, their kindness more moving than her own anger, their care and concern stronger than any need for revenge. There are sides to be chosen and their gentle defiance encourages her to choose the compassionate, kind side. She does not want to be like the Paul Fiddlers and the aging Mr Brocklethwaites of the world.

'Forget it,' she says, regaining her composure. 'I have nothing to say to you. 'Cyril, or rather ...' she turns to the woman, and realises she does not even know her name!

'Saabira.' The woman smiles at her gently.

'And ...' Dawn turns the other way.

'Aaman,' says the woman's husband.

'Saabira and Aaman, instead of trying to cause trouble for Cyril, have helped him to make his home a better place, and in the process they now have a good, clean neighbour. Perhaps if you had tried to help rather than point the finger this whole issue would have been dealt with years ago.'

And with this she turns on her heels and marches out, past Mr Brocklethwaite, who has turned a deep red, and to her car. As she is getting in, fighting with her seat belt, she adds, 'Oh, and let Cyril know about my offer with the rabbit – just in case it is a help to him.' The last half of the sentence is aimed at Mr Brocklethwaite.

She then slams her car door shut and backs down the cobbled street at an alarming rate.

After work, Dawn relates the events of the morning to Mum, who asks questions and seems quite chatty. But she also seems to be wheezing a little and she coughs every now and then. At one point Tristan breezes in and changes the bag of saline solution that drips into Mum's arm. Less than an hour later Mum's eyes grow heavy and she falls asleep. But Dawn keeps talking anyway.

'What amazed me, Mum, was they didn't have anything in common. I mean, Saabira and Aaman must be from Pakistan or India or somewhere, and Cyril's Yorkshire through and through, you can tell by his accent. And yet they'd obviously spent a lot of their time – their whole weekend, probably – clearing out Cyril's place for him! I mean, *he* couldn't, could he? Not with a broken leg.'

Mum's mouth is open slightly and she heaves in deep breaths, even in her sleep.

'It got me thinking,' Dawn muses, wondering if Mum can hear any of what she is saying. 'Why would someone do that? It was just kindness, that's all. They saw a man struggling and their response was to roll up their sleeves and do what they could.'

Dawn looks out at the neglected courtyard garden. 'Not like you, eh, Mum?' she continues, but quietly. 'There I was, just like Cyril, unable to get out of bed. My reasons were different, that's true, and I'd not broken my leg, but what that man did to me, Mum! I didn't know a person could have such strength, and the force he used to smack me across the face, his knuckles on my nose, and … and … Well, let's just say he wasn't gentle.'

There is a bird on the stunted tree in the middle of the courtyard, so small.

'If there was ever a time to be a mum, ever a time to help, to show me that you loved me, that was it. I sort of remember someone coming in, you and a man, and I remember you making me sign something, and I had no idea what it was. I trusted you. Idiot that I was, I trusted you.' She sighs, trying to remain in control. 'A plea bargain, that's what you had me sign. A bloody plea bargain. After what he did to me! I signed, didn't I, Mum? In the state I was in, I signed at your urging, retracting my accusation of rape to lessen their countercharge from GBH to ABH. Do you even know what that means?'

She is trying to keep her voice down but emotions are surging into her chest, her limbs twitching with a rush of adrenaline. Mum does not stir. 'ABH, Mum – you can be sent to prison for that, did you know that? Ah, but you did, didn't you, because, remember, years later, I asked you, all light and jovial so you wouldn't get angry. Remember? We were eating fish and chips. The fish was in newspaper back then and the headline – I flattened it out to read it – was about someone local who had just been sent to prison for a fight over a car parking space. One driver had hit another and the second had fallen and banged his head, put him in a coma. ABH. Prison sentence. "Mum," I said, "Mum, did you know that I could have been sentenced, sent to prison?" And you got up and got the ketchup out of the fridge. "Mum, did you not think to call the lawyer, barrister, whatever he was, did you not think to call him, press the point that Mr Fiddler had been violent, at least drop both sides?" You saw the bruises yourself, and do you remember what you said? Do you?' She is leaning over Mum now, their noses almost touching, speaking with quiet, fierce anger. "Oh Dawn," you said, and you sighed, as if I was some irritant. "Let's not go over that again, nothing happened. They let you off, didn't they?" And then, and this is the comment I cannot forget, Mum, you said, "I did think to call him but I realised that he was probably having his tea when I thought of it and I didn't want to disturb him." You did not want to disturb him, Mum! Sod the fact I might be sent to prison. You. Did. Not. Want. To. Disturb. Him. What kind of mum are you? And there are these people from Pakistan helping out a neighbour for no reason whatsoever. Do you know how that makes me feel? Do you know what that says about you?'

'Everything all right?' Tristan sweeps into the room. Dawn pulls away quickly.

'Yes, fine, I was just talking to Mum, but I think she's asleep. I might go now. There's no point me being here if she is asleep.'

Mum coughs and opened her eyes.

'Hello, Iris.' He leans down the side of the bed and lifts a bag partly filled with a dark yellow liquid. 'Catheter bag okay ...' He makes a tick on his clipboard sheet, which he then rehangs at the end of the bed.

A withered hand finds its way out of the bedclothes, and Tristan takes Mum's pulse then moves on to the Geordie girl.

'Oh, Dawn,' Mum says, as if she did not expect her to be there.

'I was talking to you, did you hear me?' Dawn asks.

'No, what were you saying?' She coughs again.

'That's good, Mum, cough it up,' Dawn encourages her. It's not likely that the doctors will release her whilst she is still coughing so best to bring it all up, free her lungs so they can start healing. But Mum keeps coughing – four, five times in a row – and Dawn begins to wonder if it will be weeks, rather than days, before she is ready to come home.

'I was saying that the people who live in Little Lotherton are kinder than you can imagine. There's a real community feel there, and all that moorland that surrounds it – it's a really beautiful place.'

Mum's eyes have closed again, her mouth open, as she wheezes and struggles for breath.

Dawn gathers her things together. Bag, jacket, car keys. That's everything.

'Dawn?' Mum's voice is weak. 'Dawn, I'm in pain.'

'My heart bleeds for you,' Dawn whispers and she gathers her things and walks out into the hall, leaves the ward, escapes the building.

The emptiness that echoes around Mum's house feels normal now. There's a letter for her, and Dawn is delighted to find that it contains a cheque returning the deposit on her flat. Not that twenty pounds will go far, but it's the principle of the matter. There are also five begging letters to Mum from different charities, which she puts straight into the recycling bin. In an hour and a half June will be there to pick her up for quiz night, but to be honest she doesn't feel like it. The past is swirling in her mind and her rage at Mum will not subside.

'Cow!' She expels the word forcefully and opens the fridge, hoping to find something to eat. There is a small block of cheese, mouldy down one edge, and an open tin of tuna that has dried up and turned grey.

'What?' she asks her absent mum. 'Did you think I deserved it because I quit the job with your friend and moved to my own place? Was it because I moved in with June? You never did like her, did you? Common, you called her. Common, as if you were so much better! But that's how you saw yourself, isn't it, better than anyone else. Did you leave me to my fate because you thought it was all I was worth?'

She flings the tuna in the bin.

'It's not as if you were incapable, was it, Mum? Oh no, because when it was Amanda wanting to go to university you wrote letters and made phone calls and did all you could to help. And when she moved to Australia, who bought her ticket? Who helped her ship her things? You did! Which shows you can do these things, so why not for me, eh? Why did you just leave me to rot in my bed and hang me out to dry with the law?'

221

She cuts the mould off the block of cheese and inspects it but then throws this in the bin too.

The front room is even more still than the rest of the house. The sun fades the furnishings during the day, but at night it is a ghostly room crammed with memories. Dawn takes the sherry bottle from the sideboard and unscrews the top. She looks at the glasses, laid out on their tray. 'Who needs a glass?' she says through gritted teeth and she swigs from the bottle.

'Why?' She takes another swig. 'For God's sake, why?' She takes another long drink and begins to feel the effect almost immediately on her empty stomach, the alcohol rushing to her brain. 'Why do you not love me?'

Chapter 20

'Dawn Todman?' When the phone rang she expected it to be June saying she would be late picking her up for quiz night, so the stranger's serious voice has an immediate sobering effect. 'This is Tristan from Lotherton Dale Hospital. I was just wondering if you were coming in to see your Mum tonight. There's something we'd like to discuss with you.'

'I – er …' What time is it? Seven already! What can this mean? Surely something very serious for them to be calling at this hour! 'I'll be right there.'

She drops the phone on the kitchen table and looks madly around the room, as if discovering it for the first time. What does she need? Nothing – just go.

The door slams behind her and her fingers fumble with the key. It takes three attempts to unlock the car. 'Get in!' She forces the key into the ignition and it finally gives, and she is in and away.

At the first junction she misjudges the speed of the car approaching as she pulls out and is cursed with a blast from its horn. She raises a hand of apology but does not decrease her speed. The sherry runs thick in her blood and she knows she should not be driving.

Would Tristan have said anything on the phone if Mum has died? Ice water replaces the sherry in her veins and she wipes her forehead with the sleeve of her cardigan. Surely they would just wait till she next came in. They wouldn't scare her like this. But why else would they call? She presses the accelerator harder and takes the next corner too fast, out onto the main road. It's all straight from here, except the traffic lights. They are orange; her foot touches the floor but the car has no more speed to summon – she races through the red light and horns blare at her from all sides.

'Please don't be dead.' She makes her prayer and takes the sharp turn into the car park, narrowly missing a woman pushing a man in a wheelchair. She neither pays for a parking ticket nor locks the car door. With cardigan flapping, she runs as best she can, her inner thighs rubbing, a shoe flapping on one heel, into the building, down the corridor, past the doors to Ward Six. With a hand on the door frame she swings through the double doors of Ward Four.

There is nothing but calm. Families with flowers and resigned-looking lone men wander slowly down the corridor, peering into each room in turn for the faces they want to see. Dawn's impulse is to push past them. 'Sorry,' she mutters as she inches between them.

Mum's bed is empty. There are no sheets to conceal the old woman's small frame, just an empty bed, stripped of its linen.

'Will you let my dog out?' the woman opposite asks. Mavis, or was it Gladys?

Dawn turns sharply. Tristan is standing there smiling.

'Where's Mum?'

'Oh yes,' he says casually, 'we moved her to a single room.'

He points across the hall to where, for the last couple of weeks, the skeletal woman with the open mouth has been heaving laboured breaths, mouth open, eyes closed. In an instant Dawn knows the skeletal woman is now dead – and Mum, Tristan says, with such a light tone, has replaced her. He must be mistaken, surely?

'I think the doctor wants a word,' Tristan calls after her. 'I'll tell him you're here.'

But Dawn doesn't wait, she is in the side room, leaning over Mum.

'Mum?' Mum doesn't move. 'Mum?' she says again, and the neatly folded hands twitch on Mum's chest, her head turns to face Dawn, and one eye opens, bulging, to stare at her. The other eye remains shut.

'Dawn, would you like to come through to a private room ...' Tristan is at the door; he takes her elbow and ushers her along the corridor to a small room by the nurses' station. The blonde-haired doctor is there, one foot tapping, out of either nervousness or impatience.

'Come in,' he says, and he stands but doesn't offer to shake her hand.

'Germs,' Dawn thinks, and retracts her trembling fingers.

The room is decorated with crisp retro wallpaper in orange and brown, and the furniture is straight out of the nineteen-fifties, but all too smart, too new.

'We've moved Iris to the side room,' the doctor starts, not making eye contact. 'We thought she would be more comfortable. I just wanted to talk to you about her treatment. We've decided to take your mum off the antibiotics.'

225

'Is she better?' Dawn cannot take her eyes of the television on the wall behind him. It isn't on but she can't tell if the retro effect around it is real or trompe l'oeil, and concentrating on this dulls the effect of what the doctor is saying. She resists the urge to go over and touch it.

'The antibiotics are not being useful.'

'What does that mean?'

'It means we need to think about making her as comfortable as possible.'

Dawn's heart drums in her ears. Surely it is trompe l'oeil.

'I wanted you to know where we were at,' the doctor says.

'Of course we need to make her comfortable,' Dawn's mouth responds for her. Trompe l'oeil cannot be that good; it looks so three-dimensional.

'The thing is. There's probably not much point continuing with drugs that are having no effect.'

'She might rally on her own, you mean?'

'Er, I suppose that's possible, but I think we need to consider quality of life.' He stands. 'Don't feel you have to rush out of here, stay in this room as long as you need to.'

And it is this offer of the room to herself that makes it clear to Dawn that the doctor is delivering bad news. Mum is dying; they cannot save her. How is that possible? One minute she is at home and her legs give out, and the next she is in hospital with pneumonia and the doctors say she is dying. Or rather, they don't even say it, just imply it, and leave her to piece it together by reading between the lines.

226

'Is it the heart murmur?'

The doctor turns to look at her from the doorway. 'The heart, the kidneys, the pneumonia.'

'But she has only just got pneumonia.'

'I expect she's had it for a while.' His hand is on the doorknob; he's eager to leave, to get back to the ones he can save. Dawn closes her mouth and lets him go. Her surroundings fade and she stands mechanically and returns to Mum.

Mum is twitching and writhing and sucking for air. When Dawn draws near, one eye opens again and stares at her hard, but it's not clear if Mum is seeing her. The single eye looks wrong, open too wide, bulging a little, the white – or rather yellow – showing around three quarters of her pale iris as she defiantly struggles to focus.

'It's Dawn, Mum.'

The response is more twitching of her thin limbs; her legs kick a little and then lie still but her shoulders jerk and her hands spasm.

'Are you in pain, Mum?' There is the slightest nod of her head as she continues to rattle, trying to pull air into her lungs. No one else would have seen that nod, so how on earth do the nurses know when Mum is in pain, unless they sit and take the time to watch for these small movements? And how has this happened so quickly? Or have the signs been there, and she, Dawn, has denied them?

The corridor is empty now. In Mum's old room the Geordie woman's family are gathered around her; she is singing away. There are no nurses at the nurses' station, and the little anteroom Tristan took her to is empty too.

Where can she try next – out on the main corridor? She goes to look but on seeing no one she returns. Where the hell is everyone?

Wait. Outside Mum's door, she consciously relaxes her hands and shoulders. Why is she panicking? Why is she on hyper-alert for this woman who has been nothing but unkind to her all her life? So Mum is in pain. It's not like Mum cared when she, her firstborn, was in turmoil. Was the emotional pain she suffered then less than Mum's physical pain is now?

Absolutely calm now, Dawn goes back into Mum's new room. Mum is twitching and frowning, eyes closed. If Mum was an animal in this condition they would have put her down by now; Dawn has seen enough cases through her work to know this to be the case. They didn't state it directly, but it's clear now, they think she is dying. But some people are in that state for years. Years and years. How will she manage? There will be no choice: Mum's house will have to be sold and Mum will have to go into a home for round-the-clock care. That could mean years and years of visiting, work and care home, work and care home. Thousands of pounds draining into the system to keep her alive, and for what? At least if Mum died right now something positive would come out of her life: she and Amanda would inherit the house. From what Amanda has said recently she needs the money, and Dawn's half would be enough to buy a little place of her own, with no more rent to pay. That, at least, would mean Mum had done something positive for her. All the decades she has put up with Mum's sniping and coldness would at least be paid for by the security and comfort of a place she could call her own from now on.

A pillow sits on the chair by the bed and Dawn contemplates the white cover. This could all be over in a minute, this endless toing and froing to the hospital, the worry about the future and how to care for the old woman, the constant put-downs if she recovers. It could all be gone.

She picks up the pillow and looks out into the corridor. All is quiet. Visitors' voices drift from a distance and there is no sound of any nurses. Mum has no strength, there would be no fight. She would no longer have to struggle and gasp for breath; that all-consuming sucking of air would stop, she would no longer be in pain, and everyone's stress would be gone. All it would take would be a minute. Just a minute. She takes a step towards the bed. Mum's eyes are closed, but she is not asleep. Dawn lifts the pillow. She listens to Mum's suffering, the rattling of her lungs, the slight arch of her back with each desperate effort to inhale. It is wrong to keep someone alive like this. How can society be so merciful to animals when they suffer, but so inhuman to people? It would be the compassionate thing to do.

Dawn's chin begins to quiver. At the back of her throat, a little gulping sound escapes her. Why did Mum never love her? Why? What has she ever done to deserve such utter neglect? Her eyes swim with tears until she cannot see, and she drops the pillow to wipe her cheeks dry with one hand and puts the other over her mouth to stop any more sound, any more emotions, escaping her.

'Oh, I'll put that on the chair.' A nurse steps into the room on silent feet and retrieves the pillow, puts it back on the chair.

'She's in pain,' Dawn says.

The nurse looks into Mum's face.

'I can tell,' Dawn says.

'Then we will get something for her.' The nurse leaves and returns in a minute, pulls the bedclothes back a little. Mum flinches but does not object, her eyes still closed; she is still struggling to breathe. The nurse injects her.

'Can we sit her up a bit, she might be able to breathe better if we do,' Dawn suggests. Mum's mouth is open now, the inside of it dry, her tongue a lifeless lump, partially blocking the back of her throat.

The nurse gently lifts Mum into a sitting position, and sure enough her breathing becomes less laboured.

'You know, you should get some rest,' the nurse says. 'We'll call you if you need to come. I wish all patients had such devoted children – she must have been a good mother. But you need to take care of yourself a little too.' The nurse gives Dawn a pat on the shoulder as she leaves the room.

Mum's easier breathing seems to have allowed her to drift into sleep – that or the shot the nurse gave her.

'It's not your good mothering that makes me attentive, Mum,' she tells the sleeping woman. 'It's just I'm still hoping, Mum, hoping to be a good daughter in your eyes, wishing for a kind word, a gesture of love, a sign you care, even now.'

Dawn's voice is a whisper and tears stream down her face. There is a pain in her chest that is growing, and a tightening in her throat that threatens to explode into a wail. She does not kiss Mum's hairline; better not to disturb her.

230

The walk from the ward to the car and the journey from the car park back to home happen automatically.

Back at Mum's house her phone shows three missed calls and a text from June, but she doesn't read the message. She just wants to sleep, to make a nest in her bed and curl up into a ball.

Chapter 21

When she is jolted awake in the grey half-light of morning, it is as if Dawn has not slept at all. The events of the previous evening, which the night had mercifully driven from her mind, come flooding back in an instant, and she tries to gauge whether she can somehow sense that Mum has died in the night. Would she be able to tell if that were the case? She feels somehow that she would. She looks at the clock by her bed, which tells her it is five in the morning.

It's too early to work out the time difference with Australia but she scoops up her phone from the bedside table and calls anyway. It rings and rings and there is no answer. Any hope of sleep is mostly gone now, but she is tired right to her core and she closes her eyes anyway, willing herself back to sleep. But her eyes snap open of their own accord and the curtains Mum chose for her when she was a girl stare back.

Showering only helps her to feel a little less weary, and clean clothes do nothing to stop her feeling jaded. She pulls on her bobbly cardigan and, yawning, makes her way to the kitchen, where she rifles through the cupboards, hoping something will tempt her for breakfast. Nothing does. It's too early to go to the hospital so she begins to text work, explaining why she won't be in. It seems so irrelevant that halfway through she gives up.

Early-morning television is full of joyful young people effervescing self-consciously, so she switches it off and stares at the ornaments lined up on the mantelpiece next to the pieces from around the world that Amanda has sent to Mum, her cheap token from Greece on the end. The Eiffel Tower leans at a slight angle, and she wonders if Amanda would notice, if she ever came back. Probably.

When she cannot stand the tension of waiting any longer, Dawn puts on her coat, slings her bag over her shoulder and heads out to the car. Needless to say, she arrives at the hospital long before visiting hours but the rules no longer seem to matter.

Even though she knows the route to the ward with her eyes shut by now, she takes a wrong turning and ends up at the cafeteria, which is open and fairly full of exhausted-looking doctors and nurses sipping coffees and looking blankly ahead of them, or talking quietly. She orders a coffee for herself and takes it to a table by the tinted window that looks out across the moors.

Somewhere in that direction is Little Lotherton, and for a moment her befuddled brain is granted relief from thoughts of Mum as she begins to wonder how Cyril is doing. She should help him get some furniture. Kind as they are, his neighbours, Aaman and Saabira, will not want him with them permanently, and when his leg is better he will want his own space, won't he?

'Such kindness,' she says, breathing out into her coffee, and she drifts into a little daydream in which she is living in one of the cottages in Little Lotherton, spending her time with people who look out for their neighbours, giving a home to the big rabbit, feeling a part of the community. Dawn wonders what Saabira's story is, and she indulges in a fantasy in which she is sitting at Saabira's table hearing tales of Aaman's and Saabira's country of origin, and of Cyril's life. Her coffee drains slowly so the last mouthful is cold, so lost is she in these pleasant thoughts, somewhere between waking and sleep – to counteract the recent, relentless focus on Mum and her ailments, Dawn realises.

By the time she emerges from her half dream, the caféteria is almost empty. This must be the lull before morning breaks, before visitors arrive. There is no clock on any wall to tell her the time but it still feels early, or perhaps that's just because she has not had enough sleep and feels like she should still be in bed. Now she is here she wants to put off seeing Mum. If she is dead, Dawn does not want to know, and if she is alive and still struggling for each breath she does not want to see that, or hear it!

'But this is why you are here – come on, get a grip,' Dawn counsels herself, then she takes her empty cup and puts it on the counter and forces her steps in the direction of Ward Four.

Dawn has never seen the place so busy – it must be doctors' rounds. Nurses hurry up and down the corridor; a man in a white coat pushes a medicine cabinet. Perhaps that means it is later than she thought, and she walks more quickly. The door to Mum's room is only open a crack. She holds her breath as she enters. Mum is lying there, still but for her labored breathing, her hands neatly folded on her chest. Her cheeks are concave and Dawn is vaguely aware that the hydration drip must have plumped her face; that is all gone now. She can't tell if Mum is sleeping or only semiconscious; her chest lifts and falls, accompanied by that sound of a desperate sucking of air, the fight for life.

234

'Morning, Mum,' Dawn says softly and she lightly strokes the thin skin on the back of one hand, noting the bruising where the intravenous needle was taped on. It is like a small purple egg under the yellowing skin.

The hand twitches as if waving off a fly.

'It's me, Mum, Dawn.'

Mum's head does not turn but that one eye opens again and her breathing becomes even more strained. The hairs rise on the back of Dawn's neck as Mum's struggle for breath becomes more laboured.

'Are you in pain, Mum?' The eye closes and the head nods almost imperceptibly.

'I'll get a nurse.

In the corridor everybody is busy. As she steps out, Tristan is coming out of the room opposite, where they put Mum when she was first admitted.

'Excuse me, Tristan. Mum is in pain,' Dawn says, and to her surprise he stops ticking his chart and leaves the portable medicine cabinet with another nurse and comes into the room to look at Mum.

'I'll be right back,' he says, and returns in a minute or two with a syringe.

'Has she been this agitated all night?' Dawn asks.

'No, she's been really still,' he says, and leaves.

'Then is it because I'm here?' Dawn asks after him, but he doesn't hear. She turns back to the bed.

'Mum, you're fine, don't worry,' she says, trying to soothe her, but the lie feels too big. Watching her struggle for every breath is gruelling, and after three quarters of an hour Dawn needs a break, so she returns to the canteen for a second coffee.

'What would you do, Saabira? What can anyone do?' She sends her thoughts across the moors and takes another sip of her second coffee.

There's nothing anyone can do. Not the doctors, not nurses, not magicians. This is it. Mum is going to die, and the only question is how long does she have to struggle, how long does she have to be in pain? How long does Dawn have to watch this ordeal, and is she doing more harm than good by being here if Mum gets agitated when she arrives? Does Mum know she is dying? Maybe if she knew she would stop fighting, let herself go. Could it be a kindness to tell her?

As she considers this, Dawn wonders if she could do it. It might distress Mum even more to know – might do harm, not good. But to watch her like this, hour after hour in pain, seems cruel, and time goes so slowly when you are in pain.

Dawn recalls petting a dog once, outside a supermarket. It was tied to railing whilst its owner was shopping, and Dawn didn't recognise the warning signs until it was too late, and the animal snapped at her. She withdrew her hand sharply but the dog's teeth had already punctured her skin, so it was not so much a bite as a tear. The pain was excruciating. She grasped her injured digit with her other hand and started walking as fast as she could, until her lungs hurt, but she could not stop moving; the pain was so intense that she needed to be doing something, anything to divert herself. When the initial shock and searing pain reduced a little, her pace slowed, but the ongoing pain was all she could focus on. How long that pain had lasted! The minutes like hours, the hours like days. In the end she had gone to the hospital, where they told her they did not stitch dog bites as it made them scar, but when they saw the ragged tear they gave her a local anesthetic and stitched it anyway. Oh, the relief of the anaesthetic! Her body relaxed as the pain lessened, and she was surprised to find how tense she had been. Mum has been in pain for days now, not just hours, as she was.

Maybe it would be a shock to Mum to know she was dying, but maybe in the long run it might make her suffering shorter. It would be a kindness. But it would also be hard.

Dawn leaves half her second coffee and walks slowly back to the ward. All the time she has been debating and sitting in the café, Mum has been gasping and twitching in her agony. When she reaches Mum's bedside it's clear that the shot that Tristan gave her has made little difference, if any.

There is a nurse just outside the door.

'Excuse me, I know you are busy, but I think we can say my mum is dying.' The nurse's eyes widen, her lips part as if Dawn has spoken of the unmentionable. 'So for mercy's sake, please, at the very least, ensure she is not in pain,' Dawn says. The nurse, on silent feet, steps over to a woman in a medical coat by the nurses' station and mutters quickly and quietly and points at Dawn, who goes back into the room.

The nurse appears at the door again, her hand on the frame, but she doesn't come into the room. 'I think they are going to give you something, Iris,' she says.

Sure enough, the woman in the white coat appears, carrying a metal kidney dish and a syringe. She pulls the covers off Mum's ever-shrinking frame and gives her a second injection and leaves the room again without a word.

She must do it. She must tell Mum to let go. It feels cruel but it could be kind. The battle between feeling it would be a kindness and feeling it would be one of the toughest things she has ever done rages inside her head, and with each minute that passes Mum twitches in pain, and she wheezes with each breath.

Dawn leans down, close to Mum's ear, takes a breath. It's now or never; she must get it out or she'll lose her nerve.

'Mum, do you know you are dying?'

Mum stiffens, then her head turns and that one eye opens again and she stares right at Dawn. It's not clear what the look means; the mouth still hangs open, the tongue almost black and solid at the back, cheeks sunk in. Then Mum's brow tightens and the smallest of frowns appears briefly. Dawn leans forward and places a kiss on her forehead.

'I love you, Mum, you know that, don't you?' And she could swear Mum dips her head in acknowledgment. 'But don't be scared to die, Mum. They say that you are drawn to a white light, that the feeling is pure love and you'll no longer be in pain.'

Mum continues to twitch, her eye closed again. Then she stops breathing. Dawn waits, her own breath shallow. No one could hold their breath that long. Dawn sits back and studies Mum's face, trying to understand, and then, with a massive sucking sound, Mum breathes again. Relief floods her; her words have not killed her mother, but still Mum's breath rises and rattles, and the woman suffers on.

'Mum, you need to let go. Let yourself drift. Give up this fight. Your body is done for, but your spirit is strong, your spirit will continue, but this body you've been living in is all worn out.' Still Mum heaves and jerks.

'Amanda will be fine, Mum.' A shoulder shift. 'I will be fine, Mum ...'

And at these words the twitching suddenly stops, but Dawn repeats herself. 'I will, I'll be fine. I'll miss you but I'll be fine and your spirit will live on ... Just your old, battered body has had enough, so let go, Mum, just let go.'

The wheezing stops. The chest does not rise. She becomes still. Dawn feels sure that this is the moment and her chin wobbles.

The speed with which Mum sits up in bed jolts Dawn backward. Both Mum's eyes open, and Dawn stares back as Mum's blackened mouth contorts. The rattle in her chest sounds like pure pain. The twisted-up lips are unreal. She seems to stare right into Dawn's heart. Then she sinks back. The pillow cradles her head. Her chest does not move. Her eyes are closed. Dawn waits.

She waits one minute. Another minute. Mum does not move, does not breathe.

It is over.

The wave of sadness that hits Dawn is unprecedented. It is too great for tears. Too big to voice. But with the sadness comes relief at the knowledge that Mum is no longer suffering.

She stands and opens the window. She doesn't know why, she just feels an impulse to do so.

In the corridor there is no one to be seen, not a doctor or nurse in sight, and Dawn is convinced they know. They are either giving her space or they don't want to deal with the death. Either way, she doesn't care. She walks out of the ward, leaves the hospital, drives slowly home and rings Amanda.

Chapter 22

Dawn listens to the now-familiar sound of Amanda's phone ringing. She tries to frame how she will break the news as she waits for Amanda to answer, but when the voice comes on the other end of the line, she just blurts it straight out.

'Hi, she's gone.' There is silence on the other end of the phone, in which Dawn imagines Amanda trying to keep her composure, fighting any reaction. The clock in the kitchen ticks loudly. Outside, the binmen scrape Mum's bins along the road.

When at last Amanda speaks, her voice is loud, practical, emotionless. She gives reasons why it would be difficult for her to come over, and explains that there is a company that will deal with the whole issue, will take the body away, cremate it, and send back the ashes.

Dawn had not thought this far ahead, had not even begun to consider the logistics, but it seems Amanda has. None of them are religious, Amanda argues – and what's the sense in spending thousands on a funeral, she adds, that would be attended by a handful of people at most. She has clearly done her homework.

After the call is over the ping of Dawn's mobile snaps her out of her stare: a message from June.

U ok? it asks, but she cannot answer. Amanda's practicality, her lack of emotional response, has numbed her. She won't come back for any reason, it seems. She made it clear that Dawn can deal with the contents of Mum's house as she sees fit; there is nothing she wants. The kitchen clock keeps ticking. Dawn surveys the room, noting Mum's reading glasses and a book, a murder mystery, by the letter rack on the side that is stuffed with charity letters, each marked with a scribbled cross or a star. It is going to take weeks to clear the house. Why delay? She pulls the letters out and briefly goes through them before taking them out to the recycling bin. They hit the bottom with a hollow thud.

Wandering from room to room reveals the enormity of the task ahead. Amanda said she will organise the cremation, that it was the least she could do, and it could all be done by phone. But the house, that is a bigger job, there is just so much stuff.

She takes the stairs slowly; there is no need to rush. Mum's bedroom door stands open. The bed is neatly made, the towel on the towel rack by the bedroom sink has been smoothed and hung evenly and the room smells of Mum. No, that is not true – it's more of a generic smell, of old people, faintly fusty and slightly perfumed. She opens the wardrobe door and the smell of Mum becomes stronger. She cannot help herself, she buries her face in the clothes that hang there and breathes in the familiar smell.

Then she turns to look at the bed. One side of the mattress is indented with Mum's shape. She lifts the covers to see the impression more clearly, and then before she knows what she is doing she curls up in the space and pulls the covers over her head, remembering a time when she was maybe four, or six, when she had been unwell in the night and had tiptoed into Mum and Dad's room. Mum had half woken and instead of getting up had grasped her hand and pulled her in with her, spooned her, her own knees against the back of her daughter's, arms around her. Dawn is there again now, all protected and cared for, a child with her mother.

Her shoulders shudder, and deep childlike sobs escape her as she hugs the pillow and bundles Mum's nightdress against her chest.

Evening is creeping into the room when Dawn finally wakes, distantly aware of a banging sound that echoes through the house. The unfamiliar sound is repeated and appears urgent. Why is she in Mum's bed? She throws Mum's nightgown from her, pulls the bedcovers straight and, rubbing her face with one hand, runs down the stairs down as quickly as she can, keeping a firm grip on the banisters with her other hand. Again, the banging at the front door. *Why don't they ring the bell?*

The front door needs unbolting and the security chain removing. It is so seldom used that it takes a hard pull to dislodge it; the recent rain has swollen the wood and jammed it in the frame.

Dawn peers out at the intruder.

'June?'

'Your bell's not working. I tried the back door. Are you okay?'

'Come in, then.' She steps to one side and is about to bolt and lock the door again, but she changes her mind.

243

Mum is no longer here to scold her if she leaves it unlocked.

'Cup of tea?' she asks, going through to the kitchen and putting the kettle on.

'You okay?' June repeats. 'How's your mum?' The second sentence is said quietly, the words separated.

'Dead.'

'Oh …'

'Tea?'

'Yes.'

'Earlier today.'

'Right.'

She makes the tea, relishes the feeling of rebellion when she drops the teabags in the sink, rather than straight in the bin. The teaspoon follows them, landing with a clatter.

'So come on, are you all right? I've called you a hundred times.'

Dawn looks at the ceiling, accessing her feelings, her thoughts, her gut reaction. 'I'm fine,' she says.

'Seriously?' June looks around the kitchen, helps herself to sugar, sits at the table.

'It was tough, the end. She was in pain, it was horrible. But, in the end I talked her to death.'

June sniggers, involuntarily, but stops herself and stares wide-eyed at Dawn.

'It seemed like she was hanging on, and for what? So I told her to let go. But get this – she fought on until I said, "Mum, I'll be okay." That was when she stopped fighting.'

'Really?' June leans her elbows on the table, her mug of tea clasped in both hands.

'I swear it! When I said that, she changed. It might be wishful thinking but I think she was hanging on for my sake.'

June says nothing.

'It's possible, isn't it?' Dawn asks.

'You know, you and your mum had a strange relationship, like a couple of schoolboys picking at scabs until they bled, never allowing any healing.'

'I was not!'

'Well, you could have stayed away … I never did understand why you had anything to do with her after the whole business with – well, you know.'

'With Fiddler.'

'If we'd been in touch at the time I would have done something.'

'I should have sent a letter addressed to "June Clatterworth, somewhere in Thailand".' Dawn snorts a laugh.

'I would have come back.' June stares at her.

'I know you would.'

'So you're okay?'

'Sad, I suppose … freefalling with no parachute … But a weight has been lifted. I just woke up when you banged on the door and I could feel it, this whole place in me that has felt dark and heavy for years … it's gone!'

'To be honest, I'm not surprised. Dreadful woman.' June slurps her tea.

A wave of the hurt Mum caused begins to flood over Dawn, and for some reason she thinks of Saabira.

'Not all bad. No one is all bad,' she says quietly.

'Does Amanda know? When's the funeral.'

'Yes, and there won't be one.'

June puts down her tea, raises her eyebrows.

'It's a practical matter. We aren't religious, nor was Mum, so, apparently, you can just ring up a company and get them to do everything. Amanda's sorting it.'

'When is she coming over?'

'She isn't. She's got the boys to think of, and work, and it costs so much. Besides, what would she come over for, exactly?'

'For you! Has she not thought about what you need, that you've done all this on your own, that you might need a little sisterly support?'

'You know, I don't suppose we'll talk much again, me and her. We may be sisters by blood but – well, she's been away so long, she has a whole other life, and to be honest I really don't need to be reminded of what I am not.'

'Now that's your mum talking. You're every bit as good as Amanda. Better.'

'She's a doctor, married with two boys and a loving husband. I'm spinster, an old maid, who works for the council.'

'What you do is not who you are,' June says. There's deep kindness in her voice. 'Besides, you've never been allowed to blossom. Keeping up this pretence of being less than Amanda, and for what, to keep your mum happy?'

Dawn absorbs these words in silence.

'All I can say is, watch this space,' June continues. 'I think you'll blossom now, Dawn. You can be exactly who you like, now – no conforming to other people's ideals.'

'Oh damn!' Dawn exclaims, breaking the calm that has settled in the kitchen. 'That reminds me, I've not told work I would be off.'

'Forget it, they won't sack you when your mum's just died. Do it when you're ready.'

'I'd better.'

'Do you want to?'

'No.' Dawn gives a hoarse laugh and takes another drink of tea.

'Then leave it for now. If ever there's a time to put yourself first, it's now.'

They lapse into silence. June's presence is comforting, supportive.

'Will you sell the house then?' she asks after a while.

'I guess so. Amanda says she's broke. Braxton has laid off some of his workers and her hours have been cut. I don't think they can afford their house, but maybe with half of whatever this is worth she'll be okay.'

'I see work's started next door.' June is looking straight ahead, staring through the serving hatch to the dining room that was kept for visitors. 'The whole street's being done up, it seems – this whole area, in fact. It'll be because of the new school. This place should be worth a pretty penny, I would think. A doer-upper. They always have people fighting over them, thinking they're getting a bargain.' She pauses. 'Are you sure you're okay?'

Dawn looks up at the ceiling again, closes her eyes, tries to gauge her response to this in all the corners of her gut and her heart and her head, and then a laugh escapes her. 'Yup, still fine.'

'Oh, I brought you something!' June says suddenly, and she takes her big bag off the back of her chair, puts it on the table and fishes about inside to withdraw a tiny plastic trophy. 'We won the quiz!'

'What! And you waited until I wasn't there to do it?' Dawn takes the cheap silver cup from her, holding it between finger and thumb. 'It's not mine really, then.'

'Nonsense!' June laughs. 'We're a team, and we'll share it. Have a month each, pass it around. Actually Hilary wanted you to have it. She's been calling you too.'

Dawn nods. 'I expect the battery will be dead.'

The final word hangs in the air. The plastic silver cup sits in the middle of the table.

'I suppose it's sad, however awful she was as a mum,' June sighs.

'I've been thinking about that, how people either choose to be kind or to moan and point fingers. It *is* a choice, you know. Some people choose to only see the good, be gentle with others … And I've come to the conclusion that they are the happy ones, not the moaners.'

'True.' June nods.

'I think Mum just got into a way of being and couldn't change. She must have been so unhappy keeping it up.'

'Well, I for one won't waste my energy feeling sorry for her.'

'Then you are choosing to be like her.'

'Me like your mum? God forbid.' June laughs. 'But, yeah, you have a point. I suppose I should feel sorry for her, but I find it hard to forgive what she did to you.'

'Try. These last couple of days I saw her less and less as my mum and more and more like a little old woman just like any other, struggling with life, grieving her husband. Wishing both her children were nearer. You know, maybe she was angry that Amanda moved so far away and had grandchildren she never met. She couldn't take it out on Amanda, so maybe that's why she was the way she was with me?'

'It still doesn't excuse her lack of action over the Paul Fiddler thing. Surely she should have taken greater care of you in case you went away too?'

'Who knows what was in her own past that made her so useless over that.'

'No, sorry,' says June seriously. 'I have children and I would lie down and die for them rather than see them hurt. You're going too far with this now.'

'Maybe. But hey ho.' And with this, she stands and, picking up the trophy, she beckons June, leading her down the hall to the television room.

'What mischief are you up to?' June asks, a giggle in her throat.

Dawn grins at her, clears all the little brass ornaments off the mantelpiece, and puts the trophy in their place.

'There!' she says triumphantly.

Chapter 23

Dawn puts the kettle on again and makes a fresh pot of tea, and they chat about nothing in particular until Dawn starts to yawn. Embarrassed, she puts her hand over her mouth. 'It's not that you're boring me,' she says, 'just ...'

'Silly!' June replies, 'I think we know each other better than that. You need some sleep. Tell you what, how about I take the day off tomorrow and we can do something? Either have some fun or find a way to pay tribute to your mum?'

'Yeah, I am tired – but I'd better go into work tomorrow.'

'Don't push yourself or you'll end up needing more time off.'

June stands and washes her mug at the sink, then dries it and puts it away. She fishes out the teabags and throws them in the bin. The way she does it seems automatic.

'Actually, I have an interesting case at work, and it will take my mind off Mum,' Dawn says.

'Well, text me if you change your mind. I don't open till ten these days, no point.'

'Things are okay, though?' Dawn yawns again.

'Fine, just that people don't seem to buy flowers before ten, so what's the point?'

June gives her a tired smile and now, as they are both standing, she throws her arms around Dawn and hugs her.

'And when you start clearing this place out you let me know, okay? I am here. Ready to roll my sleeves up.' She pulls away and looks Dawn in the eyes.

'Thanks,' Dawn says. Maybe in extreme situations people are all the same. Maybe they all roll their sleeves up. Saabira with Cyril, June now. Everyone but Mum. Mum didn't roll her sleeves up when Dawn needed her – she washed her hands.

'Yeah, thanks, June.' She tries to convey the depth of her gratitude in these few words.

'Okay, well, I'd better get home and see if Steve has got the boys to bed. More likely it will be mayhem.' She takes her car keys from her bag. 'Will you sleep all right? You can always come to ours.'

'No, I'm fine.'

'I'll call you tomorrow,' June shouts as she walks down the path and opens the car door.

Dawn waves and watches her drive away. As she turns to go back into the house an owl calls, punctuating the silence of the night.

A stern look and a crooked, waving finger summon her into Ms Moss' partitioned office early next morning. Dawn knows what is coming – a show of strength and superiority.

She lets Ms Moss strut around her office for a while, hands on hips, delivering her lecture about responsibility and dedication, teamwork and so on.

Finally, Ms Moss stops and looks at Dawn sitting in the low chair opposite her desk.

'So! What have you got to say for yourself?' she demands, and for a moment Dawn feels bad using Mum's death as a weapon in this battle. But at the same time it is delightfully satisfying to watch Ms Moss blanch, stammer and then mutter her condolences before suggesting compassionate leave.

'No, you're all right,' Dawn replies. 'I'll let you know if I need time off. Can I go now?'

She stands and leaves Ms Moss stammering, her face turning from white to red.

She sits at her desk for an hour or so, trying to look busy, then goes for a coffee.

'Dawn, I'm so sorry, June told me,' Hilary greets her.

'Thanks.'

'How are you feeling?'

'Fine, as if nothing has happened. I've not lost much, I suppose.'

'It might hit you at odd times, when you least expect it. I expect you'll feel tired, mostly. Here.' She passes a coffee over the counter, and with it a business card. 'Cheapest probate going,' she says, tapping the name on the card. 'Thought it might be useful.'

A man in a suit comes in and waits to be served. Hilary takes his order while Dawn hovers by the counter.

'Oh, thanks for the trophy!' she says when the man has gone, and she sips her coffee.

'Ha, pathetic thing that it is!' Hilary laughs.

'It has pride of place where Mum's brass ornaments used to be, on the mantelpiece.'

Another two suited men come in, followed by three women. One she recognises, from accounting, perhaps, but the others are new faces. There has been another internal reshuffle, it seems. More people come in – the morning rush. She finishes her coffee with two more swallows.

'I'll catch you later,' she says, but Hilary is busy at the till.

On the way back to her desk she goes to the toilets and catches sight of herself in the mirror. It is the briefest of glimpses and just for a moment she sees Mum staring back out of the glass.

'Ha!' Her response is half laughter, half cringing. At least it will give her something to talk to Mum about tonight; it's sure to amuse her.

'Oh.' The realisation hits her. There is no Mum to tell. Who else could she tell? There is no one, no one else would be interested. But the moment of grief is as shallow as it is brief and by the time she is at her desk she has moved on, forcing the feeling away.

'Emails, so many emails.' She deletes all the spam and circulars, answers the next three, which are routine, then opens the next:

Hogdykes Abattoir is due for its annual inspection for compliance with the Welfare of Animals at Markets Order 1990.

Dawn tuts. She is sure this is not her responsibility. But no one ever wants to do it and it always seems to be her that ends up organising the inspection, and usually being dragged along with the health and safety officer, for no apparent reason. She has been up there the last three years in a row. Someone else needs to go. Someone else can deal with the men there. The workers seem to think they are immune to the outside world, stuck in some sort of 1970s bubble where they can make sexual innuendos and smoke whilst they work because that is manly. At the very least she will take a tape recorder this time and if they step out of line again with their sexist remarks she will make a formal complaint.

Or maybe not. What if the whole Paul Fiddler thing comes to light and the council finds out, at last, that she lied on her job application ...? But there must be someone else she can hand the responsibility to. She forwards the email to a colleague and dismisses it from her mind.

There are many more emails to deal with, and she sits and works her way through them until the card Hilary gave her, which she tossed on her desk, catches her eye. With a glance over her shoulder to reassure herself that Ms Moss is not watching, Dawn dials the number on the card and explains the situation. The man on the other end of the line reassures her that it can all be dealt with very easily and goes on to explain that their fees can be taken out of the value of the estate, so there is nothing to pay up front. The voice is gentle and reassuring and has a local accent. She replaces the receiver with a feeling that she has really accomplished something, even if it was only a phone call.

The next few days pass in a blur of boredom, punctuated by waves of sadness that come and go. The sadness is not for the loss of Mum, but rather over the pettiness of the woman and the lost potential, the mother she could have been. Hilary was right; the engulfing emotions, when they do come, come from nowhere, but they only last seconds and then they're gone again. Even so, she is surprised to experience them at all.

Clearing out Mum's clothes is easier than she anticipated. In amongst the stacks of neatly folded jumpers on the shelves in the built-in wardrobe, she finds, Mum had not one but three bags of clothes, unworn, still with their labels on, completely forgotten. Maybe she can take them back. Or give them to charity. She puts them to one side to take to the Oxfam shop and keeps going.

Sales tags also dangle from some of the dresses and blouses, and on a stout hanger is a thick crew-neck jumper in navy blue. Pinned to it is a square of paper, on which is a note scrawled in Mum's handwriting. *Dawn, Xmas?* it reads. Oh God, Dawn thinks suddenly. Christmas is going to be so desolate! Most likely she will spend it entirely alone, with no one to cook her Christmas dinner, or to pull a cracker with. For a moment she yearns for Mum, but as soon as the feeling sweeps over her she is aware that she has fallen into some idealised dream again, of an invented Mum who never was. Christmas with her may have been better than other days but Mum still moaned. Maybe Christmas would actually be better alone. At least there would be no soggy sprouts.

She distracts herself from her thoughts by pulling the thick jumper from the hanger. Discarding her bobbly cardigan, she pulls the jumper on. It is stiff and coarse but the shape suits her and it is so warm. Too warm, in fact, and she pulls it off and puts it to one side before continuing the clear-out. On the floor of the wardrobe is a good-quality pair of shoes, and Dawn discards her slippers to try them on. She and Mum have always been the same size but these are way too small; even if she could get them on they would be too tight. She tries another pair, and they are the same. Presumably in recent years Mum's feet have shrunk, along with the rest of her.

This thought brings up a mental image of Mum as a wizened little old lady, no longer the formidable tyrant she grew up with. When did her shrinking take place? Mum's physical change took place slowly, of course, over years, but at no point did Dawn's internal image of Mum really change; until just now, her mind had preserved the old, outdated image of Mum – overbearing, authoritative, a tyrant.

Suddenly she is cast back to a Saturday, some years back. They had gone to a trade outlet, Mum's idea of heaven, and no doubt where many of these unused clothes with their labels still on have come from.

The place was like a warehouse, and on the second level were a café and a restaurant.

'Coffee time,' Mum announced, and Dawn followed, pushing the trolley past the household section with its sets of gleaming pans and stacks of dinner plates. It was late for elevenses – nearly lunchtime – and there was a queue at the restaurant.

'Let's go to the café, it will be less busy,' Dawn suggested.

'I prefer the view from the restaurant,' Mum said, and it was true that the view of the Yorkshire Dales through the enormous windows was spectacular. But Dawn was tired and she needed a coffee and a sit-down.

'Yes, but I want coffee, I'm flagging.' It was not meant to be a challenge – more of a request.

Mum straightened her back at this and took a step closer, whispering fiercely, 'You need to learn some patience!'

That was when Dawn first became aware that Mum had shrunk, when she hissed those words in her ear. She was an inch or more shorter than Dawn, and as she spoke Dawn looked down into her upturned face. Her mouth was pulled hard into a tight line, her eyes glaring, daring Dawn to challenge her authority, and the thin skin on her forehead puckered into a frown.

Dawn looked down at an old woman who was desperate to maintain control. She recognised how afraid Mum was of any loss of power, and she knew in that moment that she could shift the balance in their relationship if she wanted to: take control, snuff out her bullying behaviour. But she didn't. Somehow, the one thing that would be worse than Mum pushing her around would be to see Mum crushed, a simpering person for whom she would be a carer. It was one thing to tolerate a bully and another thing to show kindness to such a person. That would be loathsome, and with this thought she gave way, as always, and allowed Mum to maintain her control, or the illusion of it at least.

And she continued to do that from then on, pushing away that image of the shrunken version of Mum.

She checks the labels on three skirts that look brand new. If they are designer she will take them to the Nearly New shop where they will give her something for them. One is a UK size twelve, one a fourteen and one a sixteen. She can remember Mum wearing them all, in no particular order. Mum's love of chocolate and cakes was matched by a steely determination, when necessary.

But the labels confirm that, although practically unworn, they are cheap, so won't be worth selling, and she throws them in the Oxfam pile, Then she looks at all she has done, compares it to all that is still to be done and decides she needs a coffee right now.

She sits in Mum's chair downstairs, puts the television on for a bit of company and gets engrossed in a Technicolor film.

Back at work on Monday, it's all the same old, same old, and even quiz night does little to cheer her up, and much to June and Hilary's disappointment she says she might give Monday nights a miss for a while. Tuesday comes and goes, and the watercolour class is cancelled because the tutor is ill. On Friday, her half-day makes no difference to her mood and she spends the afternoon thinning out Mum's possessions in the downstairs room where Mum would entertain guests, on the rare occasions when she had visitors.

'Round and round.' Dawn stares at the bedroom ceiling on Saturday morning. 'Round and round until we are dead.'

And then, aware of the danger of this negative thinking, she decides to get up and enjoy the day any way she can. She will not turn into a younger version of Mum. The clearing out of the house can wait; she will do something fun, and just for her. She has found the motivation but is left with the question – what to do just for fun? For so long it has been work, and Mum, and conforming to Mum's impression of her. The decision also leads to another question, an odd one: 'Who are you?'

But the questions are lost in more clearing and the weekend comes and goes.

Chapter 24

The sun streams through the gap in the curtains on Monday morning, and before Dawn opens her eyes she feels an unaccountable shift in her mood. She didn't think she was grieving, not even really sad; she thought the weight of Mum had gone, but this is something new: a positivity, a lightness, and she is awake – wide awake. Washing her hair in the shower – normally a chore – is effortless today, and she even takes the time to shave her legs, which is long overdue.

The kettle boils quickly as she gathers together her bag, car keys and phone. After a quick coffee and a glance at the wall clock, she unlatches the back door to go to her car but then stops.

'Sod it,' she exclaims. 'I'm not wasting this energy on work.' A little thrill passes through her, a chill of excitement. She has never taken a day off, not even on the occasions when she has felt unwell, but today is different. She leaves the door latched and looks around her. Still so much to do, but she will not clear the house either. No! Today something big is going to happen, she can feel it.

Wandering through to the television room it occurs to her to watch the morning news but that would risk being sucked into daytime TV and that too would be a waste of the day. Something else.

'Got it!' she exclaims finally, and she pulls the directory out of the drawer beneath the telephone.

'Hello, I'm Matt,' the man, or rather boy, who knocks at the door an hour later informs her. His suit is smart but doesn't fit very well, and his tie is silk and his shoes very shiny. His hair is slicked back but a wisp at the front will not stay put and hangs in a curve over his forehead. He pushes it back self-consciously every now and then. He smells of cigarettes and aftershave.

'Hi, come in.' Dawn stands to one side and he enters, hands in his pockets, his chin lifted. 'You want to look around by yourself or do you need me?'

'I'm fine by myself if you like.' The way he speaks is slightly over-enunciated, like he is trying to suppress his accent. He strides into Mum's best room, making appreciative noises. Dawn decides she needs a second coffee.

'You want coffee?' she calls.

'No, you're all right. Er, thank you, but I'm fine,' comes the reply from the direction of the television room. Then there are footsteps on the stairs and the creak of boards overhead.

Five minutes later he is in the kitchen.

'Well?' Dawn says.

'Seller's market in this road. The new school, you know, we can't keep up with demand. And this place is a doer-upper's dream.'

He looks up sharply after he has said this, and he colours slightly. 'I mean, everyone wants to make the place their own, and this has so many original features, unspoilt,' he adds.

Dawn stands so that she is talking on a level with him.

'I think you'll get over two-fifty,' he says, and although she doesn't think she displays any reaction to this, he immediately adds, 'Were you expecting more? We might be able to squeeze two-seventy but then you are competing with four-bedroom places and things that have been done up ...' He speaks quickly.

'Actually, I feel very lucky to be in this position at all, but whatever it gets I need to split it with my sister. I guess I was thinking that half of two-fifty will only get me a flat,' Dawn says. 'Not that I have anything against a flat,' she quickly adds. This man-boy, if he is not still at home with his mum, will live in a flat, and she has no desire to cause offence. 'It's just that I've been here for a while, and sort of got used to it.'

He doesn't need to know all this but she cannot stop herself. 'I would like a garden, I guess.' The image of Cyril's fat rabbit comes to her. It doesn't have to be a big garden, just enough for her and a rabbit.

'Okay, got it,' he says as if he understands her life completely. 'You might be pushed for a house for that price, unless you move a distance. I mean, it depends where you want to be?'

Dawn shrugs. She hasn't really considered this. Near June, perhaps.

'Actually, if you like the country? I mean out a bit, in the moors?' His eyes light up and he takes his hands out of his pockets.

'If it's commutable.'

'Hmm.' His hands go back in his pockets.

'But tell me anyway – did you think of something?'

'After this I have to go and photograph a place that's just coming onto the market. It's in your price range, needs a bit of work, and only two-bed, not three. It *is* small, backyard more than a garden, but the rear of the property abuts the moors.'

It sounds heavenly, the way he describes it, but Dawn is wise enough not to get her hopes up too much, and she nods and says nothing.

'You could follow me there, have a look?' His hands are out of his pockets again, his fingers flicking against each other. She can imagine how good he would feel if he took on a property and made a sale to the same person, all before he goes back to the office – the thrill of the game for him, no doubt, and an opportunity to brag to his colleagues.

'Sure, why not?' It's as good a use of the day as any, and she has to start somewhere, get her eye in, and get a realistic idea of what to expect. 'Whereabouts is it?'

'Small place called Little Lotherton. No one's ever heard of it, not even them that live around here.'

Her heart misses a beat, and on the third beat the voice in her head tells her it's too far to commute, she must be realistic. But then people who live in London sometimes commute for hours. She saw a programme where one woman took two and a half hours each way to get to her job – Little Lotherton wouldn't even be an hour. But then the woman on the television did a job that paid well and was worth the commute. Her job in the council seems hardly worth getting out of bed for some days.

'Do you know it?' the estate agent says. He seems oddly sensitive to her feelings. 'No worries, I'm sure we can find you something else.'

'No, I don't object to seeing it.' She tries not to sound too keen.

Hands come out of pockets again, this time with his car keys.

'Great!'

He would be a very bad poker player.

'Do you have a car? You want to follow me?'

'Sure.' Dawn tries her best to keep calm but her heart is racing. An hour is not too far.

Matt drives very fast and Dawn struggles to keep up, but she knows the way and is not concerned. Maybe she will see Saabira again, Cyril, even the dogs.

'You haven't even seen it yet,' she tells herself as she stops at a pedestrian crossing. 'It's probably a dump, and if it isn't someone will buy it before Mum's house sells.'

She pulls up at the bottom of the road that forms Little Lotherton just as Matt is putting the key in the door of the fourth house on the left. Not quite opposite Saabira's.

She closes her car door and walks up the cobbled street. Parking would be a problem, and if she were to park at the bottom hauling her shopping would get tiring. She steps up to the house. The windows need repainting, and the front door too.

'Come in,' Matt says. It smells slightly sweet and slightly decaying, the smell of old age, the smell of Mum.

The single room downstairs has a wood-burning stove on the left-hand wall and a kitchen opposite. Cosy, but big enough. Exposed beams run the length of the room, the plaster between them painted white. The back wall has a central door and a window on the kitchen side. To the left, a panelled section with a door in it hides the stairs. The sofa, pulled up in front of the wood-burning stove, has knitting left on it, and in front of the kitchen counter is a wooden table.

'It needs modernising, of course,' Matt says and opens the back door. The moors fill her senses – the rich chocolate brown of the autumn bracken, the call of a peewit. The clouds are forming and breaking, tumbling across the stark horizon, and the smell of heather and peat blows into the house.

'It's just beautiful,' she whispers to herself.

Matt is handling some horse brasses hanging on a nail by the back door. 'Really?' he asks, as if he genuinely believes she is not serious.

'I'd better look upstairs.' The stairs are steep and the carpet is threadbare. Upstairs, the bathroom has a free-standing old cast-iron bath and the taps are the old-fashioned type with cross-grip tops. One bedroom is a good size; the other would only fit a single bed, but then what more does she need?

'Oh my giddy aunt, it's perfect,' she exclaims, despite herself, looking out of the window. On the horizon to the left is the outline of Greater Lotherton, the church spire dominating, and to the right, nothing but moorland as far as the eye can see.

'Worth an hour's commute,' she confirms.

Matt comes in with his camera and Dawn returns downstairs and takes a seat on the sofa. She can see herself here, toes in front of the fire on a frosty day, or with the windows all open, the back door too, when it's warmer.

'So, what do you think?' Matt says when he's finished upstairs.

'Will they take offers?' she asks. No point in being stupid; she will need cash for new furniture. If this place were hers she would not just make do with what furniture she has, she would choose carefully.

'I'm sure, put an offer in and we can start the process.' Matt is grinning from ear to ear.

'Do you think it will get much interest? I mean, will it still be on the market long enough to sell my mum's?' Dawn knows she is letting her excitement show, but she can't help it.

'Chains of people selling and buying are common ... I don't think it will put the owner off. She's just gone into a nursing home,' he says. 'Needs the money for when her savings run out, I understand.'

Dawn understands too.

'If that is the case then I feel sure she will take an offer, since the money will just go to the government anyway. Tell her that I looked after my mum so she didn't need to go into a home, would you? Tell her it's only because Mum left me her home that I could afford this one.'

Matt is too young to understand all this; he won't go through it himself for another few decades, but there's no harm in appealing to the seller.

'Sure,' he says nonchalantly. 'So, what shall I offer?'

'What did you say it was on the market for?'

'Hundred and ten.'

'Then offer a hundred, but I want it taken off the market if she agrees.' She listens to herself, wondering where all this confidence has come from. This talk, as if she is knowledgeable. All the house-buying and house-selling programmes on television, perhaps? She is amazing herself. Matt seems to think the way she is speaking is normal. He has not raised his eyebrows once, nor has he sniggered. He is seeing all that she is saying as quite reasonable.

'Right, well I have to get back to the office now that I have these photographs, so I'll put your offer to her.' He sounds so pleased with himself. 'Of course, it's early days, and she may want more people to see it.'

Getting a bit full of himself now, Dawn surmises.

'Do whatever you have to do.' Dawn tries to play it cool, and makes for the door.

'I'll tell her all you've told me, though, it might make a difference, make you seem more human.'

More human! Cheeky monkey! Dawn steps out into the street and looks across the road, hoping, maybe, for a sighting of someone – Cyril, Aaman or Saabira. Some reassurance that all this is real. But all is quiet, and a breeze blows off the moors, bringing with it the earthy smell of sheep. It all feels a little like a dream. This is not her street, these are not her friends – yet.

Without a further word to the estate agent she heads for the top of the road. Against the far corner of Brocklethwaite's house is an old cast-iron gate that leads onto the moors. Keeping an eye on Brocklethwaite's front door, she heads for this gate. As she gets close, she realises that Brocklethwaite's is not the last house after all; opposite, hidden by the old mill wall, are three more cottages at right angles to the little main street. These homes have proper little gardens in front that are full of flowers. The cast-iron gate gives with a push and scrapes on the stones beneath it. Dawn closes it carefully behind her and takes a step out onto the moors. The breeze lifts her cardigan, billowing it at the back. She should have worn the blue crew-neck jumper. The wool may have been coarse but it was tightly knitted and would have been perfect.

There is a path trodden in the bracken, perhaps a sheep track. She follows this up a slow incline until she is looking back down into Little Lotherton. It is indeed a tiny one-street village in the middle of nowhere. A little further on and she can see the back of Mr Brocklethwaite's, Cyril's and Saabira's houses and the others further down, but no sign of any people. Has she really just made an offer on a house here?

'You're mad,' she tells herself. 'Something will go wrong with probate, you're not in a position to make such an offer, and if you were you would tire of the commute.' She looks up at the scurrying clouds. 'You can't just up and move to a new place and expect the people to be your friends. Oh my giddy aunt, what have you done! You're living in a fantasy world.'

She retraces her steps at twice her previous speed. Maybe Matt is still there, photographing the outside, or making notes back at his car. She must retract her offer; she needs to be realistic.

She is sure the curtains twitch as she trots past Mr Brocklethwaite's. Matt's car is still there; she slows but waves at it and keeps walking. She is almost close enough to tap on the back window when the engine starts and it lurches off, leaving her standing with her arm in the air.

Chapter 25

'You didn't!' Hilary says as she pours coffee the next morning. Dawn couldn't wait till her usual break time to impart her news – she just had to tell someone.

'I did – oh my giddy aunt, I did! I meant to ring and cancel the offer when I got home but when I got in I heard a dripping sound as soon as I got in the back door and thought there was a leak. It turned out to be the upstairs tap I'd just not turned off tight enough, but it distracted me long enough to forget, and then I started to clear things, took a load of really old bedding to the charity shop and – well, I forgot. I can't believe I forgot. I'll do it as soon as I get back to my desk.'

'But why do you want to cancel your offer? Have you decided you don't like it?' Hilary pours herself a coffee and comes out from behind the counter, only to have to return to serve someone else.

'No, I love it. I mean it was perfect – cosy, homely, and the position, moors all around it.' The view from the upstairs window forms itself in Dawn's mind.

'Perfect for our Sunday walks? So why would you retract your offer?'

'It's difficult to explain. I mean, someone like me doesn't get a home like that.'

'Why on earth not! You want a biscuit?'

'No, thanks. People like me, well, we just don't … We live in damp flats.' She laughs, but there is nothing very funny about the flat she lived in for the best part of sixteen years.

'What on earth do you mean, people like you?' Hilary dunks her biscuit in her coffee.

'You know what I mean. Some people get all the luck, and others have to make do and be happy just scraping along the bottom, that's just how life is.'

'What utter crap!' Hilary snaps, and Dawn looks up at her; she's never heard Hilary use an expletive before. 'Oh, I know it's tempting to think like that, makes life a lot easier, takes away the chance to go make a cock-up of things. I mean, if you never dare you'll never lose, right?'

Hilary dunks her biscuit again and the end falls into her coffee, and she is distracted for a moment, fishing it out with her teaspoon. She puts it in her mouth and a piece of the soggy mess hangs on her lower lip as she continues to talk. 'I thought like that for years. Stayed with Barry for the kids, thought that was my lot in life. A drunken husband on the weekend, someone to pick up after during the week.' She wipes her lip with the back of her hand and wipes her hand on her apron. 'I thought, just like you, that was my lot in life.'

Dawn frowns. That *is* Hilary's lot, isn't it? As she struggles to find a sensitive way to say this, Hilary puts down her coffee and shifts her chair a little closer.

'I kicked him out a few weeks ago.'

'No!' Dawn exclaims. This information comes as a shock. Hilary is Hilary, has always been Hilary, with her miserable marriage – one of the few things she has disclosed – she appears to get on with life, steady, certain, unchanging.

'I did!' Hilary is quietly triumphant. 'He came in drunk, as usual, late one Sunday night, decides he is Casanova, and this time I thought, why the heck should I, so I pushed him into the spare room, and the next night I told him to sling his hook!'

'When was this?' Dawn cannot believe Hilary has kept such a momentous occurrence to herself.

'The night we won the quiz. You weren't there – because of your mum, I guessed at the time, but I was thinking of you, or your mum's ill health, and suddenly life seemed too short.' She half smiles and adds, 'I mean, if we can win a quiz we can do anything, right?'

Dawn stares at Hilary wide-eyed, lost for words.

'Are you okay?' Dawn asks finally.

'Scared to death. Haven't been on my own in my life, ever! From Mum's to Barry, no time out in between. But then I thought, how hard can being alone be? Since day one he was out most of the time, so most of the time I was on my own anyway. What will I miss?'

'And what do you miss?'

'Not a lot.' Hilary grabs another biscuit from the counter. 'But I've come to the conclusion that us bottom-dwellers are not born that way. Life pushes us there and it's up to us to pull ourselves up.' Hilary sounds emphatic. 'I like your new look, by the way – a bit of a rebellious change, eh? Jeans to work, that's right against regulations?'

The cottage in all its beautiful shabbiness comes to mind. Maybe she *can* live there, maybe …

Hilary continues, 'So, talking of a change, the day after that I applied for a job in Debenhams, stocking and hosiery.'

'You didn't!' Dawn is snapped out of her dream.

'And got it. Gave my notice in here and I'll be gone in a month!'

Dawn's first thought at hearing this news is for herself, and she is a little ashamed at her selfishness. Her own job will become so much less bearable if there is no Hilary to chat to, to break up the monotony and have a laugh. She tries hard to imagine how Hilary must be feeling.

'Are you sure?' she asks.

'Sure about what? I'm not sure about anything. How can you be? There are no guarantees. Maybe the new job will be as lifeless as this one, maybe not. Maybe I'll miss washing Barry's shirts and ironing them, but I wouldn't bet on it. I'm a good deal older than you, mind, and I see the remainder of my years and I don't want to waste them frozen in fear of things that may never happen.'

'You're not that much older than me!' Dawn protests.

'I reckon I've fifteen or twenty years on you, Dawn. So take my advice, buy the cottage, if it's what you want.' She pauses and then looks towards the door. 'Oh, here they come, accountants one and all! D'you think when they're training there's a system where they root out the ones with a sense of humour and kick them out?' She sniggers and goes back behind the counter, plastering on a forced smile.

Dawn watches her banter and joke with the suited men and women, all of whom respond warmly. If they have no sense of humour, they are doing a good job of hiding the fact.

Back at her desk there is the usual flood of emails, and in amongst them one with the subject *Hogdykes Abattoir*.

'Here we go again,' she sighs, and she clicks it open. She reads the contents aloud, under her breath.

Update on Hogdykes Abattoir. It is no longer necessary to inspect the premises.

Dawn feels nothing but relief; it means she will not have to go this month. In fact, maybe it is something more permanent, in which case she might never again have to visit that horrible place. She is about to click away when a name near the bottom of the email catches her eye. She skim-reads to this point.

It is expected that Mr C Sugden will apply for change of use.

She gasps. Is this the same Sugden – Cyril? And if it is, what on earth has he got to do with the place? She reads the whole message but learns nothing more. Using a password that should have been revoked years ago, she accesses the planning department's system, but finds nothing helpful. This is far more interesting than what she is supposed to be doing. 'What's going on?' she asks herself, and then she marks the email as unread and opens the previous email about the abattoir. She leaves this open on her screen; if anyone looks at her station they will assume she has gone to carry out some task related to the inspection.

She's out and down the stairs to her car in minutes. She sets off in the direction of Greater Lotherton and takes the turning to the old mill. It sits alone in a wooded, bowl-shaped landscape, practically hidden from the road. The mill itself is beautiful – an old woollen mill, probably, with a stone-flag roof that has moss growing around the edges, and the structure itself is solid granite with a token relief carving to accentuate the edge of one of the side doors. The men are all standing outside, smoking, in their dirty, blood-stained white coats. Dawn takes off her shoes in the car and puts her walking boots on; the place is muddy, and where it isn't muddy it's slimy with God only knows what.

'Oh, here she comes, looking for a date,' one of the men sneers as she climbs out of the car. There's a sharp breeze; she has the navy jumper from Mum's wardrobe in the car but she will not put it on now. Any sort of dressing or undressing will provoke a barrage of sexist comments. Some come her way anyway.

'You can inspect me anytime, love,' a dark-haired man guffaws.

'I hear there is no reason to inspect at all,' Dawn answers. 'I hear you've been kicked out.' She cannot help but take pleasure in saying this.

'Dirty trick, if you ask me,' a grey-haired man says. 'Who the hell is going to give me a job at my age?'

'Or any of us,' another agrees.

'So what happened?' Dawn asks, trying to sound casual, disinterested.

'New owner, apparently. And you won't believe who it is.' The young man grinds his cigarette end into the mud. 'That bloody halfwit Septic Cyril.'

'Cheeky beggar, working here pretending to be one of us, and all along he had this up his sleeve,' the grey-haired man grumbles.

'Not such a halfwit then,' Dawn suggests.

A man in a shabby suit comes out of the carved doorway. 'Eeh, that's typical of your type, never thinking of the worker – the whole lot of us on the dole.' Dawn recognises him as the foreman.

'So a change of use for the old mill then?' Dawn says, trying not to make it obvious that she is fishing.

'Aye, and guess what to!' It seems Dawn isn't the only one who doesn't know, as they all turn to look at the foreman. 'To a bloody animal sanctuary! What the hell is the world coming to if animals are more important than people, eh?' The men murmur their agreement.

'Maybe he'll take you lot in,' Dawn says.

The men turn to stare at her, eyebrows raised. A sideways smile sneaks onto the face of the dark-haired one. 'He might even give you a cage to yourself,' she adds, looking pointedly at the foreman, which draws open laughter from the men.

'Well, he's not got the place yet, so you can bugger off.' The foreman steps towards her. The men hang back, curious to see how this will play out.

'Happy to oblige,' Dawn says and retreats to her car. Once her door is shut she finds her hands are shaking. But she stood up to them, she found out what she wanted to know, and no harm has come to her.

'Well done, Dawn,' she says to herself as she pulls out onto the main road. A sign points to Greater Lotherton. So

Little Lotherton must be close – maybe this will be a quicker way to commute?

With this as her excuse she turns in the direction of Little Lotherton and is surprised at how quickly she finds herself at the end of the one-street village, coming the opposite way from her usual direction. And there is the house again. It is every bit as cute as she remembers. It might be worth talking to Cyril or Saabira, who might know the owner and know whether the price she is asking is about right. But really, she knows this is an excuse to see them again, see if she has romanticised their kindness or if they are genuinely friendly people. Best to know, really. Better to make a bit of a fool of herself by knocking on their doors than committing herself to buying the cottage and regretting it in the future.

The whole situation feels overwhelming, but she thinks of Hilary and the courage she has displayed. Knocking on the door will do no harm. She parks up and gets out of the car, takes a step towards Saabira's house. Then she hesitates. Maybe it's not a good time. Maybe Cyril is the one to talk to; there was a softness about him she felt she can relate to. But as she draws nearer she realises she can see into the front window and all the way through to the one at the back. She must offer to help with getting him furniture – that's a nice way to break the ice.

'Good thinking, Dawn,' she says to herself, but as she mutters this a bigger picture begins to form in her mind. The old mill becoming an animal sanctuary. Something clicks inside her.

She knocks on Saabira's door; maybe Cyril is there. Wherever he is, she needs to find him.

'Hello,' she says when Saabira answers. 'I saw next door is still empty, so I wondered if Cyril is with you?'

'Yes, he is, come in.' Saabira speaks politely but she appears wary. Two of Cyril's dogs stare out from behind her legs.

'Morning.' Dawn is a little taken aback to find both Aaman and Cyril sitting at the kitchen table. Even more surprising is that Cyril has a baby on his knee as he eats. Her stomach gives a little twist; it is all so alien, and the temptation is to run.

'I'll just get down to it, shall I?' she says, fighting her internal response, her desire to return to safe ground. 'Health and Safety also cover what was Hogdykes Abattoir. Well, them men down there are not backward at coming forward and they told me all about your bit of luck, Cyril, and how you've given them notice so you can set up an animal home. The whole bunch of them out of work. That's true, is it?'

Cyril nods but doesn't speak. Dawn pats one of the dogs that are sniffing round her legs.

Saabira gets a mug down from the hooks under the kitchen cupboard and puts it on the table. The implication is that Dawn should sit, and she steps into the house. With a nod, Aaman pours the tea, and Dawn, not sure what to do, accepts with a smile and helps herself to milk from a jug by a fresh plate of hot crumpets. They smell so good. Homely and warm. Cyril is eating one and has butter dripping over his hand. No one is speaking so she continues, mostly to fill the silence.

'Well, I'll tell you something for nothing. That place was a disgrace and should have been closed years back. I can't begin to tell you how much I hated it down there. It was the men that were animals, not the other way round. And I'm not sorry they are jobless – they deserve that and more – disgusting brutes, the lot of them.' She takes a sip of tea whilst she tries to phrase what she wants to say. 'Anyway, the point is all you have to do is say the word and I'll hand my notice in.'

'What?' Cyril puts down his half-eaten crumpet, a little frown creasing the skin between his eyebrows, butter on his chin.

'Well, I thought you was going to need someone and being as, years ago, I used to work for Nine Lives Cat Rescue, and seeing as you'll need someone who knows all the health and safety regulations it could work out just fine. What do you say?' Oh my goodness. What is she doing? Her stomach churns again; she points at the plate of crumpets. 'Is one of them going begging?' she asks. Saabira, Aaman and Cyril all nod, speechless. Dawn butters a crumpet liberally, mostly to distract herself from what she is saying, but it starts to melt and she cannot resist any longer and takes a big bite.

She feels more in control with her mouth full and the words continue to flow unfiltered from her. 'With a bit of application I reckon with a bit of luck we could have it open for Christmas and then we'll be ready for all them rotten sods that takes dogs for their kids for Christmas and dump them because they find they are too much work before they even see the new year in.' She licks the butter that is running past her fingers down to the wrist and then looks up at the staring faces, painfully aware how this must appear. Cyril and Aaman look at each other, but still they do not speak.

Chapter 26

Cyril eyes her cautiously.

'I'm serious,' Dawn insists. 'I could not be more serious. I wanted to be a vet but, well ...'

'Well what?' Cyril says.

'Er.' Dawn feels reluctant to launch into her life story. 'Let's just say Mum didn't encourage me.' Cyril's stare softens; there is understanding in his eyes. Her instinct about him was right – he's been there too, experienced something similar. Sitting up a little straighter, she pulls her shoulders back, lifts her head. Aaman pours her more tea, gives a sympathetic smile and excuses himself, saying that he must be off to work. He and Saabira leave the table, Saabira takes his overcoat from a hook, leaving Dawn and Cyril alone. The baby reaches up to Cyril's face, its tiny hands on his chin.

'My mum died,' Cyril says.

'My mum just died too. I watched her,' Dawn replies. Cyril's manner is calm, as if he has all the time in the world – no, as if the only thing that exists for him is this second.

'I found my mum dead,' he says. 'And Archie.'

'Archie?'

'Cyril's friend who he lived with next door,' Saabira says from the doorway.

Aaman says goodbye to them all and leaves the house, letting in a cold blast of air. Saabira rejoins them and takes the baby onto her knee.

'I am sorry,' Dawn says to Cyril.

'Why are you sorry? It was not your fault,' Cyril says and Dawn scans his face.

'No, I meant I'm sorry you had to experience that,' she clarifies.

'Are you serious about helping Cyril with the animal sanctuary?' Saabira asks, standing, baby on hip as she clears away the used plates and knives.

Dawn closes her eyes for a second, tries to sense how she feels in every part of herself, and then opens her eyes and smiles. 'Yes. Yes I am.'

'You are not a bad person then?' Cyril asks. She cannot quite work Cyril out, whether he has mental difficulties or if it is just a typical Yorkshire abruptness, straight talking.

'Oh, I hope not,' she says, and she tries to see herself through his eyes – the woman from the council coming to get rid of his dogs and forcing him to clear his house. 'The whole thing with your dogs and the house, that was my work. I don't like my job. I think you taking in the dogs is wonderful, and I wish more people were so kind.'

'I had to do a job I didn't like too,' Cyril replies. 'I didn't like who that made me.'

'Exactly!' Dawn says, 'But an animal sanctuary, that would suit me.'

'And me.'

'You know anything about this, how to make this happen?' Saabira asks.

'I know how to make a change of use application, and how to get it to the top of the pile. And there are grants, money we might be able to get to help set up. I can also find out some of the stipulations as to how it must be laid out, the room for the animals and that sort of thing. I also know the inside of the mill, what's there at the moment. Do you have a piece of paper?' she asks Saabira.

Dawn sketches a plan of the mill and shows Cyril how she would split the areas up if it were up to her. The afternoon flies by.

'If we are going to run it as a business we could have a petting farm, with fluffy animals, rabbits … You'll need a full-time administrator is my guess, someone to do all the paperwork and that stuff.'

'I like rabbits,' Cyril interjects.

'Well, lots of rabbits will bring mums with toddlers, especially if we have a café. There's plenty of room, we could use this front bit and put tables and chairs outside in the summer.' She points at the plan.

'A café?' Saabira turns from the sink where she is washing up. 'With food?'

'We could have, or snacks, cakes – that sort of thing.'

Saabira abandons the washing-up and sits with them again. The café seems to interest her.

'It could be a destination. You know, a place people head for on a day out … I mean, you have the top floor too. It has a low ceiling but it's full of light.' The ideas just seem to be flowing, one after another. Dawn is aware she is talking fast but there is an urge to get them out. 'You

285

could make a gallery up there on the top floor. People love art, get someone like that local bloke who took that piano to London on his raft. See if he does drawings or paintings, he could put a show on.'

'But the animals ...' Cyril's brow is creased.

'No, obviously the animals are the focus, but animals take money, for food and vets' bills. I was just thinking about how it would all be funded.'

'What you say makes sense. Don't you think, Cyril?' Saabira stands and puts the kettle on again. A little later still she makes them each a sandwich, but Dawn cannot stop planning and leaves hers half eaten. Cyril is growing more animated by the hour, voicing strong opinions about the animals and the kindness they deserve to be shown.

For Dawn, the idea of returning to the office has been abandoned – what she is doing feels so much more important. It is evening, and the light is fading, by the time Aaman comes home, and she realises with sudden embarrassment that she might have outstayed her welcome.

'Oh my goodness. I am so sorry,' she says, standing. 'I've taken up your whole day.' Cyril's face suddenly looks sad.

'You won't stay for tea?' Saabira asks as she helps Aaman slip off his coat. He kisses her on the cheek and takes the baby.

'Yes, stay to tea and tell me what you have been talking about all day,' he says, but his eyes are on his infant, enraptured.

'That is very kind of you. But I must go, I think.' She looks for a clock. She might have missed her watercolour class, but surely it is not that late already?

'Come tomorrow,' Cyril says. It doesn't sound like a question.

'Er, I have to work. But maybe I can find a way.' Dawn would love to spend all the next day making this idea of the animal sanctuary happen, but she also needs a little space to digest today's events. Best not to commit. Everything is happening so fast.

By the time she gets home it's too late for her watercolour class and there's a text message from June, which she replies to, apologising. She could just about make it if she were to leave straightaway but there is so much racing through her mind that she needs the quiet, and time to think. Taking a cup of tea through, it is almost automatic to switch on the television but she stops herself, purposefully puts down the remote and turns Mum's chair to face the patio door so she can look out into the fading light in the garden. Mum never faced her chair this way, and the view is so pretty.

The colours fade and change as the sun sets, pink hues that turn imperceptibly into dark-blue shadows. Could this idea of the animal sanctuary really work? The thought of such fundamental change to her life is disturbing. Look what happened the last time she broke away to live with June and work in the bar. She had to scurry home to Mum that time. If something goes wrong this time there is no Mum, and if she sells the house there won't even be the house to return to.

'Nothing like Paul Fiddler is going to happen if you move to Little Lotherton.' She speaks out loud to give it impact. But to pack in the council, for a promise of a job at the sanctuary – isn't that just crazy?

The sun has almost set now, and darkness creeps, inside the room and out. Instead of putting the light on, she goes up to bed. The same room, the same bed, the same curtains as when she was child.

'Come on, Dawn, you're no longer a child and there was no safety in that anyway,' she counsels herself, and Hilary's words about making her own life niggle away, battling with what she knows to be cowardice.

'How does one muster the courage to take such a leap?' she asks herself before falling asleep.

Chapter 27

'Well, you have done it!' Saabira says, hitching the baby up on her hip.

'*We* have done it,' Dawn answers, surveying the coloured flags. There are way too many for the area in front of the mill, but hey ho, she reflects – better than too few. Saabira follows her gaze.

'Not the flags!' She waves a letter. 'I was talking about your genius with the grant application. We finally have the official confirmation.'

'Oh, about time.' Dawn knew the application had been successful or she would never have quit her job. Hilary told her weeks ago; she had heard it from the women who deal with that sort of thing. Different department, same building. Fortunately Dawn still had access to that system, and a password that she should not really be using any more, so she checked on the computer before savouring the pleasure of telling Ms Moss that she was leaving.

'"Oh, about time," she says, as if it is nothing!' Aaman interrupts. He is bringing another table outside, carrying it as if it is weightless. Another benefit of working for the council – knowing where to go to borrow things. The caretaker at Greater Lotherton Village Hall has been very generous with chairs, tables and bunting.

'It's only right that some good came from working all those years in the council.' Dawn smiles, although the truth is she has amazed even herself: the grant they have been awarded easily pays for a full-time administrator for the first year.

'Well, I think with you being here full-time Cyril cannot go wrong,' Aaman says.

'I agree.' Saabira nods earnestly. 'With your admin skills and my cooking!'

Dawn feels her cheeks flush a little hot. The grant will only cover her wages. Saabira has the more daunting task of making the café turn a profit. Cyril will get the takings on the door.

She looks around for Cyril, spots him at the side of the mill, his dogs surrounding him as he throws stick after stick for them, making them run up the side of the dell between the trees. He is smiling and seems carefree. It is a good sight.

'I'd better get inside and get some of the food heated,' Saabira says.

'And I am going to put up the new sign.' Aaman takes a hammer from one of the tables. 'Have you seen it?' He unwraps a bulky, flat object to reveal a beautifully finished, gnarled section of a trunk from one of the fallen trees that surround the building, with the mill's original name painted on it – *Windy Lea Mill*.

'Oh, that is gorgeous,' Dawn says, admiring the skill with which the lettering has been applied. 'Is Neil coming today?'

'He said he had a book signing this morning, but will try to make it this afternoon. His girlfriend … I've forgotten her name.'

'Kimberley,' Dawn says.

'Yes, Kimberley is just painting the last wall in the sitting room and then she said she would come and help.'

'I still think it's weird that he is one of us now. So fortuitous that Mr Brocklethwaite moved out so they could move in.'

'I don't think it is fortuitous,' Saabira says. 'I think people draw to them what they need.'

'Well, I needed you to ring and ask him if he would exhibit here. I would have been way too shy, him being on the telly and everything.' Dawn laughs, puts the last of the unused bunting back in the box and starts arranging chairs around the tables.

'And he needed somewhere to live, and so everyone brought to them what they needed,' Saabira says.

'There is no use arguing with her.' Aaman winks at Dawn. 'She knows the mysteries of life.' He grins at his wife.

'You need to not be so cheeky,' Saabira says and she passes him his daughter, which silences him as he becomes lost in staring into the child's brown eyes.

'They have a dog and a cat, Bushy-Mush and Fuzzy-Pants.' Cyril joins them but a dog runs to him with a stick and he takes it to throw and returns to his game.

'Personally I think it makes sense that he lives in Little Lotherton. He was born near here, he said, and he has to live somewhere.'

'I hope everyone will come today.' Dawn arranges the last of the chairs. The place is looking amazing. The area at the front has been flagged for the café, with stone donated by a local quarry. The interior is nowhere near finished but she suspects it will always be a work in progress. The upper floor has been swept clean – that was Saabira's doing, and Neil has already put some of his work there for sale.

A car draws up and parks at an angle to Dawn's, taking up two spaces.

'Hi!' June walks straight up to Dawn and gives her a hug. 'I'm so proud.

'Knew you would do it!' Hilary is behind her.

'So who is who? I have heard so much about you all,' June gushes.

'Oh yes, this is Saabira, and this is Aaman, and their daughter Jay, short for Juliet. And over there is Cyril.

Hilary coos at Jay and Aaman passes her over. Jay is making sounds.

'Mmm – Mama, Mama!'

'She said Mama!' Saabira gushes.

'Actually, I think she was talking about the smells coming from the cooking. Mmm, mmm,' Aaman teases.

'Talking of which ...' And Saabira disappears inside.

'So what can we do to help?' June asks.

'Actually, I'm not sure. We need to put the sign up, but Aaman is doing that. You know, I'm not sure there is that much to do now. I'll make us all a cup of tea, shall I? Cyril, you want a cup of tea?'

Cyril nods but doesn't stop playing with the dogs, and Dawn follows Saabira inside, finds her organising the food, displaying it beautifully. She can still hear June and Hilary talking to Aaman as she gathers cups together.

'Well, Aaman, we're so pleased to meet you,' Hilary says, and she sits at one of the tables.

'And I am pleased to meet Dawn's friends.' Aaman sounds so polite.

'I'm so glad to meet you too,' June adds. 'Dawn's said that much about you.'

'Well, with her moving in opposite us I hope we will see much more of each other,' Aaman says.

'I must admit that was as big a surprise as her quitting her job. I guess some good came from her mum dying,' Hilary says quietly.

'I think it might have something to do with her mum,' June replies, 'but mostly I think it was just time for her to return to being the person she's always been.'

'Actually' – Dawn comes in with six mugs on a tray – 'it was something else.'

'What?' June asks.

'It was that little trophy sitting on Mum's mantelpiece.'

'That shiny bit of plastic from quiz night?' June laughs.

'Yup. It caught my eye one night, and it was like a sudden realisation. Whether it be quizzes or animal sanctuaries, you'll never lose if you put your energies into something you enjoy, something you are passionate about!'

If you enjoyed *The Other Daughter* please share it with a friend, and check out my other books!

I'm always delighted to receive email from readers, and I welcome new friends on Facebook.

https://www.facebook.com/authorsaraalexi

saraalexi@me.com

Happy reading,

Sara Alexi

Made in the USA
San Bernardino, CA
30 June 2018